Praise
Guises of

'Hilda Reilly has written a vivid, powerful and highly readable version of Bertha's story. The emotional turmoil of her experiences is empathetically portrayed against a carefully researched period setting and medical background. An absorbing and thought-provoking book.'
  Scientific ana Medical Network Review

'Hilda Reilly has written a novel of immense significance – a must read for anyone interested in the history of psychoanalysis.'
  Dr Terry Marks-Tarlow, author of *Clinical Intuition in Psychotherapy*

'This is a wonderful stroll through the Jewish culture of Vienna at the turn of the century, holding the hand of 'Anna O,' psychiatry's most famous patient, all the way.'
  Dr Edward Shorter, Hannah Professor in the History of Medicine, University of Toronto

'This book is a gift to anyone interested in psychoanalysis and the textures of human experience. I was moved reading it and in awe of the breadth of its scope.'
  Dr Deborah Serani, author of *Living with Depression.*

'Even famous people have day to day lives and it is in the story of their lives that we begin to feel what it might have been like to be in their shoes. Hilda Reilly gives us the gift of Bertha Pappenheim's lived experience.'
  Richard Hill, Director, *MindScience Institute*

'This is a story, and a message, that desperately needs to be heard.'
  Dr Neel Burton, author of *The Meaning of Madness*

GUISES OF DESIRE

HILDA REILLY

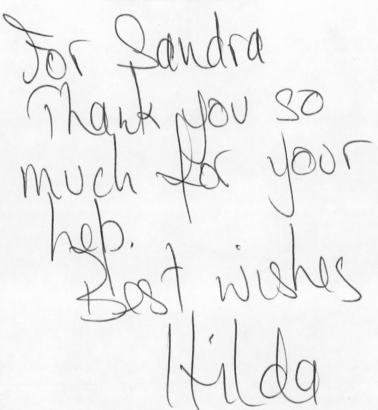

For Sandra
Thank you so
much for your
help.
Best wishes
Hilda

Dicatur Press

Published by Dicatur Press
First published 2012
This paperback edition 2013
Text copyright © 2012 Hilda Reilly

ACKNOWLEDGEMENTS

I have been accompanied during the writing of this book by a sterling team of supporters. I would like to thank my tutor, Conor O'Callaghan, and my fellow students on the 2009 Creative Writing MA at Lancaster University; Dieter Neumann of Bad Ischl and the Bad Ischl Tourist Office who provided invaluable assistance with my research, particularly during my visit to Austria; and finally Mike Handel, Kathleen Taylor, Anne Ortiz-Talvaz, Barbara Gleave and Mike Comerford who were generous with their time in giving me feedback as the novel progressed.

Carl Hansen strode to the front of the stage. The tails of his black coat swirled as he bowed, first to the right, then to the left. The audience clapped in muted appreciation, alert to the heightening drama.

Hansen took a few steps back and raised his arm in salute to the woman behind him. Illumined in the circular glow of a red spotlight, she lay across the backs of two chairs standing a few feet apart. One supported her head, the other her ankles. Her skirts swept out an arc to the floor.

'Ladies and gentleman, what you see before you is remarkable.'

Hansen's gaze scanned the audience, as if challenging them to deny it. 'But a sight even more remarkable is yet to come. If I could have just one more volunteer from the audience, please? Preferably a gentleman.'

A few hands were tentatively raised. Hansen beckoned to a portly man of middle years. 'Yes, you sir. If you please, sir.'

The man walked up onto the stage. Hansen shook his hand. 'Thank you, sir. This is most kind of you. Would you be good enough to tell us your name?'

'Frankel. Fritz Frankel.'

'Thank you, Herr Frankel. Now, before we go any further I would like you to remove your boots.'

A stage assistant scurried out from the wings with a chair for the man to sit on while he took off his boots. A second assistant produced a small set of steps which he placed at the side of the prone woman.

'And now, sir, if you would accompany me, please.' Hansen took the man's elbow and walked over to the steps. 'I would like you to climb the steps.' The man looked at him uncertainly but did as he was bid. There was silence in the auditorium. Hansen addressed the man again.

1

'Now listen, sir, my next request will surprise you, but have no fear. You are quite safe, and the lady you see lying here is also safe.' He paused. There were faint whispers in the audience. The woman on the chair backs made not a move.

'Are you ready, sir?'

The man nodded.

'I would like you to place your right foot on this lady's midriff.'

The man obeyed.

'And now your left foot.'

The man hesitated, aghast.

'I assure you, sir, there is nothing to fear. See here, my two assistants and I are right by your side to support you and the lady in the event of anything untoward.'

Slowly the man raised his left foot from the steps and placed it beside his right foot. He was now standing upright, high above the stage. The woman on the chairs was bearing his full weight. Her body remained straight as an arrow, the man on top of her as steady as a mason on a scaffolding plank.

'Ladies and gentlemen!' cried Hansen, twirling round, arms aloft.

The audience roared their applause.

o~o~o

February 1880

Dear Cousin Anna

First of all, thank you so much for sending me your copy of Indian Summer, *which arrived this morning. I have not yet read any of Adalbert Stifter's books, but look forward to doing so; your high opinion of him is recommendation enough for me. Thank you also for your letter, with all the latest news of the Karlsruhe family. I was especially entertained by the antics of little Wolf and Rebekka. How lucky you are to have so many nephews and nieces. With children one can never be glum for long.*

And now I must tell you about the latest entertainment here in Vienna. I am sure you will already have heard about this art of hypnotism which has been causing such a stir through half of Europe.

2

Well, tonight, with Papa, Mamma, Willi and Miss Thomson, I attended a performance at the Ringtheater by Mr Hansen, a hypnotist from Denmark. The theatre was quite packed, and with such a babble of excited chatter at the end of each act that the compère struggled to restore calm for Mr Hansen to proceed with the next. I declare I have never seen a theatrical event give rise to such amazement.

Now this is what happens. For each act, Mr Hansen invites members of the audience to take part. Those who step forward he puts into some strange mental state by obliging them to fix their gaze on a piece of glittering glass and by passing his hands repeatedly over their cheeks and foreheads. The trance achieved, he is then able to induce in them a variety of absurd beliefs and to persuade them to behave accordingly. Thus, for example, we watched a grown man eating a raw potato with gusto, having been told it was a pear; another sitting astride a chair, rising and falling as if he were on a cantering horse; and a third quaffing a large glass of water in the belief that it was champagne, and then reeling around the stage as if intoxicated.

Of course, there are sceptics who say that these volunteers are accomplices of the hypnotist, planted in the audience in advance, and that the whole enterprise is merely a new branch of the conjuror's art, based on artifice and illusion. I do not believe so. Nor, it seems, do many physicians. Indeed, we saw a number of doctors, some quite eminent, in the audience tonight and as we were leaving we met our own Dr Breuer in the foyer. He talked with Papa about the possibility that hypnotism could have a healing power in the case of certain diseases, although how this can be so I confess I have little idea.

Oh Anna, it is at times like this that I feel so ignorant. How I should have loved to be able to study the natural sciences and to learn the why and wherefore of things. Papa frequently tells me that there is little purpose in fretting over what cannot be changed and no doubt he is correct. But I find the thought of little comfort.

I wish that we lived closer to each other, you and I. Then I could attend your literature courses and take part in your amateur theatrics and all those other interesting things that you do. But you are far away in Karlsruhe so I shall just have to content myself with hearing about your activities when you write. Dearest Anna, I enjoy your letters so much.

With fondest love
Bertha

Bertha stood up and moved over to the window. Looking down from the third floor apartment she watched a carriage pass – theatregoers, probably, heading homewards from one of the venues in the nearby Ringstrasse. The horses tossed their heads and whinnied, their breath condensing in the cold night air. The first flurries of a snow storm flecked the cobblestones, muffling the sound of the hooves.

Bertha turned back into the room and started to undress. She loved her bedroom, had chosen the décor herself: pink-papered walls with an arabesque tracery of cinnamon and gold, a wine-red woolwork carpet dotted with rosebuds, and cream-coloured chintz curtains. The furniture was all of rosewood, except for the sleigh bed which was of solid mahogany. At one side of the bed was a low upholstered chair in floral chintz, at the other a small round table draped with white lace and covered with silver-framed family photographs. The wardrobe and the dressing table stood in the alcoves at either side of the white tiled stove. Against the opposite wall were an escritoire, with matching hardback chair, and a red velvet chaise-longue. The window facing the bed was flanked by bookcases crammed with books in German, English, French and Italian. Bertha had created for herself more than a bedroom; she thought of it as her boudoir, a place of privacy where she could shed all social masquerade along with her clothes.

Boudoir. Bertha considered the word as she unbuttoned the bodice of her brown tussore dress. Her fingers lingered on the last button. How odd to think that the word came from the French *bouder*, which meant to sulk. Her room was not designed for sulking in. On the contrary, it was the setting where she felt most free.

She took off the dress and hung it up in the wardrobe. Closing the mirrored door she caught sight of her reflection. For an instant, she saw her white lace petticoats transformed into the dress of a ballerina. She raised herself to her tiptoes and twirled. She was Giselle, returned from the grave and dancing with Albrecht. She had seen the ballet in the Opera House the previous week; the music had been running

4

through her head ever since. She sang it to herself. 'Tra la la la, tra la la la.' Swaying in front of the mirror, it was not herself she saw reflected but Albrecht, begging her forgiveness. Granting it, she made a final pirouette and danced off into the forest at the other side of the room.

Still humming, she unlaced her corset, removed her petticoats, chemise, stockings and drawers and pulled her nightdress over her head. She sat down at her dressing table and took out her tortoiseshell combs, freeing the dark brown braids piled on the back of her head. How tiresome to have such unruly hair. She started to disentangle it. As she did so, the facial pain which had been nagging all evening worsened. It scythed viciously up the left side of her nose and into her forehead. She laid down the brush, reached out for her bottle of chloral hydrate and poured a measure into a glass. She swallowed it in a single gulp, screwing up her face as the acrid liquid scorched her throat. Then she slipped into bed.

The children clamoured for more.

'What else, Papa? What else?'

Dr Josef Breuer had been describing how a man from Mr Hansen's audience had tried to shave another man with a piece of wood, believing it to be a razor, and then dandled a bundle of clothes on his knee, thinking it a baby.

'What else, Papa? Show us.'

Dr Breuer stood up and danced round the breakfast table, cradling a walking stick, to show how a tall fat fellow had done a polka with a broom handle. The children screamed with delight.

'Papa, can these hyposits like Mr Hansen make people do bad things?' Baba asked. 'Could he make a good person steal, or murder someone? And if he could, would it be the hyposited person's fault or would he be let off going to prison because he couldn't help what he'd done?'

'Hypnotist, stupid!' shouted Robert. 'Not hyposit.'

'Hush now, Robert.' Dr Breuer sat down again. 'That's no way to speak to your sister.'

He turned to his daughter.

'I don't think so, Baba. But in any case hypnotism should only be attempted by people properly trained in its methods.'

'I know how to hypnotise,' said Robert. 'We've been doing it at school. We got Karl to lie on two chairs and stay stiff and Franz sat on him and Herr Muller came in and shouted and Karl and Franz fell on the floor. But only because Herr Muller came in. And Herr Muller gave them both detention and...'

'And quite right too,' said his mother. She leaned over and straightened the bib of four-year-old Johannes who had porridge dribbling from his chin.

Robert turned towards Margarethe who was sitting beside him, crumbling a bread roll and dropping it into her milk. He picked up a spoon and held its convex side in front of her face, fixing her with a menacing gaze. 'Look at the spoon,' he ordered. 'Keep your eyes on the spoon. Sleep. You are going to sleep, going to sleep.'

'No, I'm not. It's morning and I'm going to school.' Margarethe was only eight, and frowning at all the strange talk going on around her.

'Stop teasing, Robert.' Mathilde Breuer took Johannes onto her knee. 'Come on now, all of you, it's time to get ready.'

The children's governess appeared in the doorway. Robert, Baba and Margarethe ran off to get their coats.

Mathilde refilled her husband's coffee cup. 'Josef, do you think it was fitting for you to attend Mr Hansen's performance. What are your patients to think if you appear to be impressed by these charades?'

Dr Breuer helped himself to a *kaisersemmel* and bit into it, wondering how best to answer this question. For all the pantomime and showmanship associated with the stage hypnotists, he believed that there could be something to it, something of medical value. They might laugh now at the goings-on surrounding Mesmer and his associates a century ago, with their wands and tubs of water, and their notions about magnetic fluids, but recent research indicated a possible neurological basis to the phenomena. Professor Czermak's hypnotic experiments on animals a few years ago had been

6

impressive and more recently the physiologist Heidenhain had come up with a persuasive theory involving cortical inhibition. Just a couple of weeks ago a patient of his own, Franz Brentano, had visited Heidenhain in Breslau and come back with convincing reports of what he had seen. A philosopher like Brentano was not someone likely to have the wool pulled over his eyes easily. There was also the clinical evidence: reports of surgical operations carried out on hypnotised patients without them feeling any pain, and of hypnotic procedures having a curative influence in cases of hysteria.

It was too complicated to explain all this to Mathilde. Dr Breuer himself had no fears about negative opinions. Although a modest man and not yet forty, he felt secure in the solid reputation he had built up in his professional practice. Most of his patients were also his friends – wealthy professionals and intellectuals, many of them medical men or scientists, who shared his own liberal and enquiring outlook.

'Don't worry,' he said, and drained his coffee cup. 'Half the doctors in Vienna have attended Hansen's show, and the other half intend to do so.' He stood up, brushing some crumbs from this beard. 'And now, I must start my rounds.'

'Well, well, well!' Mr Pappenheim laid down the *Neue Freie Presse* and peered at his wife over the top of his pince-nez. 'I see that the Danish hypnotist has now been banned from practising his art on our stages.'

It was Friday, early evening. The family were gathered in the drawing room, whiling away the time until the Shabbat meal. They had all bathed and put on fresh clothes. Bertha wore a dark blue silk dress with a looped overskirt, Mrs Pappenheim grey taffeta. Earlier in the day, the two women had supervised the housemaid and the cook in the cleaning of the apartment. It had been dusted from top to bottom, the bed linen changed, the kitchen and bathroom scoured, the floors swabbed and the window panes buffed till they sparkled. Bertha had polished the silver *challah* tray, the Shabbat candlesticks and the *kiddush* cup.

Mrs Pappenheim looked up from *Frauen Illustrierte*. She had an oval face, the shape accentuated by a downward tilt of both the eyebrows and the mouth. The lower lip jutted out slightly. Her hair was dark and drawn back into a chignon on the nape of her neck. 'Really, Siegmund? Why is that?'

Mr Pappenheim consulted the newspaper again.

'Apparently the Public Health Officer had received a number of complaints.' He scanned the column. 'From people worried about possible dangers – I must say it doesn't surprise me – so he asked the Faculty of Medicine to look into the matter.'

Bertha lifted her head from the bookmark she was crocheting. 'How fortunate that we attended his show last week, then. Otherwise we shouldn't have had the opportunity.' She snipped a strand of thread. 'But what dangers could there be, Papa? Surely it's only harmless entertainment? And don't they say that it might even help in

8

curing illness?'

'What rot you talk, Bertha.' Willi turned round from the window where he had been gazing down into the street. 'Where have you been these past few weeks? What about all those schoolchildren running around trying to hypnotise each other and getting over-excited?' He moved over to the fire and leaned against the mantelpiece. 'There have even been people who've been hypnotised and found themselves stuck there. Why, just the other day I heard a story about a pharmacist who hypnotised his fiancé and had to call in a doctor to bring her back to normal.'

'My goodness!' said Mrs Pappenheim. 'Fancy that.'

'And there's talk about ways in which a hypnotist might take advantage of young women....'

'Willi!' snapped his father. He cast a glance in Bertha's direction. Willi bent down to throw a log on the fire. Mrs Pappenheim cleared her throat.

'So what did the Fac people have to say, Papa?' Willi asked, straightening up again.

Bertha turned back to her crochet.

'Well, they invited a commission – including some very eminent people, I must say....' Mr Pappenheim ran his eye over the list of names. 'There's the physiologist Brücke, Professor Meynert, Moritz Benedikt and a few others. They were asked to look specifically at, let me see, yes, here it is – "the possibility of detriment to an individual's health by pressure on nerves and vessels in the neck, or by being rendered unconscious, or by being sat upon while in a state of tonic spasm". I suppose that last one refers to the business with the woman supported between two chairs. I must say, it didn't look very safe to me. Anyway, the upshot of it all is that the commission responded affirmatively to all three questions. Hansen's show has been closed down and the man has left town.'

Bertha was no longer listening. She slipped her hook automatically through loop after loop of cotton thread, dwelling on her brother's question. Where had she been the past few weeks? Where had she ever been? Oh, lots of places to be sure. Riding most mornings in the Prater, evening concerts, sometimes a play, social visits to family and old school friends. But it was all so passive. What was the point of it all? What was the point even of fashioning this stupid bookmark? Merely a waste of time and energy. '*A thing of beauty is a joy for ever,*' Papa had said, quoting one of her favourite English poems, when she had complained to him with this same question. Yes, she loved beautiful things, but they lacked substance. They provided pleasure, but not satisfaction. What single useful subject had she learned at school? None. What good were the four languages she had learned other than to clothe her ideas differently, like so many different outfits to be worn on the various days of the week?

The voices of her father and younger brother, authoritative and assured, continued to provide a backdrop to her thoughts.

'Yes, I agree with you, Willi, that the Dual Alliance helped to strengthen Germany's defences but what did Austria gain from the bargain?'

'Well, you see, Papa, you have to consider…'

A joy for ever! A beautiful bookmark! She hated Papa when he said things like that. She had loved him so when she was a child, had even felt that she was his favourite. He was forever bouncing her on his knees, joining in her play, singing nursery rhymes with her, even remonstrating with Mama if she rebuked her for boisterousness. 'Let her be,' he would say. 'She's only a child once.' He hardly ever called her by her name, only by terms of endearment: poppet, rosebud, cherub, pumpkin. With Willi he had been more sober. He was still more sober with Willi – look at them now, deep in earnest conversation – but the pet names were no longer a source of emotional satisfaction and she found the consoling remarks belittling. It was how one might treat a family dog, fondling it, laughing at its antics, tossing it a bone and expecting it to be content.

At least she had her writing. This was something which she could indulge in privately, and perhaps publish, even if she had to do so under a male pseudonym. But why should she

10

have to pretend to be a man? She glanced with covert resentment at Willi, a short, plump young man with red hair and a stubby beard, standing in front of the fire with legs apart, hands behind his back. She particularly disliked his voice. It had a slushiness to it, like footsteps in wet snow, as if his tongue was too big for his mouth. To Bertha's ears it always lent his words a disagreeable pomposity.

She must submit her stories to some magazines. She set about composing a letter. *Dear Sir, I have been an avid reader of* Die Gartenlaube *for some years. I particularly enjoy the short stories and have ventured to pen some tales of my own….*

'Willi, I don't think you appreciate how important it is for the European countries to resist the growth of Russian influence.'

The crochet hook darted back and forth. *Dear Miss Pappenheim, Our editors have read your story,* Der Magische Spiegel, *with great pleasure. We are pleased to inform you that we shall be publishing it next month. For this we will pay you a fee of ten gulden.* Bertha's thought paused. She had no idea how much she could expect to be paid for a story. No matter. The important thing was that she would be paid something. The crochet hook flew on. *Moreover, if you have written any other stories we invite you to submit them.*

'Granted, Willi, however I still maintain that Bismarck …..

Dear Miss Pappenheim, I have the honour of informing you that the Board of Die Gartenlaube *would like to offer you the post of Prose Fiction Editor. We believe that your qualities as a writer, your vivid imagination, your felicitous turn of phrase, your sensitive delineation of character, make of you a person admirably suited to the task.*

The letter would arrive when all the family were together at breakfast. She would know at once what it was; something about the solid buff envelope would speak of its importance. Now she was slipping her thumb under the flap, removing the headed notepaper and absorbing the content; glancing at her father, mother and brother in turn, fancying how each would respond to her news.

'Have a look at this, Bertha. You might like to take it along with you to the sewing circle. I think it's very fetching.'

11

Mrs Pappenheim held out *Frauen Illustrierte* and pointed to a picture of a boy in a sailor suit. 'There's a pattern included so it should be quite simple. I daresay the orphanage would be delighted to have a set of little suits like this.'

Bertha glanced at it. 'What a good idea, Mamma. Yes, I'll take it.'

'I suggest you use a strong twill fabric. Something very hard-wearing in any case so that the suits can be handed down as the boys grow out of them.'

'Of course.'

Bertha continued to crochet. She would have little time for her charitable activities when she had real work. No more sewing circle. She set about furnishing her office at *Die Gartenlaube*. An oak kneehole desk, a green leather chair and a large brass lamp with a globe of frosted glass. A silver pen and ink stand. A few Makart prints on the walls – nothing too pretty or frivolous. The overall effect would be of elegant sobriety. Her job was to read the stories submitted and select those good enough to be published. She no longer wrote short stories herself; she was now working on a novel. And she had the services of a stenographer.

'Bertha, have you given Ilse the shopping list for tomorrow?'

'Yes, Mamma.'

'I hope you remembered to tell her that she must go to Gruber's for the fish. The pike she bought last week wasn't quite fresh.'

'Yes, Mamma.'

'In future I'd like you to pay a little more attention to the quality of the provisions Ilse buys. It's the only way to ensure that we're getting the best'

'Of course, Mamma.' Bertha bent her head over the crochet, pretending to search it for flaws. Her mother turned back to her magazine.

'But wasn't Austria adequately compensated for lost territory by the Treaty of Berlin?' Willi moved away from the fire and threw himself down on the sofa as if throwing down a gauntlet to his father.

Mr Pappenheim frowned, gathering his thoughts. 'I think, Willi, that you'll find…'

Bertha tied off the end of one thread and looped another into her hook. Her position at the magazine would have an impact on her social life, of course. She would mix with journalists, artists, musicians – the sort of people who sat around for hours in the Café Griensteidl. She would join them. She had never been there, had only glimpsed its interior from the outside. 'Fast', her mother called it. But her mother need never know. She pictured herself at a table, sipping coffee, discussing literature with a journalist in a brown velvet suit and a Rembrandt hat. She quoted a couple of lines from 'All Night in Dreams' to illustrate a point she had just made about the poetry of Heinrich Heine: 'You say to me secretly a soft word, And give a garland of cypress'. Laughing, the man in the velvet suit completed the verse: 'I wake up and the garland is gone, And the word I have forgotten'. A chess match was underway at the next table. On a dais at the back of the room a pianist played 'Where the Lemon Trees Bloom'.

'Bertha, dear, put your work away.' Mrs Pappenheim rose from her chair. 'It's eighteen minutes to sunset.'

Bertha lifted the lid of the sewing table and put her materials inside. Mr Pappenheim folded his newspaper. He stood up, a tall, lean man with a ring of sparse grey hair around a bald crown and a bushy beard. He put his right hand to the back of his head to check that his *yarmulke* was firmly in place and led the family through the double doors separating the drawing room from the dining room.

The table was already set for the Shabbat meal. Taking a lighted taper Bertha and her mother each lit one of the candles standing on it. They drew their hands over the candle flames and towards themselves several times, then covered their eyes.

'*Boruch atoh adonoi eloheinu…..*' The two women murmured in unison.

The blessing over, they stood silently, heads bowed. This was the time for private prayer, the time when women pray for health and happiness, for family welfare. Bertha waited, with mind blank, for her mother to finish. When she had done so, the family exchanged the traditional greeting: *Shabbat shalom*. Then together they began the *Shalom aleichem*, a song of welcome to the Shabbat angels. After it, Mr Pappenheim blessed and embraced each of his children and recited the biblical verses in praise of the virtuous wife.

'Who can find a wife of excellence? Her value far exceeds that of gems. The heart of her husband trusts in her, he lacks no gain. ….'

Bertha wondered what she might in turn expect from a husband. God forbid that he should be one of those who consider a wife to be a housekeeper, a social accessory, a governess for their children or, worst of all, a child herself.

'... She puts her hands on the spindle, and her palms grasp the distaff….'

And what if she should find herself married to a man of dull intellect, or a man whose horizons extended no further than the balance sheets of a family business? Could she be happy with a man like Papa perhaps? He was so kind and she loved him dearly yet she sensed somehow that she would want more in a husband. But where was the choice? She was twenty-one. Most of her school friends were already married and so far her parents had not found a single suitor for her. Her thoughts drifted back to the man in the brown velvet suit in the Café Griensteidl.

'…Her husband is well-known at the gates, as he sits with the elders of the land….'

He was a journalist. He wrote theatre and opera reviews for the *Neue Freie Presse*, and poetry. Yes, he must write poetry. He didn't earn much money but no matter. She would have a large dowry.

'She opens her mouth with wisdom, and the teaching of kindness is on her tongue.'

He would have no objection to her working. Like Cousin Anna in Karlsruhe who ran courses in literature, and even gave lectures.

'….Give her praise for her accomplishments, and let her deeds laud her at the gates.'

Unsuitable, Mamma always said when mention was made

of Anna's work. Little better than a governess. A governess! As if Anna could be compared with someone like Miss Thomson. Anna, with her energy always at the ready, like a jack-in-the-box on its coiled spring, her decidedness which swept aside all obstacles, and dreary Miss Thomson from Leeds in England.

Miss Thomson was not with them this evening. She never joined them for the Shabbat meal, preferring to have a tray in her room. Bertha was glad of her absence. There was something about her that she found oppressive: a faint air of dejection, a narrowness of expectation. It was not helped, of course, by the fact that she always dressed in black, like a widow, and wore her hair scraped back so tightly into a bun that the very skin of her face seemed to be pulled backwards.

Miss Thomson had been with living with the family for the past seven years. She had come just after Bertha moved up into Miss Baxter's class for English. Bertha had been thrilled at the prospect of having an English governess, expecting someone chic and dynamic and charismatic, just like Miss Baxter whom she believed to be the model of English womanhood. Bertha was the only girl in her class to have an English governess. How she boasted to her friends in advance of Miss Thomson's arrival, and how mortified she felt on that day when Miss Thomson first escorted her to school. Just like that gloomy Queen Victoria of England, Heidi Muller said – squat and dumpy and with a face like a bloodhound. As for her hat! The other girls all laughed. They teased Bertha about it for weeks.

Head bowed, Bertha scanned the table from the sides of her eyes. Everything was in place and as it should be, as it was every Friday evening: the spotless white table linen, the best china and cutlery, the flickering candles, the two loaves of plaited *challah* covered with an embroidered cloth, the flowers, and the *kiddush* goblet, the symbol of the vessel into which the divine blessings are poured. Her father was filling it now with wine, and saying the *kiddush* prayer over it.

The man in the brown velvet suit would be Jewish, of course, otherwise her parents would never agree to it. But not

15

so observant. They would still have the trappings of the Shabbat meal, for example – the candles, the *challah*, the best tableware, perhaps even some of the songs, but not all this endless praying.

'....*Baruch ata Hashem, mekadeish ha-Shabbat.*'

'*Amen.*'

Mr Pappenheim drank half of the wine in the goblet and poured the remainder into three glasses for the others. They then took it in turn to wash their hands. Using the pewter basin and cup placed on the table for that purpose they each poured three cups of water over the right hand and then over the left, murmuring the ritual prayer from the book of Psalms as they did so.

When they had finished and were seated at the table Mr Pappenheim removed the cloth from the *challah* bread and recited the blessing over it. He cut the bread and gave each a slice. They dipped it in salt and ate it.

Later that night Bertha sat at her escritoire, suffused with a mix of freedom and guilt. Tonight all work, even the lighting of her gasolier, was forbidden. How distressed her parents would be if they found out what she was doing. Yet what silliness to believe that it was somehow reprehensible to light a lamp on Shabbat and all those other taboos.

Bertha looked over the story she had started the previous evening. As she read, her tensions subsided. She was caught up in the mood of her tale, a fable in which a brother and sister strayed from their home and into an enchanted forest, a world of ice, frost and snow, but nonetheless warm and balmy. Penetrating deeper into the wonderland they came across a cottage made of ice and packed snow. At the door stood an old woman clad in black.

'Come here, children,' said the old woman. 'What a beautiful little girl you are,' she said to the sister. 'But you, boy, are an ugly little boy.'

With that, the old woman yanked the girl inside and slammed the door shut against her brother.

The boy returned home. Fearing that his parents would be

16

angry with him for abandoning his sister in the forest, he told them she had fallen into a river and drowned.

The girl remained with the old woman who kept her imprisoned in the ice cottage. The woman fed her with sweet berries which grew beneath the blanket of snow. She slaked her thirst with icicles which melted as soon as they touched the tongue and ran down her throat in a warm, lemony-tasting flow.

As the boy became a man he began to regret the loss of his sister. He returned to the forest to look for her and found the ice cottage. His sister was inside. She was now a beautiful young woman. He put his hand on hers, he kissed her cheek. Her body was warm to the touch. But she was still, her eyes unseeing. Her heart had frozen.

3

July 1880

Dearest Anna

At last! We are in Ischl. I have been intending to write to you every day since we arrived but truly, I have been so busy. We have been here for only ten days and already I have had more excitement than in ten months in Vienna. And we are to stay for ten weeks more! I shall horde each precious memory, like a squirrel its nuts, to sustain me throughout the dreariness of winter.

It is six years since we last holidayed here. I was only fifteen then. Too young, said Mamma, for the evening social activities. I used to listen every night to the music floating over from the Esplanade, imagining how it would be when I was older, what I would wear, how my hair would be dressed, how I would dance till I was footsore and exhausted. Now I am older – and it is such fun! Especially as I have a new friend to share it with. The Goldschmidt family have rented the apartment below us and Klara Goldschmidt is just six months younger than me. We have done all sorts of things together – walks in the woods, hiking up the mountains, swimming in the lakes. It is like having a sister. Is this how it would have been if Henriette or Flora had lived, I wonder? Probably not. By now they would have been married and taken up with babies and husbands and all manner of domestic cares.

Yesterday we climbed halfway up the Jainzenberg which gave us a splendid view of the Traun valley, and also the Kaiservilla lying at the bottom. We hoped to catch sight of the Imperial family who arrived two days ago for their annual holiday but they were not to be seen. Next month it is the Emperor's fiftieth birthday and Ischl is sure to be ablaze with celebrations for it. We would have gone further, only Miss Thomson, who is always with us on these expeditions, pleaded fatigue. It is tiresome to have her in constant attendance, but Mamma insists it is not fitting for two young women to be cavorting – Mamma's word! – around the countryside on their own. Klara does not mind as she finds Miss Thomson hilarious, with her execrable accent, her silly hats and her

18

absurd attachment to Percy, that horrid little poodle of hers. Klara and I always talk quietly when she is with us so that there is little chance of her understanding what we are saying. So it is just as well that she has the wretched dog to talk to.

This morning Papa, Mamma, Miss Thomson and I went boating on the Traun. Willi had risen early to go hunting in Langbath with some young men he met in the Café Ramsauer yesterday. I am a little worried about Papa as the boating expedition seemed to exhaust him. Yet he has done little but rest since we arrived. Perhaps he is still getting accustomed to the mountain air. Myself, I find it invigorating, each breath a stream of pure energy, intoxicating as a flute of champagne.

I have brought Indian Summer *with me to read again while I am here. It is the perfect holiday companion, I find; the prose is so serene and leisurely, and of course the setting is almost identical to that around Ischl. Heinrich's interest in nature, his attention to the merest detail, have encouraged me to open my eyes wider to what is around me on my walks and to see things as if in a brighter light.*

I wish you could join us here, but I know that you have already arranged to go and stay with Uncle Fritz in Frankfurt. Please write to me with news of everything that you are doing there!

With fondest love
Bertha

Bertha looked out over the garden. She was sitting on the balcony of their third floor apartment in the Villa Bellevue. A wide sweep of lawn, bordered with clumps of pink and white phlox, purple rhododendrons and scarlet hydrangeas fell away from the villa and down towards Kaltenbachstrasse. Two tall pine trees stood sentinel at the top, one at each side of the house. Just beyond the river rose the Siriuskogel, and to the right of that, even higher, Mount Katrin. Wherever she looked there were mountains, their great bulks surrounding the little town like the tiered slopes of an amphitheatre.

It was strange that she should feel so much freer here than in Vienna. The hills were so close, so embracing. Yet it was a comfortable containment, a solid barrier which seemed to mark the frontier between two worlds. And it truly was another world here. Of course, the fact that it was the summer

19

residence of the Imperial family made all the difference. They too must feel it to be another world. In Vienna they were rarely seen, their lives hemmed in by protocol and ceremony, whereas here they mingled freely with the townsfolk. Why, that very morning Mamma had reported seeing the Empress and the Archduchess Valerie at a table in the Hotel Elisabeth, drinking coffee and eating pastries just like any mother and daughter. No wonder so many musicians and artists and other famous people came here for the summer season. There was so much to do that at times the town seemed to be but one gigantic stage and the Esplanade an extended dance floor.

At the thought of dancing, Bertha began to tap a foot, humming to herself the first few bars of The Blue Danube. She would be dancing tonight, at the Kurhaus ball. She imagined it now, herself light as a fragment of thistledown, borne on the surface of the music, rising and falling with the tempo of the waltz, the skirts of her ball gown swirling around her. A warm excitement coursed through her body, the touch of her partner's arm steering her through the throng of dancers without collision, as if she were a magnet of identical polarity to all the others.

Which of her partners was she dancing with? Which would she prefer it to be? Her dance card for the evening was already almost full. How she would love it to be Herr Brull. The summer villa of the Brulls, a Jewish family from Vienna, was just a short distance from Villa Bellevue, further along Kaltenbachstrasse. The son, Herr Ignaz Brull, was a renowned concert pianist, and was beginning to make his mark as a composer. There was no fiancée yet, according to Klara, although it was high time; he was well over thirty. Not that Klara was interested. He was too old, she said, and his shoulders were sloping, which she found unbecoming in a man. She preferred men with a more military mien. Bertha thought Herr Brull was of an ideal age. She started the dance again, in the arms now of Herr Ignaz Brull. What did the slope of his shoulders matter when his very soul must be participating in the rhythms and the melodies of the music?

The house concerts of the Brull family were the talk of

Ischl. Their guests included Herr Brahms and even the Waltz King himself, Herr Johann Strauss. Bertha hoped that the Pappenheims would be invited to attend. Papa was already acquainted with the elder Brull. They were both merchants and moved in the same business circles in Vienna. Now, being such close neighbours in Ischl, an invitation would surely not be long in coming. She would become a regular guest there, with Mamma and Papa. But not Willi. He cared little about music and in any case had plenty of other activities with his silly friends.

Bertha's dancing stopped. Now she saw herself sitting at a small round table in the Brull salon, Ignaz at her side. Herr Brahms was at the piano, his large leonine head bent over the keyboard, long blond hair swept backwards, the tips of his waxed moustache just visible from behind. Although she could not see his face she knew that his eyes were the colour of lapis lazuli; she had glimpsed him several times in the Café Walter where he took his coffee every afternoon. He was playing his own Sonata No.2, the sharply contrasting notes of the right and left hands cascading up and down in clashing cadence. Ignaz was bending forward to whisper to her. He was taking a rose from a vase. He was offering it to her.

And what if? Why not? A few years slipped by in the space of a second and now she was mistress of the villa, hosting, with Ignaz, a house concert. Herr Strauss was about to play, adjusting his violin under his chin.

'Bertha, at last! I've found you.' Klara burst out onto the balcony, her hair streaming out behind her. 'We must start to get ready for the ball.'

Bertha turned round. 'But it's only four o'clock. It doesn't start for hours yet.'

'But getting ready is all part of it,' cried Klara. 'Choosing our dresses, doing our hair, talking about who we will dance with. I declare that the ball starts now.'

She grabbed Bertha's hand and pulled her inside. The drawing room was empty. Mr and Mrs Pappenheim had gone to the synagogue. Willi had not been seen since early morning, and Miss Thomson was in her own room. Klara carried on into Bertha's bedroom which opened from the drawing room. 'Now,' she said, 'what are you going to wear?' She threw open the wardrobe doors and started rummaging among the dresses.

'Klara! You're rumpling my clothes.'

'I'm looking for something which will show you off to perfection at the ball.'

Klara pulled out a high-necked blue silk with a lace collar and stared at it with pursed lips.

'Haven't you got anything a little more décolleté? You know, like the dress I wore to the Warburgs last week.'

Klara had looked splendid in that dress, Bertha remembered: body-hugging yellow silk with a train fanning out behind her. But then, Klara looked splendid in everything, though Bertha could not quite determine why. If you considered each of her features singly there was nothing especially attractive. Her eyes were narrow and just a shade too close together, her nose long and her lips thin. Yet there was something about the way in which they all worked together when she spoke or laughed or smiled, even when she directed her gaze at something. And her build, tall and slender with a small bosom, almost boyish, was enhanced by the current fashion for sheath dresses. Even Bertha, barely five feet tall, could have looked elegant in one. But her mother would not allow it. They were not seemly, Mamma said. At the Warburgs, Bertha had worn a dress of dark-green tulle with an overskirt heavy with rows of ruching and big satin bows. She had felt squat and clumsy beside Klara.

Oh no, Klara was pulling that very dress out of the wardrobe now, holding it up against her chest and pirouetting in front of the cheval mirror. To her chagrin, Bertha saw that on Klara the dress would have looked quite presentable. She had the height to carry it off.

'Drab.' Klara tossed the dress onto the bed. 'The colour reminds me of graveyards. Moss on tombstones.'

Bertha sat at the dressing table toying with a comb while Klara continued to inventory the contents of her wardrobe, keeping up a stream of chatter that required little reply from

Bertha. Bertha envied Klara her non-religious family. It seemed to her that Jews like the Goldschmidts had the best of both worlds. They had the cultural enjoyment of the festivals and the sense of fraternity with other Jews, but were not bound by all the rules of religious observance which Bertha felt so hemmed in by. The Goldschmidts did not even keep a kosher kitchen, Klara had told her. Mrs Pappenheim had, of course, forbidden Bertha to eat anything in their apartment. There was never any arguing with Mamma about fashions or what other people did.

'We are not other people,' Mamma was fond of saying. 'We are Jewish.'

Klara had finished with Bertha's dresses and was talking about marriage now. She plumped down on the bed. 'What do you think it'll be like when you're married,' she asked. 'Will you be able to do what you like? Wear what you want? Will you have to go on pretending or will you be able to be your true self?' She lowered her voice and gave Bertha a knowing look as she emphasised the last two words.

Bertha considered. Her parents would choose her husband, of course, so it was sure to be someone who shared their ideas. 'That will depend on who I marry, I suppose. But I should hate to spend the rest of my life living a lie. Better never to get married at all.'

'Oh no, Bertha! You don't want to be a spinster!'

'Why not? I could become a nurse, like Miss Nightingale, or....or....'

'Or what? Women can't become anything. They just have to be what they are.'

Bertha turned her head away and gazed out across the garden. It wasn't true what Klara had said. There was Cousin Anna in Germany, and Betty Paoli the poet and Louise Otto-Peters the writer. But there was no point in telling Klara about them.

'In any case,' Klara continued, 'what about the pleasures of married life?'

'What pleasures?'

Klara laughed, a tinkling giggle. 'Oh, Bertha, you innocent

23

little goose!'

The foyer hummed with laughter and inconsequential chatter: cries of delight from friends encountering each other, gracious introductions as strangers were presented, compliments on the ladies' dresses, checking of dance cards. Through the open doors of the ballroom came the sound of the orchestra playing the overture to Strauss's *Carnival in Rome*, softly and tentatively, as if just coaxing their instruments into life.

The Pappenheims stood with the Brull family, sipping champagne. Ignaz Brull had just invited Bertha to partner him for a waltz. His younger brother Eugen was now booking her for a mazurka, the only dance left on her card.

As Bertha chatted with the two young men she noticed that she was directing her conversation more towards Eugen, responding to his remarks rather than to his brother's. Somehow she found it easier to talk with him, not because she found him more interesting or agreeable than Ignaz – on the contrary – but because she felt relaxed with him. With Ignaz there was an undercurrent of tension.

Bertha scanned the dresses of the other women in the room. Klara was looking magnificent in yet another figure-hugging silk, sapphire blue this time. Most of the younger women were dressed in similar style. She herself was wearing a pale aquamarine gown with a cream-coloured lace overskirt topped with swathes of material draped round the waist. It had a sash across the chest and down the sides to which were attached a number of large taffeta roses. It had looked pretty in the dressmaker's pattern book; at least Mamma had managed to convince her it did. Now she was not so sure.

The orchestra had stopped playing. A percussionist was hammering out a prolonged roll on his drum. Men and women were forming pairs and moving to towards the open doorway. The Radetzky March began and the guests proceeded into the ballroom. Bertha was on her father's arm, behind them her mother on Willi's.

Cascading bouquets of white lilies trailed from the balconies above, tall green palms stood against the mirrored walls, light sparkled from the frosted white globes of the chandeliers. At the top of the salon they turned, the men to the right, the ladies to the left, and marched back to the other end where they rejoined their partners. In groups of four they swept back through the room again, the men stiff and straight in their black tail-coats, the women fluid in their flounces and trains. The melange of the military and the romantic had a strangely thrilling effect on Bertha and she found her mood changing with the music as it alternated between softly seductive and boldly exuberant, as if she too was an instrument, controlled by the conductor's baton. She no longer worried that her dress might be unbecoming, thinking instead of the dance she was to have with Ignaz Brull. She was glad it was to be a waltz, so much more intimate than something like a galop or quadrille.

The march ended and there was a lull before the first dance. Mr and Mrs Pappenheim sat down at a little side table in an alcove, on a sofa of yellow brocade. They would be spectators from now on, Mrs Pappenheim said. Dancing was for younger people. She smiled at Klara's father as he claimed Bertha for the Tritsch-Tratsch polka, sweeping her off and round the room so masterfully that her feet barely touched the floor. Bertha was quite out of breath by the time it finished but no sooner had she sat down with her parents than she was claimed for the first waltz by Horst Botstein, a boy from Willi's set with a pimply face and a braying laugh whom she detested. She had accepted with bad grace when he asked her to partner him earlier on; Mamma had rebuked her for her rudeness afterwards. Now she tried to smile as he led her on to the floor. At least she was getting it over with early on. To her surprise she found that Horst was an accomplished dancer, guiding her with smooth aplomb. She even began to enjoy the waltz, and began to anticipate how much better it was going to be when she was in the arms of someone she really liked.

For the next dance, another polka, she was partnered by Gustav Kohn, the young man from the villa next door. As she danced past the alcove where her parents were sitting, she caught sight of her father leaning back, his eyes closed. Her mother was bending towards him, an anxious look on her face. When the dance ended she stopped to talk with Klara, then saw her mother gesture for her to come over. Papa was tired, she said, they would have to leave.

'But it's only…'

'Bertha!' There was a warning note in her mother's voice.

Bertha glanced at her father. His face was drawn and his shoulders bowed. He had a hollow look in his eyes.

'What about my partners?'

'Willi will let them know what's happened. Come along now.'

Bertha sat at her bedroom window, looking down towards the River Traun. The window was wide open, the night air warm and scented. Faint sounds came from villas nearby: laughter, a snatch of song, shouted goodbyes, the slammed door and the clip-clop of a departing carriage. The gas lamps lining the Esplanade glowed like a necklace of jewels.

The ball would still be in full swing. She had been so annoyed at having to leave early. They hadn't even had supper. 'I'll ask Ilse to prepare something for us when we get in,' Mamma had said. As if that would be any compensation for the feast they had already glimpsed being set out in the dining room. And she had missed the opportunity of dancing with Ignaz Brull who had been scheduled as her next partner. They had met him on the way out and she had to make her excuses and tell him that she had to go home, like a child sent early to bed.

Willi, of course had stayed. No question of him being expected to forgo the evening's entertainment. Not that Bertha could see what entertainment there was for him in a ball. He didn't like dancing. So he said, anyway. He and his boorish friends would be standing in a corner now, getting drunk on champagne and laughing at all the girls they could find fault with. That was their enjoyment. A big nose, a thick waist, a dowdy dress – all grist to their mill. Hateful beasts!

Klara would probably be dancing with Max Reinhard.

26

Bertha had seen from Klara's card that he had booked her for at least half of the dances. Klara had pooh-poohed the idea when Bertha said that Max must be sweet on her but Bertha had noticed that she had blushed, which was unlike Klara.

Bertha remembered their conversation from earlier in the day. How unfair of Klara to call her a little goose. And innocent! What did Klara know that Bertha didn't? 'Innocent' was the word they used at school to refer to girls who *didn't know* – they always gave the key words a special breathless emphasis in speaking of those things – who still thought that babies were brought by storks or angels.

Bertha had known since she was thirteen. Heidi Muller told Renate Grunwald and Renate told the rest of the Jewish girls. But none of them believed it. Heidi Muller was a Catholic and they decided that she was pulling their legs. Most of the girls in Bertha's school were Catholic and the Jewish girls often felt out of things. It was just like Heidi to try and make them believe something disgusting like that and then laugh at them for being so foolish as to believe it, they said. Later that year, in December when the Catholics were preparing to celebrate the birth of Jesus, the subject came up again. Mademoiselle Lamartine, the French teacher, had been talking to them about Christmas and she spoke about *la Vierge Marie* and how her baby Jesus was born in a stable.

'Please, Mademoiselle, what does *'vierge'* mean?' Heidi Muller asked, darting a sly and triumphant look at the Jewish girls who she knew hadn't believed her about that.

Mademoiselle's face had gone pink. 'You'll learn about that when you're older,' she said, and hurried on to talk about three kings who had come from far away to give presents to Jesus.

After class Heidi told Renate what it meant so Renate looked the word up in a dictionary but she only found other words, like 'chaste', which none of them understood, or 'intercourse', which they thought meant the same as conversation. Claudia Hahn had asked her mother about it and reported back that her mother had said it meant an unmarried woman but that couldn't be right because Mary was

27

married to Joseph. Then Renate pointed out that, according to the Catholics, the father of Jesus wasn't Joseph, but God. That meant that what Heidi said couldn't be true because God didn't have a body and you needed a body to do what Heidi said. Renate put this to Heidi but Heidi just said it was a miracle. After that they had forgotten about it for a while, what with all the excitement of Christmas and Hannukah, which were at about the same time that year. But in January Claudia, whose father was a doctor, said she had looked up one of his books about female diseases – she had wanted to find out more about what had begun to happen to her every month – and it was all true. There were even diagrams. Some of the girls had pestered Claudia to draw the diagrams for them but she said they were too complicated. Bertha noticed, however, that Claudia's face was turning red and decided that she was too embarrassed. Bertha was not surprised.

After that they were more sober and fearful when they talked about it. That was why married people slept in the same bed, they said – it always happened at night, when you didn't have any clothes on. 'Not even your nightdress?' Bertha had said. 'Surely not?' Heidi said that it hurt horribly and the Jewish girls thought that she was just trying to frighten them. But Renate said that it must hurt. How could it not, when you thought about it? Bertha preferred not to think about it. Heidi said it hurt only the woman. Men enjoyed it. In fact they enjoyed it so much that they often went to special women – they were called prostitutes – who let them do it to them in exchange for money. This was what Claudia said, anyway. She had read about it in another of her father's books which talked about the horrible diseases men got from these women and then passed on to their own wives.

So, Bertha decided, there was no reason for Klara to call her an innocent little goose. But she still didn't know what she could have meant about the pleasures of marriage. She tried to visualise herself married. She would be in charge of her own house rather than under the constant supervision of Mamma, which would be a good thing. And she would be able to dispense with Miss Thomson. Other than that there was little she could see that would afford pleasure. Then there was that side of marriage. But perhaps she wouldn't have to do it. Some married couples didn't have children. That must be because they didn't want to do it. Or if the man did, he could go to one of those prostitutes.

In the meantime, there was the pleasure of dancing. Bertha closed her eyes and started humming Roses from the South, the waltz for which Ignaz Brull was to have partnered her. She leaned back and felt his arms around her.

By the next day Bertha's disappointment over the ball had diminished. She spent the morning playing quoits in the garden with Klara and then went back in to change for a lunch party at the lakeside villa of the Mayers, friends of Klara's parents. She would wear her pink muslin, she decided as she ran up the stairs. It was too hot today for anything heavier.

She hoped Papa would be up by this time. He had still been in bed when she went out. It was unlike him. He usually rose before everyone else in the family, particularly when they were in Ischl where he loved to go walking in the woods before anyone else was abroad. Mamma had assured her that he was perfectly well, that he needed to take advantage of their time in Ischl to relax as he worked so hard during the rest of the year in Vienna, but he had been resting for almost two weeks now and he just seemed to be getting more exhausted. It would be so tiresome if he were to be ill.

She let herself into the apartment. The drawing room door was slightly ajar. Through it she glimpsed her mother, seated at the table in the middle of the room.

'Here I am, Mamma.' Bertha walked through the door. 'I must tell you, we ….' She stopped. At the other side of the table sat a man she recognised as a doctor who lived nearby. A medical bag lay at his feet.

Mrs Pappenheim turned round.

'Bertha dear, Dr Bettelheim has called in to see Papa. He's developed a slight fever.'

'Oh! What is it, Dr Bettelheim? Fever? What do you mean?'

'A summer cold, perhaps. I've prescribed some medicine. Your father should be back to his usual self in a day or two.'

Dr Bettelheim promised to look in again the next day and took his leave.

Bertha sat down beside her mother.

'A cold, Mamma? Do you really think that's all it is? You don't think…?' Bertha thought back to Henriette's illness, and to the first symptoms which had lingered for months before it became clear what was causing them. And Papa hadn't been himself for several weeks now. She looked fearfully at her mother.

'No, Bertha, I don't.'

'But so many people…. I mean, what if…. Oh, Mamma, please don't let Papa be really ill.'

'Bertha, I don't want to listen to such talk. You heard what Dr Bettelheim said. It's just a summer cold.' Mrs Pappenheim lifted a copy of *Frauen Illustrierte* from the magazine rack. 'Now why don't you go and change your clothes? I expect Papa will be up by the time you get back from the Mayers.'

4

July 1880

Dear Cousin Anna

   How things have changed since I last wrote to you. Then I was full of gaiety and anticipating a summer sparkling with excitement. Now I am filled with dread, fearful of what each new day might bring. When I received your letter telling me how you would have loved to join us here, were it not for your visit to Frankfurt, I could have wept. If only you could be here!

   I mentioned Papa's fatigue to you in my last letter. It turns out that it is much more than that. I will not go into all the details. It distresses me too much. Suffice it to say that during the last two weeks Papa has transformed almost beyond recognition. He is confined to bed. He has lost all appetite. He coughs continuously, bringing up quantities of foul-smelling pus, and is racked with chest pain. The fever never leaves him and he is so drenched with sweat that the bed linen must be changed several times a day.

   What else can it be but tuberculosis? Dr Bettelheim, who has been caring for him, never mentions the word, of course, at least not in front of me. He speaks only of an infection, with inflammation of the lining of the lungs. But Papa is now in such a grave state that he is to have a surgical operation. Mamma wrote to Dr Breuer in Vienna and Dr Breuer has arranged for a lung specialist to travel to Ischl to perform some kind of drainage. He is expected tomorrow morning. I do so wish that we were in Vienna, or that Dr Breuer was here. We are used to having him treat us and he would surely know what is best. Mamma says it would not make any difference because what Papa needs now is a surgeon, and for his general care Dr Bettelheim is just as good as Dr Breuer. I hope she is right, and I must try to believe what Dr Bettelheim says. It is an infection. Let us not try to put any other name to it. It is merely an infection and infections can often be cured. Anna, please reassure me that I am right in thinking this. You are so wise and knowledgeable I will put my faith in whatever you tell me.

With much love
Bertha

o~o~o

Bertha now exchanged night for day. She sat with her father during the hours of darkness to allow her mother nights of uninterrupted rest. At first she had been unable to sleep during the day. She lay in her darkened bedroom, worrying about her father, but alive to the sounds from outdoors and fretting about the activities she was missing. That morning, after lying restless for three hours, she had taken a draught of chloral hydrate. Now, twelve hours later and at her father's bedside, she was still drowsy. She felt herself drifting off, floating on the arm of her father, her ball gown billowing around her. But her father's arm, instead of wafting her in fluid waltz motion was suddenly rigid, the sleeve of his black tailcoat stiff. She turned her face up to his and her body convulsed in a jerk. She was staring into the empty eye sockets of a skull. She snapped awake, her heart thudding. She dared not look at her father in the bed. Had her dream become reality? She closed her eyes to shut out the shadows cast by the nightlight glowing on the table and by the shifting shapes of the curtains fanned by a faint night breeze. Only when she became aware of her father muttering in his sleep did she open them again. She looked at him. His lower jaw lay slack, his breath bubbling and sour.

Bertha turned her head away and settled it into the crook of her shoulder with her arm draped over the back of the chair. She started to sink back into the same dream. Her father's black-sleeved arm extended towards her in invitation to the waltz. Bertha's body flailed in a second jerk, her eyes startled wide open. It was no dream. There was no black-clad arm. Instead a black snake slithered out from the wall and towards the bed of her sleeping father. She wanted to scream, to waken her father, to beg him to save himself, to get out of the bed, to flee. She had no words. No sound came from her mouth. There was only a drumroll in her ears, a crescendo of

32

heartbeats. Bertha tried to stretch out her right arm, to grasp the snake before it reached her father. The arm would not move. She felt a numbness in it, a tingling sensation. She tried again. The fingers began to respond, then took on a life of their own as they reared up, little black snakes with death's heads at their tips. Bertha felt for an instant her heart stop. Pray, she must pray, pray for help. Still no words would come.

Now I lay me down to sleep, I pray the Lord my soul to keep. An English prayer Miss Thomson had taught her. Oh yes, that's it! *May God guard me through the night and wake me with the morning light.* She began to babble out loud in English. 'Thank you, God, for giving me these words, thank you for showing me the way. Dear God, please save Papa. Please don't let these snakes…'

A shrill whistle blast pierced the room. Bertha looked down. There were no snakes. The whistle blew again as a train approached the station, the train from Vienna which was bringing Professor Aschenbach for her father.

The following morning Professor Aschenbach arrived at the apartment at ten o'clock, after putting up at the Hotel Bauer overnight. Dr Bettelheim accompanied him.

Bertha stood at the foot of the bed with her mother and Willi while the doctors examined her father. Like twin vultures, Bertha thought, as they bent over him, bald heads rising out of hunched black-clad shoulders, beaky noses pointing out from broken-veined rough-skinned cheeks, withered eyelids fluttering as they gave each other knowing looks. Hands, a tangle of ropy purplish veins, as spare of flesh as talons, explored her father's chest, tapping it to assess the quality of the sound, applying the stethoscope front and back. They murmured to each other, their exchanges peppered with unfamiliar terms. Pleura. Axilla. Expectoration. Intercostal. Surely if it was something straightforward they would use ordinary words like 'chest' and 'cough' and 'lungs'. Oh dear God, now they were pushing a needle into him, between his ribs. Professor Aschenbach was drawing something out. The syringe was filling up with a yellowish fluid. Bertha turned her head away. She caught Willi's eye. No, she mustn't let him see her flinch. She turned back again. Professor Aschenbach had emptied the fluid from the syringe into a bowl. He swilled it around, eyeing it keenly, then lifted it to his nose, sniffing as if savouring the bouquet of a freshly opened bottle of claret. How could he bear to inhale such a noisome odour? Even from where she stood Bertha was almost vomiting from it.

'As I thought.' Professor Aschenbach laid the bowl down on the bedside table.

The examination had confirmed Doctor Bettelheim's original suspicions – a subpleural abscess. The doctors were now going to proceed with the drainage. Professor Aschenbach explained what was involved. Dr Bettelheim would anaesthetize Mr Pappenheim – they had brought all the necessary equipment – and he himself would perform the operation. A small opening in the chest, the insertion of a tube, aspiration of the purulent matter. It would all be over very quickly and Mr Pappenheim would already be greatly relieved by the time he recovered consciousness. Would the family members like to remain in the room? Willi begged to be excused. He had an engagement in town; in any case he would only be in the way. Selfish milksop! Bertha had seen how he had kept his eyes averted throughout the examination, passing his hand constantly over his nose, trying to ward off the fetid odours. So much for all his cosy confabs with Papa about politics and business. What use was he when he was really needed?

Willi backed out of the room, muttering something incoherent.

Mrs Pappenheim, apologetic and indulgent, excused him. 'He's still only a boy.'

Dr Bettelheim had raised the lid of a black case and was removing a rubber bag with tubes attached to it. Professor Aschenbach had opened his bag, revealing a set of knives and other sharp and pointed instruments.

Bertha moved over to the window. She would not watch this. She looked out. A beautiful summer's day. The Kohn family next door were preparing to set off for a picnic. An open carriage stood ready for them in the street. The

34

coachman was helping the maid to load the hamper. The two little girls ran out of the house shrieking, chased by their black spaniel. Their mother, shielded from the sun by a pale pink parasol, shooed them into the carriage. Their father, following behind, scooped up the dog and handed it in after them.

The room was filling with a strange odour. Sweet and sickly. Like rotten pears. She half turned. Dr Bettelheim was administering the anaesthetic. Her father was already unconscious, a rubber mask over his nose and mouth. Professor Aschenbach was selecting an instrument. Bertha looked quickly away again. Willi had just come out of the house, straw boater perched jauntily on the back of his head. He started to walk down Kaltenbachstrasse, twirling his cane, as insouciant as a spring lamb. How dared he!

That horrible smell. She was feeling faint. The ether must be leaking somewhere. They could all fall unconscious. She looked round again, for reassurance. She could see only the two doctors huddled over her father's body. Suddenly there was a faint gurgling and a swooshing and a stench which swamped the ether smell. Professor Aschenbach was holding a large bowl to the side of her father. It was filling up with a thick, frothy liquid. The bile rose in her throat. She averted her eyes, looking towards her mother. How could Mamma sit there, impassive, observing this vile butchery without a flicker of fear or disgust?

She looked down into the street again. She must think about something else, anything but the scene in the room behind her. The Kohns' carriage had gone. She wondered what Willi was doing. With his stupid friends, probably, those cocky young men he spent all his time with, giving each other knowing looks, laughing at things she didn't find amusing.

A sharp, clean smell cut through the putrid emanations of ether and pus. Professor Aschenbach was washing out the cavity with antiseptic solution, explaining to her mother that this would have to be done regularly over the next few days. Dr Bettelheim would visit daily, he was saying, but Mrs Pappenheim might also like to engage the services of a nurse. A drain would be left in place, with a dressing on top of the wound which would need to be changed several times a day.

'There is no need,' Bertha heard her mother say. 'My daughter and I will do the nursing. If you could just tell us what is required.'

Bertha listened, aghast, to the doctor's instructions. Again she felt bile rise in her throat. Why couldn't Mamma have agreed to hire a nurse?

A bell sounded in the street below. The local dairyman was coming up Kaltenbachstrasse with his cow. He stopped outside the house as Ilse came out with a jug. Bertha watched as they stood in laughing banter, then the dairyman squatted down by the swollen udder. Seizing a teat, he propelled a jet of milk into the jug. Bertha heard again the gush of infected matter from her father's chest, smelt the noisome odour. She closed her eyes, revolted at the thought of drinking the milk, revolted at the thought of ever eating or drinking anything again.

Her mother was thanking the doctors. Dr Bettelheim had removed the mask from her father's face and was packing his equipment. He and Professor Aschenbach would sit with the patient for a while, he said, until he came round and they were sure that his condition was satisfactory.

Mrs Pappenheim turned to her daughter. 'Bertha, I think you should go and get some sleep now. You'll be sitting up again at night.'

Bertha dashed from her father's room to her own, borne on a wave of relief. She lay down on her bed. It was over. The tension in her began to wash away. The room was dim, cool and fresh, the light filtered through the slats of the half-closed blinds. She closed her eyes. But as soon as she did so the scenes in the sickroom reared up again before her. The rubber mask over her father's face, the syringe thrust into his chest, the knife slashing in between his ribs, and that awful stuff that had come pouring out. Surely there must be something terribly wrong for him to have so much nastiness inside him. And even though it had been drained away now, what was to stop whatever it was that had caused it doing the same again? Professor Aschenbach had talked about hope. With full rest and a good diet, he had said, we may hope for improvement. Why had he said improvement? Improvement wasn't the same as being better. He had also talked about the mountain air and the fact that Papa was away from his affairs in the city. But that hadn't stopped him deteriorating so dramatically in the time that he'd been here in Ischl. What good had the rest and mountain air done him in the past few weeks?

Bertha jumped up. She had to talk to someone. She would go down to Klara.

She tiptoed along the hall, towards the front door. She turned the handle quietly, opened the door and stepped out. But no! She was in the room occupied by Miss Thomson.

The governess sat by the window, Percy on her knee, a glass of water in her hand. The dog's long pink tongue slurped in and out of the water, slithering over the rim of the glass. Bertha felt a fresh gush of bile. She pressed her hand to her mouth and rushed from the room, out of the apartment. She ran down to the floor below and rang the bell.

Klara opened the door.

'Bertha, whatever is wrong?'

'Oh, Klara, I'm so frightened.' Tears started to flow. 'Papa is so ill with his lungs and I'm afraid he's going to die.'

'Bertha, you mustn't upset yourself like this.' Klara took Bertha's arm and drew her inside and into her bedroom. She sat her down on the bed and settled down beside her. 'Now tell me all about it.'

Bertha recounted the doctors' visit, the anaesthetic, the rubbery apparatus, the sinister bag of instruments, the cutting of the chest, the worrying conversations conducted in grave voices, the sickroom duties that she was going to have to carry out.

Klara took both of Bertha's hands in hers. 'Bertha, listen to me. You know that Professor Aschenbach is the best doctor in the whole of Austria for lungs. Lots of people get better from illnesses like this. Just wait, by the end of summer when it's time for you all to go back to Vienna he'll be as well as ever he was.'

'But my sister Henriette, she died from tuberculosis. And

37

we've heard of so many people now in Vienna who have had it and died.'

'Bertha, no one has said that your father has tuberculosis. And even if he has, this isn't Vienna. This is Ischl , which is the best possible place for anyone who's ill.'

Bertha felt some of Klara's cheerful confidence begin to flow into her. She listened to Klara prattle on about the pure air and the spas, the baths full of salt and sulphur and all manner of good things. It was true. And it was fourteen years since Henriette had died. Doctors had discovered so many new treatments since then. Why, every day there were new discoveries.

'Perhaps you're right.'

'Of course I'm right.' Klara jumped up. 'Come now, let's go out into the garden and have a game of quoits.'

Bertha dried her eyes and followed Klara downstairs to the quoits pitch at the bottom of the lawn. Once outside her spirits lifted further. The grass was newly mown, its scent still lingering; the bushes blazed with summer colour and the sun shone gaily overhead. The glacier-clad peaks of the distant Dachstein massif stood out clean and pure. A bee, hovering over a yellow rose, buzzed soothingly. The scenes of sickness indoors were a world away.

'Here, you can start.' Klara passed Bertha a handful of quoits.

Bertha took aim and tossed the first of her rubber rings. It fell short of the hob. Her second overshot it. She stood aside to let Klara take her turn. As she waited she looked back up at the house. Surely it was wrong of her to be out playing, amusing herself, when her father was so ill.

'A ringer,' shouted Klara. 'Two points for me.'

If Mamma knew that she was out here instead of resting in her room…. Well, if it was all right for Willi to be out larking around town so could she.

Now it's you again, Bertha.' Klara put her hand on Bertha's arm and shook her gently. 'Bertha, what's wrong?'

'Nothing. I'm just waiting for you to take your turn.'

'But I've taken my turn. Look, I've got a ringer. Didn't

you see?'

Bertha looked over towards the hob. 'Oh, yes. Yes, of course.'

'Right, so it's your turn now. On you go.'

Bertha picked up a quoit. She felt the hard rubberiness of it in her hand. Like the rim of the mask over her father's face. There was even a faint whiff of rubber – or was it ether? – wafting up through her nose, making her gag. She threw it hard, away from her. It flew over the hob and into the bushes at the other side.

Klara laughed. 'You'll have to go and find it now. Mind you don't tear your dress on those roses.'

Bertha stepped carefully through the shrubs. As she bent to pick up the quoit a black snake slithered towards her from under a rose bush. The arm she had stretched out for the quoit turned rigid. Bertha stood still. Time stood still. The bee continued to buzz but Bertha no longer heard it. Nor did she hear Klara call her name.

Klara ran up from behind. She called to her again.

'Bertha, why are you standing there with your arm stretched out? You've been standing like a statue.'

Bertha turned round. 'Have I?'

It seemed to her that she had just woken from a dream. But she could not have been asleep. She was in the garden with Klara. But what was she doing here, in the midst of the rose bushes? She looked at the ground. A blackish branch, long and straight, lay at her feet. Beside it lay a quoit. She remembered now. They were playing quoits. She bent down, her arm loose again, and picked up the quoit. She felt dazed and lethargic, and as if she was shrouded in a veil, cutting her off from the rest of the world. She must explain to Klara, tell her that she needed to rest. But she could not quite find the words.

'K…K…' The name. What was her name? Bertha shook her head, trying to clear the fuzziness. 'K… Klara. Erm, I…'

'What is it, Bertha? Are you all right?'

'I, erm, bed. Need rest.'

'Of course, Bertha. Let's go back in.'

The two girls walked back into the house. Klara took Bertha's arm and tucked it under her own. Bertha said nothing more. Even Klara was silent. They exchanged brief good-byes at Klara's door.

Bertha let herself into the apartment quietly and went to her room without seeing anyone. She lay down on her bed and sank into a profound sleep.

5

August 1880

Dearest Anna

Thank you for all the kind letters you have been sending. It is good of you because I know that Uncle Fritz must keep you very busy. Is he still trying to find a husband for you? You told me he is lonely in Frankfurt. Perhaps he thinks that is because he is unmarried himself and deduces that the only way to avoid loneliness — for everyone — is to acquire a spouse. But I know that you have always set your mind against marriage, preferring to follow your vocation in teaching. You are so fortunate to be able to choose between them, although not, of course, as fortunate as men, who may have both.

We are still in Ischl, as you know, and will stay for three weeks more. I do not know whether I shall feel worse or better when we are back in Vienna. Lovely as Ischl always is, it is so hard to be all the time indoors, knowing that outside life is going on as usual, that others are hiking up the hillsides, boating on the lakes, attending concerts. How I long to exchange the fetid air of Papa's sickroom for the earthy odours of the meadows, the fragrance of the alpine flowers, the clean, fresh scent of the pine trees. And the music. How I miss the music. Often in the evening I hear in the distance an orchestra playing at a summer ball and I feel myself swaying to the rhythms of the dance. I try to appear happy and gay for Papa's sake, to pretend that all will soon be well again, to ignore the blood-stained phlegm, the wheezy breath and the constant fever that tells me otherwise. But I cannot.

I will say no more for fear that you will think me a selfish and unnatural daughter.

With fondest love
Bertha

o~o~o

Bertha picked up *Ischler Wochenblatt* and saw that it was dominated by the week's main event – the Emperor's birthday. She had been so excited about it during her first visit to Ischl in 1871: the parades through the town, the uniformed bands, the pageants, the fireworks, and the air of febrile gaiety which swept over the populace like a forest fire. On the 18th of August, they had been allowed into the Kaiserpark – the only day of the year when it was open to the public. People had come from all over the Salzkammergut region, many of them in traditional costumes. She had been entranced at the sight, as if she was in a foreign country. She was twelve at the time. She remembered the dress she had been wearing. Yellow organza – she had loved the slippery feel of the material between her fingers, could feel it yet – with a scarlet sash and matching ribbon in her hair. The Emperor had mingled with the crowd, shaking hands and thanking people for their birthday greetings. She had stood only a few feet away from him, marvelling at the proximity, as he accepted a bunch of flowers from a little girl, bending down and murmuring gruffly to her, his grey mutton chop whiskers almost touching her hair. She would have liked so much to have had a bouquet to give him herself.

Bertha tossed the paper onto the drawing room floor. She wanted to read no more about the Emperor's birthday.

It was a month now since Papa's operation and it seemed to have made little difference. He rarely left his bedroom and required constant nursing care. Mamma was with him now, helping him with his inhalation treatment. Ilse had just carried in a bowl of steaming water exuding a sulphurous smell.

Bertha heard a door opening and the yapping of Miss Thomson's dog. They must have come back from their walk. Bertha got up and went out to the balcony which ran the width of the drawing room. She had established it as her territory since her father's illness. Papa was in bed most of the time, Willi spent all day out of doors and Mamma was either with Papa or engaged in domestic business with Ilse. Miss Thomson never went onto the balcony uninvited, seeming to regard it as a private family space on which she should not

42

encroach.

Bertha sat down in one of the wicker armchairs. The sky, overcast in the afternoon, had begun to clear, revealing tracts of blue, but the sun was already sinking low. The birthday celebrations were more subdued this year. A torrential downpour had caused flooding in the town and many of the festivities had had to be cancelled. Some of the summer residents had gone further afield to celebrate, and Willi had taken advantage of the opportunity to go to St Wolfgang for a few days where there was to be a lamplit pageant on the lake. Bertha felt both relieved at his absence and resentful at his freedom to carry on as normal. She herself had done little in the past month. Mamma sometimes encouraged her to go into town with Klara and Miss Thomson, to take coffee in the Café Zauner or the Hotel Elisabeth, or to go walking in the woods. But when she did so, she felt guilty about leaving Mamma on her own. Not only that, she found that she no longer enjoyed Klara's facile chatter and would end up feeling irritated with Klara for her insouciance, irritated with herself for being unreasonable and even more irritated than usual with Miss Thomson for just being there.

Tonight there was to be a fireworks display for the Emperor in the meadow at the base of the Siriuskogel. Papa had promised to get up for it. They would have a splendid view from the balcony, he said, as good as a front row seat in the theatre.

Theatre! That was another thing she was missing. Herr Ignaz Brull's opera, *The Golden Cross*, was being performed in the Kurtheater by special request of the Emperor as part of his birthday celebrations. The Emperor himself would be attending along with King Carl of Rumania tomorrow evening. Were it not for Papa's illness Bertha would have been there. It was all too aggravating.

Miss Thomson was in the drawing room now, sitting in a chair by the stove, stitching at something, Percy at her feet. Bertha watched her from the corner of her eye; she did not want to look directly. What must it be like to be in her position? At the thought, she began to feel sorry for Miss

43

Thomson, and then remorseful about her own feelings of irritation with her. There seemed to be little in the governess's life which could afford her pleasure, other than the affection of her little dog. This thought made Bertha feel even gloomier, and then again irritated with Miss Thomson for being the source of this gloominess. She turned her head away.

In the west the sky was streaked with shades of sunset.

The Goldschmidts had also gone to St Wolfgang. They were staying at the Post Hotel, Klara had told her, perched high up on the hill overlooking the lake so they would have the best possible view of the pageant. Bertha imagined them now, on the terrace of the hotel, an orchestra playing in the background, waiters circulating, chatter and laughter. Klara would be toying with her fan. It was never still when it was in her hands. Wasn't she worried about giving out the wrong messages, Bertha had asked her once, noticing that Klara had inadvertently pressed the half-open fan to her lips – an intimation that the owner was willing to be kissed. Klara had merely laughed.

The sunset sky was darkening now to shades of damson and fig. In the drawing room Miss Thomson continued to sew by the light of an oil lamp. She always refrained from lighting the gasolier when she was in the room on her own, as if it was a profligacy to which she was not entitled.

A cannon boomed – once, twice, three times – the sound multiplying as it ricocheted from hill to hill. At the same instant, a ring of bonfires high on the Siriuskogel blazed into life, their flames garlanding an illuminated display in the shape of the Imperial crown standing on the summit. As the echoes faded away, the massed bands gathered together in the meadow began the opening bars of the Kaiserhymne. Now the voices of the regimental choirs were coming in. Bertha could not make out the words but the melody carried from across the river, becoming louder as groups of people throughout the town joined in.

The Kohn family next door had been sitting out on their lawn with guests. Now they were all standing to attention,

44

singing the anthem. A couple of carriages travelling along Kaltenbachstrasse stopped. The occupants – a group of young people in evening dress – spilled out onto the road and lent their voices to the chorus. The first fireworks whooshed skyward, exploding into a constellation of multi-coloured stars. The Kohn children shrieked anew with each exuberant cascade.

Bertha still sat alone on the balcony. Papa didn't feel quite well enough to get up, her mother had said. It would be better if he just stayed in bed. Mamma would sit with him till Bertha came in. Even Miss Thomson hadn't wanted to come outside. Fireworks made her feel nervous, she said.

The Kohns and their friends were organising an impromptu concert now. Gustav Kohn had brought out his violin and was setting up his music stand. Gretel Kohn was preparing to sing a song. The maid was bringing out another bottle of wine. The two younger children were protesting as their governess led them away to bed.

'Bertha, dear.' Bertha turned her head. Her mother was standing at the French windows. 'Papa is dozing. Would you go and sit with him for a while? I'd like to rest now.'

6

5 September 1880

    Siegmund a little less tired today. We have tried to build up his strength so that he can participate in the Rosh Hashanah activities, even if it is only for the evening meal. Dr Bettelheim visited this morning and expressed himself tolerably satisfied with the patient's condition. I have asked him to write to Dr Breuer with a full account of the treatment so far so that the handover of care can take place smoothly on our return to Vienna.

    Frau Rackman brought our dresses for their final fitting this morning. Bertha's was rather loose in the waist – she has lost weight even in the week since she was measured. Fortunately Frau Rackman was able to adjust it on the spot. Willi has just brought his suit back from the tailor, made from his own choice of material. I find it a little loud but thought it better not to make any comment. Siegmund decided just to have a new dressing gown this year as getting fully dressed is too exhausting for him.

    Reb Goldin has offered to come to blow the shofar *for us tomorrow as Siegmund is housebound. Willi will join a group from the synagogue at the riverside in the afternoon and represent the whole family for the* taschlich.

    Willi has borne up well under the burden of his father's illness. It would have been a pity if he had not been able to make the most of the opportunities for enjoyment he has here as he will have to buckle down to his studies when we are back in Vienna next week. Bertha has been of great support to me in nursing Siegmund. I cannot criticise her regarding the exercise of her duties, although I have to say that she has been moody and irritable of late. Of course, she must be missing Klara since the Goldschmidts went back to Vienna at the end of August.

o~o~o

The apartment had a depleted air. All the Pappenheims' personal possessions, apart from a change of clothing and some essential everyday items, had been packed. The trunks stood in the hallway, ready to be taken to the station the next day.

Mr Pappenheim sat out on the balcony in an invalid carriage with a rug over his knees. The doctors had advised him to expose himself to the fresh air as much as possible before returning to Vienna. In the drawing room Bertha, Mrs Pappenheim, Miss Thomson and Gretel Kohn sat around the card table preparing for a game of Tarock. Mrs Pappenheim shuffled the cards as they tried to decide which version to play. Mrs Pappenheim favoured Königrufen but Miss Thomson begged for something more straightforward.

Bertha looked out through the window. It was early afternoon and the sun stood high overhead. She stared up at the summit of the Siriuskogel, remembering the blaze of the bonfires and the drama of the music and the fireworks. But it brought her no pleasure, only feelings of regret that she had not been able to enjoy them. Finally, she heard the others settle upon the Slovenian rules.

Mrs Pappenheim won the first two contracts. Bertha took the third with a king of diamonds and led next with a two of spades. Miss Thomson won the trick with a ten of spades, then led with a Tarock XII.

'No, Miss Thomson.' Mrs Pappenheim lifted the card and handed it back. 'You may only lead with a Tarock if a Tarock has already been played in the game. Correct me if I'm wrong, but I don't think we've seen a Tarock yet in this game.'

'I've never heard of such a rule, I'm sure,' said Miss Thomson. She frowned at the card which had been returned to her, as if holding it responsible for the error.

'It doesn't apply in all versions,' said Mrs Pappenheim, 'but as we're playing the Slovenian we should abide by it.'

'Why does this game have so many rules?' asked Gretel. 'It makes things so complicated.'

What a duffer Gretel was, Bertha thought. If only Klara were still here. Card games were fun with Klara. She had a way of keeping up a pert commentary on the proceedings which made everyone laugh, even Miss Thomson. Then Bertha caught sight of her father and realised that Klara's presence would not make any difference. She had no inclination to laugh now.

Rosh Hashanah had been terrible. Papa had insisted on getting up and coming into the drawing room, wheeled in his invalid carriage, his new dressing gown – a dark chestnut-brown silk – accentuating his pallor. Then Reb Goldin arrived with his *shofar*. The great bellowing blasts, so impressively sonorous in the synagogue, had been deafening in the domestic confines of the drawing room. Bertha had felt her ears might burst with the force of them. Worse followed with the recitation of the *Netaneh Tokef*. When they came to the lines: 'Who shall live and who shall die? Who shall have a full life-span, who shall not?' her eyes had filled with tears. She knew at that moment the answer to that question for the coming year. She had kept her eyes closed, head bowed. Papa must not see her tears.

'Well, then,' Mrs Pappenheim said, 'let's just ignore the rule this time.'

Bertha checked the cards in her hand. Miss Thomson laid down her Tarock XII again. Bertha won the trick with a Tarock XX, scooped up the cards and led with a king of hearts.

Bertha thought again about the words of the New Year greeting: 'May you be inscribed and sealed for a good year.' It had been so difficult for her to say them. Inscribed in the Book of Life, it meant, yet Papa would be dead by next Rosh Hashanah. The singing of the *avinu malkeinu* had been even more agonising. Papa's voice, previously a strong baritone, always deployed with pleasurable gusto, was now no more than a whispering whistle. The melody was bleak, the rhythm slow and repetitive. No matter what the words were, to Bertha's ears it was a song of grief and mourning. She had thought it would never end.

'Gretel, you ought to have played that card in the last contract,' said Mrs Pappenheim as Gretel led with a four of hearts. 'You must follow suit if you can.'

'But I trumped it with a Tarock,' said Gretel. 'Really, this game is so confusing. I can never understand which card I'm supposed to play.'

'I'm inclined to agree,' said Miss Thomson. 'I prefer whist myself. It's much more straightforward.'

Bertha slammed her cards down on the table. 'Let's stop playing then.' Every time they played Tarock, Miss Thomson sooner or later made this same complaint. Why didn't she just refuse to play if she felt like that? In fact, why didn't she just go back to England where she could play whist as much as she liked? 'What's the point of it if we're going to do nothing but argue?'

'Bertha!' Mrs Pappenheim darted her eyes out towards Mr Pappenheim as she spoke. Bertha glared. Gretel clutched her hand of cards, scrutinising them as if reading a book. Miss Thomson's face took on the blank expression it always acquired when family confrontation threatened.

Mrs Pappenheim gathered up the cards. 'It's a shame to sit inside on such a fine afternoon. Miss Thomson, would you accompany Bertha into town? Coffee at the Elisabeth. You too, Gretel. There's no need to add up the scores, I suppose. It's been such a short game.'

Mrs Pappenheim went out on to the balcony to join her husband. The girls waited in silence while Miss Thomson went into her room to fetch a hat.

On the way into town Bertha walked slightly ahead. Gretel liked spending time in conversation with Miss Thomson as she was curious about life in England. Bertha was happy to leave them to it. She had enjoyed Gretel's company earlier in the summer. Gretel was only seventeen, a tall gangling girl with a coltish gait not yet constrained to adult deportment. Her fair hair was always braided and twisted into a coil on the back of her head, a crimped fringe hanging untidily over her eyes. She treated Bertha with an admiring respect, all the more gratifying in that she seemed to find Klara intimidating. Bertha had felt protective towards her, but lately she was finding her naivety and artlessness irritating. Her stream of

49

foolish chatter, her agitated jabbering about everything and nothing, set Bertha's nerves ajangle. Now she was flattering Miss Thomson, complimenting her on her knowledge of English literature because she had read *Oliver Twist* and *Great Expectations*. What did Gretel expect? The woman was English, after all. And you could hardly say that reading a couple of novels by Charles Dickens constituted a knowledge of literature.

Bertha quickened her step. They were on the Esplanade now, with the river to their right. There was the spot where Willi had come to perform the *taschlich*. The thought of it triggered another surge of anger in her. Willi was always so pious when it came to religious ritual. Casting his sins into the water, indeed! If only his faults could be got rid of that easily.

The street was quiet, the cafes almost deserted. Most of the summer residents had gone and there was a flatness in the air as if, with their departure, the town had lost its magic, like Cinderella after midnight.

'Miss Bertha, this is not a race.' Miss Thomson stopped to catch her breath as they arrived at the door of the Hotel Elisabeth. Gretel laughed and said that decidedly she was not a successful person as she had won neither the card game nor the race into town. Bertha said nothing and led the way to the salon overlooking the river.

They took a table by an open window and ordered coffee and pastries. Miss Thomson was asking Gretel about life in Ischl during the winter. Did the river ever freeze? It was not unknown for the River Thames in England to freeze, she said. The last time it happened was in 1814 and then the ice was so thick that it had even been able to bear the weight of an elephant which was led across it. Gretel gasped and said that she could not imagine such a thing.

Bertha pushed aside her plate, her apple strudel only half eaten. Miss Thomson, who always ate with a frank gourmandise which Bertha found off-putting, had already finished her chocolate cake and was wiping her lips with her napkin while suppressing a burp. Gretel was toying with a doughy concoction filled with whipped vanilla custard and raspberries.

The lakes often froze, Gretel said. Lots of people went to Wolfgangsee or Langbathsee to skate. They travelled in horse-drawn sleighs. But she had never gone. She preferred to stay indoors when it was very cold. She stabbed her fork into her pastry. A jet of yellowish custard gushed out, striated with raspberry juice.

Blood-stained mucus dribbling down Papa's chin!

Bertha turned her head away and looked towards the bridge opposite where a band of *klezmer* musicians, clad in shabby black coats and round black hats, had just stopped. They shouted to each other in Polish-accented Yiddish, laughing, as they prepared to play. The two violinists and the cellist tuned their instruments, the flautist gave a few tentative toots and the fifth, who was only a boy, adjusted the strap of his dulcimer around his neck. Then they were ready and their demeanour changed as they began to play, plunging into the solemnity of *avinu malkeinu*.

The first few notes triggered for Bertha the memory of her father trying to sing it two days previously. She could hear the eerie chesty sibilance of his voice now, mingling with the haunting threnody of the *klezmerim*. And a single line of the hymn ran through her mind repeatedly, in time to the music. 'Our Father, Our King, send a complete recovery to the sick of your people.' What was the point of all the singing and praying? None of it made any difference. No matter how fervently they might sing *avinu malkeinu*, Papa would still die.

Gretel was spearing a morsel of dough with the fork now, dipping it in the custardy liquid, raising it to her lips.

Bertha averted her eyes. She felt the apple strudel begin to rise in her throat. She swallowed, stared at the marbled wall, and the marble – a mottled pinkish beige, with a faint tracery of red – came alive. It seemed to rise and fall, in time with her breathing. Her breath quickened, the movement of the marble with it. She must stop looking at the wall.

She dragged her eyes sideward, directing them to the interior of the room, to the pillar in the centre. The pillar was made of the same marble. It too was pulsating. A gigantic

51

lung. It was about to burst. Her lungs were about to burst.

Bertha jumped up, threw down her napkin, rushed to the door and out into the Esplanade. She did not hear the startled cries of Miss Thomson and Gretel. As she emerged, the boy who had been playing the dulcimer came up to her, his hat held out for money. The rest of the *klezmerim* were still playing: a spirited dance tune now, the sort of thing they played at weddings. Merry and frenetic, it seemed to mock Bertha's anguish. Then the cellist and one of the violinists laid down their instruments and joined with the dulcimer player in a circle dance, shouting for joy, clapping their hands and stamping their feet. The remaining violinist and the flautist played faster and louder.

Bertha ran, the music pursuing her. Up Wirrarstrasse, past the Kurhaus, running till she could bear the pain in her chest no longer. She stopped for breath and bent over, her hair tumbling down over her shoulders. The combs had fallen from it. She set off again at a rapid trot, gasping, half sobbing. The frenzied *klezmer* music still rang in her ears even though she knew she could no longer hear it.

Heads turned as she passed.

'Well, I never!' A couple of women coming out of a milliner's looked askance. 'What on earth?'

Left along Salzburgerstrasse, past the parkland around the Hotel Bauer. Only when she reached the slopes of the Kalvarienberg did she stop again. She had left the town behind her now. She began to climb steadily upwards, through the pine trees, until she came to a clearing, a small tract of meadowland, thick with gentian, forget-me-nots and red campion. She sank to the ground and wept.

7

November 1880

Dearest Anna

I can scarcely believe that it is two months now since we returned to Vienna. When I think back to Ischl it seems only yesterday that we were there, and yet each day of those two months has felt like an eternity. It is as if my life is suspended. That is what happens, I know, when there is illness in the family, but knowing it does not make it any easier.

Mamma and I are still busy looking after Papa, although our duties are now lighter as Mamma has engaged two nurses so that there is always someone with him, day or night.

Willi is of little use and Papa's illness has changed nothing of his daily routine. He says, of course, that caring for the sick is women's work. Does he not realise that caring for the sick entails more than the physical tasks of changing dressings, putting fresh sheets on the bed and serving medicines? Papa — and Mamma and I also — need moral support, the support that comes from knowing that we are all willing to help each other in whatever way we can. Do I even have this with Mamma? I don't think so. She is dutiful, to be sure, she does everything that is necessary. But she is so…. the only word I can think of is resigned. I have the feeling that she already thinks of Papa as…. Oh Anna, I can't write the word.

I understand that Mamma is worried about Papa. We are all worried about him. And now she is worried about me too because I have a cough. It's nothing, I tell her. It's just a cough. She worries also because she thinks that I don't eat enough and that I'm always tired. Of course I'm always tired. We're all tired with looking after Papa and worrying about him. And how can I think about eating when I'm so worried? She complains too about my behaviour. She accuses me of being moody, of being absorbed in my own thoughts. She says that sometimes when she speaks to me I don't reply but remain shut away in a world of my own. I don't know if this is true, but don't you think that it would be hardly surprising in the circumstances?

But enough of my sorrows. Although confined to the house myself at present, I do so enjoy hearing what others are doing and your letters are a particular pleasure to me. How I laughed as I read about the fun you had performing Siegfried's Horns. *I had not realised Sachs' plays could be so amusing. It even made Mamma smile when I read it to her.*

We both send our best love to all the Ettlinger family.

Your loving cousin

Bertha

o~o~o

It was past midnight. Bertha had just turned out the gasolier. She no longer sat up with her father throughout the night as she had done in Ischl. Yet the nights brought her no repose. Her anxiety about her father increased once the household had gone to bed, as if she feared that his state would worsen without a family member watching over him. She often got up in the early hours and tiptoed along to his room, listening at the door to reassure herself that he was still alive.

Her face ached. The neuralgia had abated during the summer. Now with the cold weather it was back again. She would take some chloral. But first she must check on Papa. She got up quietly and crept along the hallway.

A blade of light was visible at the edge of her father's door. She bent and put her ear to it. She could hear no sound from within, only the soft thudding tick-tock of the tall mahogany clock at the end of the hall.

Something was amiss. On previous nights she had heard her father clearly, the whining sough of his breath, the burbling wheeze. She pressed her ear closer. If there was anything wrong the nurse would be doing something, surely. But there was no sign of movement. The room was quiet and still.

Bertha's heart thumped. It was racing now with the ticking of the clock, overtaking it, leaving it behind.

What was that? Very faint. A guttural rasp.

He was still alive!

But it could be the nurse. Asleep. Snoring.

54

Bertha's hand trembled as she put it to the door, ready to push it ajar, peek inside.

Suddenly a hand seized the neck of her nightdress, twisting it, pulling her backwards. Another hand gripped her shoulder and started shaking her.

'Get back to bed,' hissed Willi. He pushed her along the hallway. 'You've no business here. Prying! Snooping! Get back to bed.'

Willi grabbed her again and shook her even harder. He opened her bedroom door. As he did so, Bertha turned her head and saw the nurse standing in the open doorway of her father's room. Her lips were moving. She was saying something. Bertha could not hear what it was. She could not hear anything at all, not even the ticking of the clock. Willi thrust her inside. Bertha stumbled to her bed, still trembling, whether from her own fear or from Willi's shaking she did not know.

The next morning Bertha lay on top of her bed, fully dressed. She had breakfasted in her room: a cup of black coffee and half a slice of *zwieback*. Weariness weighed her down, like a damp blanket. Even with the chloral she had found it difficult to sleep after the encounter with Willi. How dared he attack her like that! As if he did anything at all to help Papa, either by day or by night. What was he doing anyway, prowling around at that time? It was certainly not out of concern for any of the family members. More likely the need to throw his weight around. With Papa ill, he thinks he is head of the household and free to act like a petty tyrant, a plump little Napoleon Bonaparte. Thinking back over the events of the night, Bertha realised that Willi had only just got in. He was still wearing his overcoat. She had felt the dampness of rain on it when he pushed up against her, and had smelt schnapps on his breath.

Anger gave way to shame. The idea that she should have been subjected to physical attack by her younger brother! Younger! When they were children she had been able to do with him as she wished. She had always had the upper hand in all their games. He had been the lackey to her princess. There

55

had been those games they used to play with the big wooden horse on wheels. Willi was always the groom. Before Bertha mounted it she would supervise him as he brushed its mane and tail, pretended to pick stones out of its hooves, saddled it up. Then he would draw it along with Bertha riding and showering him with imperious commands. Even when they played with Willi's toy soldiers Bertha dominated, always managing to insist that her army had won. But as they had grown the balance had changed, especially once he had started to outstrip her in height. He would jeer at her, pour scorn on her – just, it seemed, for the pleasure it gave him. Like the time he had found her with his Greek primer, trying to decipher the unfamiliar characters. 'Don't bother,' he told her loftily, as if it was something that must be beyond her. And now he had had the temerity to shake her and hiss at her as if she were a chambermaid caught in some underhand act.

She should get up. The newspapers would have been delivered by now. She swung her legs over and bent to put her shoes on, then hesitated. Miss Thomson would be in the drawing room, stitching one of those samplers she was always working on for her many nieces. Better just to stay where she was. She lay back down again.

Before her father's illness, she had often gone riding in the Prater in the morning. She must go riding again. She would tell Mamma that she was going tomorrow. She would insist. She might have been there now. The trees would be glorious at this time of year – russet and gold. She closed her eyes and sensed the rise and fall as she trotted along the Hauptallee on Greta, her favourite black mare. She clicked with her tongue, signalled to the horse with her left heel and Greta broke into a canter. She felt the clean, sharp chill of the wind on her face, heard the clippety-clop of Greta's hooves and the rustle of fallen leaves.

A man's voice. Doctor Breuer. He had just come out of her father's bedroom. A few minutes later she heard her mother bid him goodbye. Bertha got off the bed and went through to the drawing room. Her mother was sitting at the occasional table in the far corner, in conversation with Miss

56

Thomson.

'What did Doctor Breuer say, Mamma?' Bertha coughed, a harsh barking sound. 'How did he find Papa?'

'Much the same.'

It seemed to Bertha that her mother's eyes only skimmed her own and then locked on to Miss Thomson's. What had the two of them been talking about, huddled together all hugger-mugger like that? Outrageous to think that Miss Thomson might be privy to more information about her father's health than herself! The woman was little more than a servant, after all. It was no business of hers.

Bertha said nothing, but fixed her mother with an enquiring stare. Mrs Pappenheim began to rummage in the key basket which lay on the table. Papa was to start a new treatment, she said. Some kind of inhalation. A sulphur gas, or some such thing. She picked out a key and checked the label. 'Ah, here it is. The linen closet. So you see, he has the best of care.'

Miss Thomson was engrossed in threading a needle.

'Oh and Bertha.' Mrs Pappenheim opened her sewing box and took out a square of batiste. 'I spoke to Doctor Breuer about your cough. He said it doesn't sound like anything serious but he's going to examine you when he visits Papa tomorrow.'

Oh, not this again. Bertha sank down on the sofa.

'Please don't fuss so, Mamma.' How she wished her mother would stop nagging about this cough. She must change the subject, talk about her plan to go riding.

'Now tomorrow I'd…..' Bertha stopped speaking, her lips and tongue static in the I configuration, her eyes fixed.

'Bertha!' Mrs Pappenheim laid aside the batiste and went over to the sofa. She sat down. 'Bertha, what is it? What are you staring at?' She looked in the direction of Bertha's gaze herself, as if expecting to see some extraordinary sight. Miss Thomson looked on, passive as a spectator at a play.

Mrs Pappenheim seized Bertha's shoulder and shook it. 'Bertha, speak to me please. Please speak.'

Bertha's features relaxed.

'… like to go riding with Klara. I haven't been for such a long time and…'

'Bertha, you know I don't think you should go riding when your father's so ill. But tell me, why did you stop talking just now? Are you unwell? Were you feeling dizzy? Please explain.'

'What are you talking about, Mamma?' Bertha coughed again. 'I was just telling you I'd like to go riding.'

'But, Bertha, you stopped in the middle of a sentence. You looked…' Mrs Pappenheim groped for words. 'I don't know…. transfixed. What was going through your mind?'

'Nothing was going through my mind. Except that I'd like to go riding.' Bertha frowned. Her mother might as well be talking in riddles for all the sense she was making, and now she was staring at her in perplexity as if she was the one who was talking in riddles.

Mrs Pappenheim got up and returned to her seat at the table. 'Oh well, perhaps it's just fatigue. You must get more sleep.' She selected a skein of red thread from the sewing box and snipped a length off. 'But I must insist that you don't go riding for the present. You may invite Klara to come for tea instead. Now why don't you go and play the piano. Leave the door open so that Papa can hear you.'

Bertha sighed. Much as she enjoyed music she hated playing it herself. All those tedious hours of being forced to sit at the piano when she was a child, drilled in scales, practising the same piece over and over again. Music could only be enjoyed when it was perfect – no false notes or wrong timing. Why couldn't Mamma have asked Miss Thomson to play instead? She was always saying what an accomplished pianist she was.

Bertha glanced crossly at the governess but went over to the piano. She could scarcely refuse when there was so little enjoyment in her father's life at present. If she could give him pleasure by playing a few tunes, so be it. She sat down, pulled out some music at random and started to play Chopin's Grande Valse Brillante in A minor.

Her fingers picked out the notes of the plangent opening

bars in a slow, mournful plod. It was more like a dirge than a waltz. One could never dance to this. The melancholy tones of loss and longing reverberated with her inner gloom, magnifying it, drawing it out. She felt tears gather in her eyes. Briefly the music skipped – almost into gaiety, a sober gaiety – for a few bars; but now it was sinking back into lethargic sadness. She could bear it no longer. She must have something more cheerful. She stopped and picked out some Strauss music.

She plunged into the merry melody of the Tritsch-Tratsch polka, giving the soaring chords verve and panache. She recalled it played at the July ball in Ischl. How commanding the conductor had seemed, ramrod straight and debonair, the orchestra springing to life at the mere flick of his wrist and the guests galvanised into a kicking, swirling mass of colour and laughter. As her hands danced over the keyboard her feet burned with a desire to dance around the room. Spurts of joy flashed through her, like little fireworks. She pressed her foot down on the loud pedal and quickened her pace. She spread her right fingers for a four-note chord.

Suddenly the black keys she was spanning rose up from the keyboard, tangling with her fingers. Black vipers! Her right arm stretched out stiff. Her mouth opened, but the scream it was to frame stayed stuck in her throat. Her left hand raced ahead over several bars while her right, fingers rigid, held down keys for notes which had already died away.

Mrs Pappenheim put down her embroidery. 'Really, Bertha, please choose a simpler piece if you can't do better than that.'

Bertha removed both hands from the piano. The right arm had returned to normal, the keys were back in place.

A dream. She seemed to have had a dream. She must have nodded off for a second. She could not remember now what the dream was. Just that it was something frightening. She was tired, so tired.

'I'm sorry, Mamma. I just don't feel like playing.' Bertha sat on at the piano, drained. 'Perhaps Papa would like me to read to him.'

'I'm sure he would. Why don't you go and ask him.'

Bertha put the sheet music away and closed the piano lid. Her head had begun to ache, her neck and shoulders too.

She braced herself as she entered the bedroom. The very air, with its mingled odours of sweat and laudanum, iodine and soiled dressings, beef tea and quinine, spoke of sickness. Her father lay wan and shrunken in the canopied four-poster bed, his features sharp under the taut skin, his shoulder blades sticking up like bird wings under his nightshirt.

'Hello, poppet.' The voice was hoarse, the eyes sunk deep in their hollows. 'Was that you I heard massacring Strauss?'

'I'm sorry, Papa. I'm not in the mood for music today. Would you like me to read to you?'

'If you like, sweetheart.' He struggled to speak, shifted his head on the bank of pillows. 'Just ... a short while.' The words were faint, a mere modulation of his breath. 'Something simple. Some poetry, perhaps.' He closed his eyes, exhausted. 'Heine. I've always liked Heine's 'Hebrew Melodies'.

Bertha fetched a book of Heine's poetry from her room. She sat down in a low chair at the foot of her father's bed, bending her head over the book to shut out the sight of the bowls and swabs, the bottles and syringes, all the paraphernalia of disease. She opened the book and started to read 'Princess Shabbat', the tale of a prince, transformed by a witch into a dog but restored to human status each Friday evening for the Shabbat celebrations. Her voice quavered at first, then grew firmer, steadied by the strong, simple rhythm of the poem.

> But on every Friday evening,
> On a sudden, in the twilight,
> The enchantment weakens, ceases,
> And the dog once more is human.

She glanced towards her father. His eyes were closed, a slight smile around his mouth. 'Are you awake?' she whispered. There was no reply. She read on.

> And his father's halls he enters
> As a man, with man's emotions,

60

Head and heart alike uplifted,
Clad in pure and…..

The words wobbled before her eyes, out of focus. Bertha strained to see but could make out only a jumble of black marks. She squeezed her eyes tight shut. It must be something to do with the headache. She imagined to herself the first line of the verse: 'And his father's halls he enters'. She could visualise the words in her mind. She opened her eyes again. 'And his father's halls he enters', she read. Her vision had cleared.

Had it even been blurred in the first place? She was so tired. Perhaps she had nodded off again, had another fleeting dream. A dream in which she had been looking at a book filled with black squiggles. She felt a cough rising. She swallowed, trying to quell it, fearing to wake her father. The urge grew stronger, scratching in her chest, rising in her throat, insistent. She slipped out of the room.

Back in her own room, Bertha lay down on the chaise-longue. The stench of the sickroom lingered in her nostrils. The wheezy whisper still sounded in her ears. She must think of something else.

She opened the book of poems again and skimmed over 'Of Pearls and Stars'. It described a love more precious than the stars, greater than the ocean and the heavens above. Could this be what Mamma had once felt for Papa? Of course not. What a stupid question. Their marriage had been an arranged one. Love came after marriage, Mamma had once said to her.

But she had not said what kind of love. Sometimes, when she was dancing, Bertha felt buoyed up by surges of excitement. Was that it? But in that case, why did she feel that way regardless of the man she was dancing with? And that feeling was surely but the palest flicker – no, not even that – compared with the emotion described in these poems.

She stood up, holding out her arms as if in the embrace of a dancing partner, willing herself to re-experience the sensations. She closed her eyes, the better to imagine herself in a ballroom, and started to hum 'Tales from the Vienna Woods', tiptoeing in triple time to the swell and the sway of her own music.

Nothing.

Opening her eyes, she caught a glimpse of herself in the wardrobe mirror, arms still outstretched, and was shot through with a flash of embarrassment and a sense of foolishness.

Bertha sat down and started to read 'Princess Shabbat' again.

> In Arabia's book of fable
> We behold enchanted princes
> Who at times their form recover,
> Fair as first they were created.
> The uncouth and shaggy monster
> Has again a king for father.

Bertha remembered how, when she was very small, her father used to recite verses from the poem on Friday evenings as they waited for the signal that Shabbat had begun. She would be wearing one of her best dresses – usually velvet – with her hair freshly washed and tied back with ribbons, and Papa would bounce her up and down on his knee, in time to the rhythm of the verses. 'My little Shabbat Princess', he used to call her. And he was her king, she had thought then, her very own king. She had especially liked the terrifying verse towards the end which spoke of the prince's shudders as he felt the icy fingers of the witch upon his heart. She would pretend to feel the fear of the prince and snuggle into her Papa for comfort. He would laugh and hug her tight.

Bertha read on to the end of the poem, seduced anew by the vitality of its rhythm. When she had finished, she lay back, dwelling on the story of the Jewish prince, revelling in the delicate tracery of images created by Heine.

I shall try a story like that, Bertha thought, something along similar lines. She got up and went to sit at her escritoire. Taking her pen and notebook she began to jot down her ideas.

A girl, Amalia, falls foul of a witch who changes her into…. Not a dog, no…. Bertha tapped her teeth with the pen. A horse? Yes. A beautiful palomino filly. She scribbled a

62

description of it – light golden coat, cream-coloured mane and tail.

The horse is allowed to turn back into a human once a year, for one of the Jewish festivals. Rosh Hashanah? No, too solemn. Simchat Torah would be better. Lots of dancing and singing.

Now she would have to describe Amalia's life as a horse. Bertha pursed her lips and frowned. Should she make it a wild horse? Or a carriage horse, trudging the streets all day, beaten by a cruel coachman? Or perhaps a horse in the Spanish Riding School, drilled in all those impossibly intricate movements?

Ah, she had it! The horse would have wings, like Pegasus in the Greek myth.

Amalia loves the power that the wings give her. She can fly anywhere. Out of Austria, across snow-laden mountains, swooping over deserts, high above tropical jungle, into the clouds even. She glories in the speed, the feeling of being above and beyond all earthbound things. Each Simchat Torah the witch waits for Amalia to present herself for her annual day of release. Amalia never comes.

Bertha continued to write. But now the words wavered as she wrote, the letters became fuzzy, indistinct.

A stab of fear. This was the second time.

She blinked rapidly and turned to look upwards, out of the window. Outside there was only a blue expanse of sky, not even the outline of a cloud to be discerned. She gazed at it, not daring at first to look back down. The she closed her eyes. Opening them slowly – just a slit – she looked towards the door and saw its solid rectangle. Sideways to the wall. The gold and cinnamon tracery stood out clear on the pink background. Finally she looked back at her notebook. The letters had fallen back into their familiar shapes, like the pattern of a kaleidoscope.

8

Bertha buttoned up the front of her blue merino dress. She fastened the lace collar at her throat.

'Well, Miss Bertha, I don't think this cough of yours is any cause for alarm.' Dr Breuer replaced his stethoscope in its case. 'The lungs are clear and there's no sign of fever. However, I shall check you again next week. Until then.' He bowed slightly and picked up his hat and bag.

Bertha watched as her mother accompanied the doctor from the drawing room. He had questioned her closely about her daily habits. Was she eating less than usual? Had she lost weight? Did she feel tired when she woke up in the morning? Did she find it difficult to fall asleep? Was her system regular? And her monthly flow? Abundant? Scanty? Then Mamma had complained to him about what she called her emotional caprices, and about her sometimes failing to respond when spoken to. What did she expect when they were all so distracted by Papa's illness? How could life carry on as normal in the circumstances?

Mrs Pappenheim was talking to Dr Breuer in the hall. Although the words were indistinct, Bertha detected an anxious tone in her mother's voice. She slipped over to the door and put her ear to the jamb.

'How am I to cope with this, doctor? My husband bedridden and gravely ill, and now my daughter.'

What could she mean? What could Dr Breuer have said that he had withheld from her? She pressed her ear closer to the crack. How exasperating! She was the patient. She was the one who should be informed of his opinions.

'And please don't tell me that the cure is marriage. At a time like this, with her father so ill….'

What could marriage have to do with this? Bertha strained to catch the deeper tones of Dr Breuer.

64

'….old-fashioned notions about hysteria…... I, for one, do not believe ……. remedied in the marriage bed.'

So, she was suffering from 'hysteria'. But what was all this talk about marriage as a remedy? Bertha thought back to people she knew who had been diagnosed with hysterical illness. There was Mamma's cousin who spent months in a clinic having hydrotherapy – ice baths and blister baths and so on. There was also some talk of electrotherapy. She hoped she wouldn't have to have that. Her schoolfriend Alice who had a hysterical cough had endured torture when doctors applied a faradic brush to her throat.

Dr Breuer's voice rumbled on.

'…. moral therapy…. allow the patient to talk freely…... emotional turmoil….And a second course of treatment…..' Footsteps obscured the rest of his words.

'But Dr Breuer…... public entertainment…... surely not suitable…. young woman in poor health.'

What on earth could Dr Breuer have said to elicit such a reaction from her mother? Bertha could not make out his reply. But she sensed from the tone that it was reassuring. How annoying to have to rely on her mother to relay the doctor's words to her.

A door opened and closed again as the voices faded. They must have gone into the parlour. Bertha hovered, wondering if she dared slip across the hall to listen at the parlour door. No. It would be so humiliating if she were caught. She returned to the sofa. When her mother came in some ten minutes later she was reading the *Neue Freie Presse*. She raised her head.

'What were you talking about with Dr Breuer? Am I allowed to know? You were talking about me, I presume.'

'Please don't take that tone with me, Bertha.' Mrs Pappenheim sat down and took up her tatting. 'It's only proper that a young woman's health should be discussed in private by her mother and her doctor.'

'But Mamma, I'm an adult now!'

'You may be twenty-one, Bertha, but until you have a husband you're the responsibility of your parents and it's up to us to look after you.'

Bertha looked at her mother's careworn face, her bowed shoulders, and regretted having spoken with asperity.

'Well, what did Dr Breuer say?'

'He feels that you're overwrought.' Mrs Pappenheim tied two threads together and tugged the knot tight. 'He believes that it will help if you can talk with him about your anxieties.' She looped the thread round her fingers and started to pass the shuttle to and fro. 'Then for this cough, he thinks it's a hysterical one and he proposes a new treatment. I don't know that I'm altogether happy about it. He'd like to put you into a hypnotic state in which by some means or other he'll put a stop to the coughing.'

Bertha sat bolt upright. So that was what her mother had been referring to when she talked about public entertainment.

'Oh, how thrilling, Mamma!'

'Calm yourself, Bertha. This is a serious matter.' Mrs Pappenheim snipped a loose end of thread. 'Dr Breuer assures me that it's a perfectly respectable procedure, although I confess that if he weren't such a highly regarded doctor I would never have agreed to it. Of course, normally your father would have discussed this with Dr Breuer but given his present state of health we feel that it's better not to burden him with it. As it is, we'll try it and see what happens.'

Bertha was paying scant attention to her mother's words. 'It must be the same kind of treatment that Cousin Anna told me about.' She perched on the edge of the sofa, taut with excitement. 'Don't you remember, Mamma? That book she read by an English woman who was cured by hypnotism. I'm sure I told you about it. It was after I'd written to Anna about Mr Hansen's performance. '

Mrs Pappenheim looked up, frowning. 'I don't recall.'

'You must do. Just wait. I'll get the letter.'

Bertha jumped up and went to her bedroom. It was all coming back to her now. Harriet Martineau, the woman's name was. She'd been ill for five years – some kind of female illness with pain and exhaustion and lack of appetite. Doctors had been unable to cure her and opiates were her only source of relief. Finally she had tried hypnotism – mesmerism they called it then – and experienced a miraculous recovery. Not only that, she found that just by imitating the mesmerist's actions she was herself able to bring about the same curative effects in others. Why, she had even taught her maid how to mesmerise and the maid had successfully put Miss Martineau into a trance.

Bertha opened her escritoire and took out a bundle of letters written in Anna's bold forward-sloping hand. She rummaged quickly through them, eager to refresh her memory with everything that Anna had said on the subject. Finding the one she wanted, written in March of that year, she took it through to the drawing room. She sat down beside her mother.

'Here it is, Mamma.' Bertha started to read the letter but found that the words, which she had just read in her bedroom, were now indecipherable. She shook her head and tried to refocus her eyes. In vain. She burst into tears.

'Bertha, what on earth is wrong?'

The letter slipped from Bertha's hand and fell to the floor. 'I can't see, Mamma. I can't read. It's all just a jumble. I'm so afraid.'

Mrs Pappenheim laid down her shuttle. 'Now Bertha, don't distress yourself. You're probably suffering from eye strain. You do far too much reading. Perhaps you need eye-glasses. We'll get your eyes checked.'

Bertha closed her eyes and lay back against the sofa. She felt the ache of neuralgia coming on, accompanied by a headache and a stiffness in her neck.

o~o~o

28 November 1880

The first day of Hannukah. It will be a quiet time for us this year. Of course, the celebration is mainly for children so we will not be much affected

Dr Breuer visited this morning and examined Bertha. He could find no physical cause for her cough and has diagnosed her as suffering from hysteria. It is a relief to know that she does not have a serious illness. He proposes to spend time with Bertha, encouraging her to talk about her worries and fears. It is all part and parcel of this fashion for 'catharsis' which has become so popular with physicians in the treatment of neurasthenia and the like. We have Professor Jacob Bernays to thank for it, apparently. His book outlining his interpretation of Aristotle's ideas on the subject has been the talk of the salons this past year, I believe. As for the hypnotic treatment he proposes, I am still in two minds about it. It will facilitate the work of suggestion that a physician normally resorts to in cases like Bertha's, Dr Breuer tells me. We shall see. Bertha became quite over-excited at the prospect and got carried away over an account of a hypnotic cure described by some English woman which Anna Ettlinger had sent her. The woman is apparently a journalist, and with political pretensions, which Anna seemed to think gave her report added credibility.

I fear that Anna often agitates Bertha with her talk about women's rights and girls' education. It is little wonder that Anna is almost forty and still unmarried. Her own choice, apparently, and a disappointing one for her parents. Of course, given the company she keeps, it is perhaps not surprising. Clara Schumann and Johannes Brahms and their friends are not the sort of people I would want my own daughter to mix with.

Tomorrow we are to visit Dr Schneider for an eye examination. It will be unfortunate if Bertha is found to need eye-glasses but health is more important than appearance.

Siegmund is no worse today. At this stage, it is the most that can be hoped for.

9

December 1880

Dearest Anna

You cannot imagine how your latest letter was appreciated here in Vienna. We had such a quiet time over Hannukah, as you will understand, but we were most entertained by your tales of the little ones and their mischief with the dreidel *games and their gluttony with the* potato *latkes. I recounted it all to Papa and he said it took him back to the days when Willi and I were tiny. It did Papa good, I think, though otherwise he is in very weak condition.*

As regards my own health, I hardly know where to begin, and I do not know whether I should be alarmed or excited. In fact, I am both.

First of all the exciting news. I am to be hypnotised!

Dr Breuer examined me last week because of this cough which Mamma has been worried about. He has diagnosed it as hysterical and proposes to treat it with hypnotism. Mamma does not quite approve but has agreed because she holds Dr Breuer in the greatest esteem. What do you think, Anna? Perhaps you do not know what to think as it is something quite new for all of us. Rest assured that I will give you a full account of everything that takes place, and then at the end you will surely be in a position to form an opinion.

And now the alarming news. Over the past few days such strange things have been happening to my body. It is as if one half of it is closing down. First it was my neck, then my right arm and now my right leg. I cannot walk without support and I can barely hold a pen to write. My left eye turns inward and I must close it when I read otherwise I cannot make out the words.

Mamma sent for Dr Breuer who came at once. He examined my limbs with various instruments, pulling and prodding and bending and pricking. He assured us that there is no cause for alarm, that these new symptoms are consistent with his original diagnosis. They are, he says, all classic signs of hysteria, as is the trouble with my eyes. This surprised me as Mamma took me to an oculist last week and he was of the opinion that there was a muscular impairment which could be due to some underlying disease, but when Mamma showed Dr Breuer the report he discounted this. The fact that I have other symptoms which are hysterical in origin is sufficient ground, apparently, to believe that the visual disturbance is also hysterical.

After the examination I had a long conversation with Dr Breuer. He wanted me to tell him about all my worries. He thinks that I have been unable to talk about them openly for fear of disturbing Mamma and Papa and that this has meant that they have had to find expression in other ways.

I felt unwilling to talk at first, all the more so as Miss Thomson was present. However, she sat by the door at some distance from us and Dr Breuer and I spoke with our backs to her and in low voices. I soon began to feel easier and relieved at being able to talk freely.

Dr Breuer encouraged me to tell him about any matters which might be weighing on my mind. Of course, the first thing I thought of was Papa. Then I felt I could not bear to talk about it because I did not want to think about it. But I do think about it. I think about it all the time. Then before I could stop myself I found that I was telling Dr Breuer about my secret wish, how sometimes I wish that Papa would die of an apoplexy or a heart attack so that it would all be over very quickly, so that we do not have to live in constant mourning even though he is not yet dead, and with him suffering so much. I told him too how I think I am wicked for thinking these things (I hardly dare confess it even to you, dear Cousin – indeed I would not do so had Dr Breuer not already assured me that it is not wicked), although I am sure it would be best for everyone, especially for Papa.

Dr Breuer said these are very natural feelings, that they stem only from concern for Papa. He also tried to put my mind at rest about my fear that Mamma would think me very wicked if she knew what I thought. Mamma has her own way of dealing with her distress which may not be the same as mine, he said, and there is no need for her to know my innermost thoughts if I feel they would upset her.

The problem is that Mamma misconstrues my innermost thoughts. She accuses me of being irritable when in fact I am just so worried I can hardly think at all. And she accuses me of ignoring her when she is speaking to me. She says I stop talking sometimes in the middle of a conversation and look as if I have seen a ghost. Even Papa has said this.

70

Dr Breuer says that this kind of behaviour is understandable in the circumstances. It is all a manifestation of my anxiety. Our conversations together will help to relieve this anxiety, he says, and thus bring about an improvement in my mood and my health.

I do so hope that Dr Breuer is right about my symptoms being hysterical. I must believe him. I must believe that I will be recovered soon.

Tomorrow we are to start the hypnotic treatment. I shall stop now and add a postscript to this letter later so that I can tell you all about it.

With fondest love
Bertha

o~o~o

Bertha tried to sit up. Her head would not rise from the pillow. She eased her weight onto her right side, trying to manoeuvre herself with the support of her right elbow. The arm had no strength in it. She shifted over to the left and managed to raise herself slightly but the lack of balance brought her down again. She reached out and yanked at the tasselled bell pull at the side of her bed.

Ilse arrived.

'Please help me to sit up, Ilse.' Bertha coughed. 'I feel so stiff. My neck... I can't move my head. And my arm.'

'Of course, Miss Bertha.'

The maid slipped her arm under Bertha's shoulders and drew her towards herself. Holding her upright, she piled the pillows up and settled Bertha back against them.

Bertha groaned and closed her eyes. 'Ask my mother to come in, please.'

'Yes, Miss Bertha.' The maid went out of the room.

A moment later Mrs Pappenheim appeared.

'Bertha, what's going on? Ilse told me you can't move.'

Bertha raised her left arm and tried to heave her whole body up; with no success.

'No, I can't move. You see? Mamma, you must do something.' Bertha's voice spiralled in panic. 'I'm so frightened. What's happening to me?'

'Dr Breuer's coming this morning. There's no need to

71

worry.' Mrs Pappenheim smoothed the bedcover and patted the pillows.

No need to worry! How could Mamma say such a thing when here she was, stuck in bed, unable even to sit up? There was every need to worry. Patting the pillows wasn't going to help.

Now she was fussing with the curtains. She always had to have them falling just so, with a pleasing fullness to the folds. 'It's probably the weather', she was saying. 'We all feel a little stiff when winter sets in. We just have to make sure there are no draughts in the room. I'll ask Ilse to find an old cushion and make a draught excluder for the bottom of the door.' She tugged at one of the tie-backs and bunched the chintz. 'And I'll get her to bring you some breakfast. You'll feel better with something in your stomach.'

'I don't want anything in my stomach!' Bertha thumped the bed with her left arm. 'Go away. Leave me alone.'

'Bertha, I know you feel ill but I can't allow you to speak to me in that way. If your father knew you were behaving like this....'

'Well, he doesn't know, does he? Go away!'

Bertha closed her eyes as tears trickled out of them. She kept them closed when Ilse brought in the breakfast tray and laid it on the table beside her bed. She did not want to speak to anyone. She did not dare give voice to the fears which were crowding in on her, increasing with each new symptom that developed. How could Dr Breuer be certain that there was nothing seriously wrong with her? How could he be so sure that her squint was hysterical when the oculist – who specialised in eye diseases after all – thought that it was possibly a sign of some other illness? There were so many sick people whom doctors could do nothing to help, people with symptoms like her own, who became confined to wheelchairs, or even permanently bedridden. How would she cope? How would Mamma cope? She might even die. Mamma would then have lost three daughters. And she was going to lose her husband soon. Mamma would be left all alone in her grief. She would have only Willi, for all the good that he would be to

72

her. Bertha began to imagine all the other dreadful things that might happen to her. She might go blind. Then she wouldn't be able to read. She would be reliant on Mamma and Miss Thomson to read to her and they would only read the silly boring books that they liked themselves. She wouldn't be able to go to the theatre, or to balls. She wouldn't even be able to crochet or sew. At the thought of this she found that these activities no longer seemed so tedious after all. Please, God, she thought, please don't let me go blind and I will never complain about sewing again. Exhausted, she drifted back into sleep.

An hour later the rasp of the opening door roused her.

'Miss Bertha?'

Bertha opened her eyes and looked up. Dr Breuer was standing beside the bed, her mother and Miss Thomson behind him. He sat down.

At the sight of him, the anxieties which had been tormenting her earlier retreated. Dr Breuer's air of grave concern reassured her without any need for words. It was an air which spoke of purposeful support, allowing no room for unease.

'Good morning, doctor.'

'Miss Bertha, your mother tells me that you have some new symptoms. Could you describe them for me?'

'I can't move my right arm at all now, or my right leg. They feel numb. And my neck is stiff. I can't lift my head from the pillow.'

Dr Breuer took Bertha's head in his hands and moved it from side to side, then flexed her arms and legs.

'I think you might feel better if you were to get up.'

'But I can't move.'

'We can help you. Mrs Pappenheim, if you don't mind?'

Mrs Pappenheim drew back the covers and helped Dr Breuer ease Bertha out of the bed. They settled her into the upholstered chair beside the bed.

'How do you feel now?' Dr Breuer asked.

'The same.'

Dr Breuer glanced at the untouched breakfast tray 'And

your appetite? Are you eating?'

'Not at all, doctor.' Mrs Pappenheim broke in before Bertha could speak. 'How she can expect her health to improve when she's denying her body the nourishment it needs, I really don't know. But perhaps she'll explain this to you, if not to me. I'll be in the drawing room if you need me.'

Mrs Pappenheim left the room. Miss Thomson moved the chair from the escritoire to the door and sat down on it. Dr Breuer brought over the chair from the dressing table for himself and positioned it so that he was facing Bertha, with his back to Miss Thomson and blocking her from Bertha's view.

'Oh, doctor, I'm so afraid that I'm going to be paralysed for the rest of my life.' Bertha stopped to cough. 'I didn't want to say this in front of Mamma.' Bertha's voice had dropped to a whisper. She was afraid that Miss Thomson might overhear and repeat her words to her mother. 'It only upsets her.' She coughed again. 'What makes you so sure that this is a hysterical illness?'

'Let me put your mind at rest about this right away, Miss Bertha. You've had a thorough examination and I can find no sign of anything other than nervous disorder. I'd like you to be able to relax more. And of course, your mother's right about eating. We must try to find ways of overcoming your aversion to food.'

Dr Breuer leaned forward with his forearms on his thighs and his hands clasped, reducing the distance between them. His eyes were a light blue, Bertha noticed, with amber glints around the pupil. There was a faint mottling of grey on the lower lids.

'How are things between you and your mother now? You mentioned last time we spoke that she complained of you being irritable with her.'

'Yes, well, you see yourself that she doesn't understand. She thinks that I'm deliberately making life more difficult for her, or at least that I'm not trying to….'

Bertha stopped, her features still, her eyes fixed on Dr Breuer's left shoulder.

'Not trying to do what? Can you speak to me, Miss

74

Bertha?'

There was no reply. Dr Breuer got up and walked round to the other side of the bed, all the time watching Bertha. He picked up a photograph of Mr Pappenheim and walked back again. Bertha had not moved. He sat down and held the photograph in front of her face.

'Who is this?' he asked.

There was no eye movement, no flicker of recognition. Dr Breuer waited.

'….make life easier for her.' Bertha continued to speak as if there had been no break in the sentence. 'I think that deep down she thinks I'm just pretending to be ill, or that I could make myself better if I tried.'

'Miss Bertha, why did you stop speaking just now?'

'I didn't stop speaking. I've been telling you why Mamma complains about me.'

'Didn't you tell me on my last visit that she says that you sometimes ignore her, that you stop speaking and don't seem to hear her.'

'Yes, that's right.'

'Well, that's what you've just done with me.'

'Oh?' Bertha frowned, perplexed. Had she had a momentary distraction? She scrutinised her most recent thoughts and could find nothing but what she had been saying to Dr Breuer about her mother. 'Why should I have done that?'

'Shall we try to find out?

Bertha nodded.

Dr Breuer moved his chair so that he was closer to Bertha and directly opposite her.

'We'll start the hypnosis now. Just a short session to see how you respond.'

Bertha looked at Dr Breuer apprehensively. 'I… I hardly know what to expect, Doctor.' She felt as if a door was about to open and she had no idea what lay on the other side. 'Can you tell me? What am I going to feel?

'That I can't say exactly,' Dr Breuer said. 'People experience the process differently. Some pass directly into a form of sleep, others have dream-like sensations or simply a very deep state of relaxation. But I assure you that there will be nothing disagreeable.'

Bertha hesitated. Dream-like sensations? It might be a bad dream.

'But what if the dream is a nightmare?' Her voice was quavering now.

Dr Breuer smiled. 'There will be no nightmare. I promise you. I'll be talking to you all the time, encouraging your body back to health.'

A memory flashed through Bertha's mind. She was four years old. Papa was tossing her in the air. As she soared from his hands she thrilled with a delicious terror: the fear of the height and the joyous anticipation of being caught up again in his arms as she came down. The two in one.

'Do you trust me?' Dr Breuer asked.

Bertha nodded.

'Now just do as I say.' He spoke slowly and quietly. 'Look at me, Miss Bertha.' Bertha stared steadily ahead, taking in the high forehead, the fine reddish-blond hair – thinning on top – the aquiline nose and the thick square-cut beard which just covered the knot of the cravat, as if imprinting them on her mind.

'Keep looking at me.' Dr Breuer paused and then carried on, his voice even quieter. 'You are beginning to feel tired. Your limbs are heavy. Your body is relaxed. You are feeling drowsy, so drowsy. Can you hear me, Miss Bertha?'

Bertha's lips moved in the faintest of whispers. 'Yes.'

'You are resting now. You are relaxed. All your cares are slipping away. You yearn to fall asleep.'

The light in the room was changing, as if an ethereal dusk was falling. The objects in Bertha's field of vision were bathed in a luminescent greyness, the man in the chair facing her transforming into a benevolent ghostly patriarch.

'We are going to work on your worries, to bring them into proportion. When your heart feels lighter, your body too will benefit.'

Bertha's eyes closed. A stream of affirmative suggestions

was coming at her, as if from a great distance, then nothing at all; only a remembered void as she came out of the trance, with Dr Breuer's voice now back to its normal rhythm and volume, the tone commanding. 'Miss Bertha. Wake up, Miss Bertha,'

Bertha opened her eyes and smiled at Dr Breuer. He smiled back at her. She felt as if she had been asleep for hours. She was still too languorous to speak.

'How long....?' she asked, unable to complete the question.

But Dr Breuer understood. 'Only five minutes.'

He understood also that she needed to be alone now. He rose, returned the chair to the dressing table and picked up his bag, each of his movements measured and unrushed.

After he had taken his leave Bertha lay back in her chair. She did not remember anything that had transpired during the hypnosis and her neck and arm were as stiff as before, but she felt deliciously rested. She sighed, closed her eyes and drifted off into a daydream; she was reclining, eyes closed, and a warm, vibrant voice was lulling her into a trance. All disquietude had fallen away, leaving her with no thoughts, only sensations of an exhilarating calm.

PS. The hypnosis is over. I hardly know how to describe it. It was not at all like Mr Hansen's performance. But how can I say that? Apart from some unsettling visual effects at the beginning, as if I was seeing through shimmering curtains of greyness, I have no memory of what happened. For all I know I may have been dancing a polka or dandling a pillow in the belief that it was a baby. This is scarcely likely, of course, as my limbs are so stiff. Yet, if Mr Hansen could transform the lady on the chairbacks into a support as strong and straight as an iron girder, perhaps Dr Breuer can return my stiffened limbs to their previous supple state. I do so hope that he can. I cannot write any more now. I still feel very strange, as if I am awake but dreaming.

10

Dr Breuer and Mrs Pappenheim stood at Bertha's bedside.

'She won't get up,' Mrs Pappenheim said. 'Miss Thomson and I have tried. She will not move.'

'Mamma, why do you say I will not move?' Bertha screwed up her eyes and clenched her teeth. 'I cannot move. How can I get up when my legs won't support me? Why do you make me feel as if I'm behaving like this to be tiresome?'

Mrs Pappenheim pursed her lips. 'Because I feel you could make more effort, Bertha, especially when your father's so ill. This indisposition of yours isn't helping him at all.'

'And you think I can help that? Do you think I have any choice in the matter? You see, Dr Breuer, how she blames me?'

'I don't think anyone is blaming you, Miss Bertha. Just one moment.' Dr Breuer turned to Mrs Pappenheim and put a hand to her elbow. He steered her towards the door, speaking in a low voice and managing to make it appear that she was leading him. They stood together on the threshold for some minutes, in close conversation. Bertha saw that they were just beside Miss Thomson who was already in place on her chair. How dared they speak within earshot of that woman while she, Bertha, was excluded?

Dr Breuer and Mrs Pappenheim exchanged a few final words and Mrs Pappenheim left the room.

Bertha glowered as Dr Breuer came back towards her. If he was going to leave her out of his conversations with her mother then she was resolved not to talk to him at all. Dr Breuer seemed not to notice her sulk, suggesting only that she might like to sit up and that he would help her to do so.

'Miss Thomson, please.' He looked over towards the governess. Miss Thomson came and stood at the opposite side of the bed.

Dr Breuer put his arm under Bertha's shoulders and started to raise her while Miss Thomson piled the pillows up behind her back. All at once, as Bertha's head came up, the pink-papered walls of the bedroom came toppling down, swooping towards her, in an eerie slow motion; with them came the heavy rosewood wardrobe, the dressing table, the bookcases and the escritoire. Her stomach lurched, her head spun, waves of nausea surged up into her throat. She shrieked, her left hand clinging tight to Dr Breuer's arm.

'What is it, Miss Bertha? What's wrong?' Dr Breuer looked across at Miss Thomson as he spoke and indicated with a movement of the head that she should go back to her chair.

Bertha kept her eyes tight shut.

'The walls!'

'What about the walls?'

'They're falling over.'

'I don't think so.' Dr Breuer placed his hand over Bertha's. 'Why do you say that?'

'I saw them. Toppling. The furniture too.'

'Why don't you try opening your eyes and tell me what you see? I assure you that nothing is falling over.'

'I can't. I'm too frightened.'

'Just try. I promise you, nothing is going to fall on you.'

Bertha waited, wordless, until her stomach had settled and the dizziness subsided, before opening her eyes slowly, still clinging to Dr Breuer's hand. At first she dared not look up but kept her gaze fixed on the bedspread. When finally she raised her head she saw that the walls were back in place. The rosewood wardrobe was in the alcove beside the stove, its mirrored front reflecting the room in its usual state: the escritoire against the opposite wall, the bookcases beside the window.

'I'm sorry, Dr Breuer. I don't know what came over me.' Bertha's heart was still racing, her voice trembling, her fit of pique now gone.

'Please tell me exactly what you saw, Miss Bertha.' Dr Breuer sat down on the hardback chair.

Bertha recounted the experience and her feelings of fear –

fear of the room falling in around her, fear that if she had imagined it then she was surely going mad. As she spoke her fears dissipated. How easeful it was to be able to confess all this to Dr Breuer. He said little, but cocked his head attentively, nodding now and again. How dreadful it would have been if the episode had occurred at some other time, if it had happened when she was alone, or when her mother was in the room.

'This is very probably related to the problems you have in reading,' Dr Breuer said when Bertha finished speaking. 'The visual disorders you describe are due to the erratic behaviour of the eye muscles which are controlled by motor nerves. You see, Miss Bertha, illnesses such as yours are due to an instability of the nervous system and to various parts of the nervous system influencing one another in an abnormal way, so it's not surprising that you have a range of symptoms. We must try to reduce the excitability of the nervous system and that way we can eliminate the symptoms.'

So it was all due to a muscular problem. Bertha sighed with relief. But what was all this talk about the nervous system?

'I do so wish I understood more about the way the body works. Could you explain to me what the nervous system is and how it works. If you have time, of course.'

Dr Breuer laughed. 'That would take a very great deal of time. But I'll give you a brief outline. Perhaps it would be better if I drew a little sketch.' He stood up and walked over to the escritoire where Bertha's notebook lay. He picked it up. 'May I?'

'Of course. That's the book I write my stories in, but use as many pages as you want.' Bertha, still shaken from her experience, was eager to have something to distract her.

'What kind of stories do you write?'

'Oh, fairy tales mostly. The kind of thing that Mr Andersen and the Grimm brothers write.'

'How interesting. You must let me read them some time.'

Dr Breuer sat down again and took a silver propelling pencil out of his pocket. Opening the notebook at a blank page, he drew a rough diagram of the brain and the spinal cord, showing pathways for some of the motor and sensory neurons.

'You see, here is your right hand.' Dr Breuer pointed to his sketch. 'Now if, for example, you hold your hand too close to a fire, a message will travel along this sensory nerve which goes up the spinal cord and into the brain. When it reaches the brain you'll be aware of your hand feeling too hot and another message will then pass down this motor nerve through the arm – you see?' Dr Breuer traced out the path with his pencil. 'And the message will cause the muscles to contract so as to move the hand away from the fire.'

'How wonderful! I had no idea. I thought the nervous system was…. well, to tell you the truth I'd never had any thoughts about it at all. How really wonderful! Please tell me some more. What about my thoughts? What can all this have to do with thinking?'

'Oh, I think that's much too difficult a question even for science to explain fully. But our thoughts are formulated in words and we do know the parts of the brain which are used for language.' Dr Breuer drew a small circle towards the front of the brain. 'Here, you see, is Broca's area which is involved in speaking.' He drew another circle further back. 'And here is Wernicke's area, discovered just six years ago, which is involved in understanding language.'

'But how does our mind link up with this system? I mean, when the nerve sends the message about the hand being hot, how does the message get from the brain to the mind so that the mind can decide whether the hand is so hot that it has to be moved, and how does this decision get sent back to the brain and the – what did you call it? – motor nerve?'

'Some people would say that the mind is simply the activity of the brain, that there is no real distinction between them. It's as much a philosophical question as a scientific one, and it's another question to which we don't yet have the answer.'

'So many questions without answers,' said Bertha. 'Perhaps I'm not so ignorant after all.'

81

'I'm sure you're not at all ignorant, Miss Bertha. But now let's continue our work on your nervous system, shall we?'

Dr Breuer stretched out his legs and leaned back in the chair.

'I'd like you to tell me more about your family life, Miss Bertha. We've already talked about your mother and father, particularly your father's illness, but I'd like to know if there any other difficulties that you have to cope with, or perhaps circumstances which we could adjust to make things easier for you.'

Dr Breuer paused, as if to give Bertha time to gather her thoughts. He got up and walked over to the window. Turning round, he half sat on the ledge, his arms folded loosely across his chest. Everything about him spoke of an easy looseness, to Bertha's eyes, his limbs like those of a string puppet, just hanging casually, as if no tension or conflict would ever tauten them.

'Tell me about your brother. How is he dealing with your father's poor health? Is he supportive?'

No! Willi was not at all supportive. Bertha's words tumbled from her tongue. It was so easy for him, out most of the time. When he was at home he acted as if he was master of the house, assuming that with their father bedridden he could lord it over the womenfolk, jeering at Bertha for being over-emotional, and always so pleased with himself: pleased because he was a man, pleased because he was studying law, pleased because he belonged to a wealthy family, pleased because he was Willi Pappenheim, in short.

'He doesn't even care about Papa.' Bertha was shrilling now. 'Oh, I'm sure he'd say that as a man he shouldn't show his feelings but I think that he doesn't have any feelings, not any good ones, at any rate. I can't tell you how aggravating it is to be made to feel inferior to a person of such mediocrity. I'm older than him, I belong to the same family, I'm more intelligent – I'm sure I am – yet I'm condemned to a life of banality, trapped here with Mamma and Miss Thomson and the maid and the cook while Willi goes off, out and about and doing just as he pleases.'

Bertha stopped and looked at Dr Breuer, a little fearfully, as if expecting a reprimand. Still the loose-limbed stance; the slightest of nods and a fractional lifting of an eyebrow: an encouragement to continue.

'If I complain, Mamma tells me that it's my duty to lead my life as laid down by all those Jewish rabbis. All the rules about what to do in the kitchen, what not to do on Shabbat, what to do to keep one's husband happy. There is so much to learn about what pots and pans to use and how to avoid breaking the Shabbat laws that there's no time for women to learn anything useful or interesting apparently. Perhaps that brain we were talking about earlier is smaller inside the female skull.'

Dr Breuer laughed. 'Certainly not in your case, Miss Bertha. I sense already from our conversations that you're possessed of a most lively intelligence.' He stood up straight. 'Now, let's do a little more work under hypnosis.'

This time Bertha felt no apprehension, only an eagerness to enter again into that soothing void.

'Let me prop you up so that you can fix your gaze properly.' Dr Breuer came over and helped Bertha sit up with the pillows supporting her. She closed her eyes, fearing that the walls might begin to topple again. She kept them tight shut, and now she was thinking not of the walls, but of the feel of firm hands holding her shoulders, and of a faint pleasing odour. She savoured it, a dry animal earthiness mingled with a hint of cigar, as she inhaled.

Dr Breuer moved down and stood at the foot of the bed. He was now facing Bertha directly.

'Look at me, Miss Bertha. Look at me. Keep looking at me. You are beginning to feel tired.'

Bertha fixed her eyes on Dr Breuer's face. It was becoming so familiar to her that she felt she could draw it from memory, with the accuracy of a photograph. The high dome of the forehead, the way the eyebrows sloped down sharply over the deep-set eyes, the mouth barely visible in the luxuriance of the beard. Large protruding ears. She imagined herself in his arms, the way she used to be when Papa tossed

83

her in the air, still tiny. Then, if she stretched out her arms, she could take hold of these ears, pull them. A laugh bubbled up in her throat.

'Look at me, Miss Bertha. You are drowsy now. Keep looking.'

The laugh dribbled away as she was engulfed in grey mist, a mist on which the contours of Dr Breuer's face remained imprinted. Already she was floating off, borne on the sounds of a rich sustaining voice taking her to a place of indefinable respite.

Mrs Pappenheim came into Bertha's bedroom as soon as Dr Breuer had gone.

'What do you want?' Bertha snapped. Her mother's presence was an intrusion; it broke a bubble of – what was this feeling? It had felt like bliss. A bubble of bliss. It had burst now.

'I've come to see if you need anything. But why did you address me in that abrupt fashion? I hardly recognise you these days, Bertha.'

'I'm tired.'

'Would you like Miss Thomson to read to you?'

'No, I'd like to sleep. Please leave me.'

Mrs Pappenheim left the room, frowning.

Bertha closed her eyes. Read to her! What fatuous novelette would Miss Thomson have proposed bringing to her bedside? She started pulling at the embroidered bedspread with her left hand, seizing ends of thread, worrying at them like a dog with a bone. She ground her teeth. She wanted to scream. She imagined it. Scream after scream after scream. Scream till she burst from the very force of it. She imagined her body disintegrating: pieces of flesh, bone, lung, liver, heart, brain, scattering hither and thither in the bedroom. Where would her mind be then?

She let the bedspread fall from her fingers, the violent emotion subsiding as quickly as it had come on. She began to luxuriate in the memory of her conversations with Dr Breuer. It was not just the subject matter of their discussions, the revelations about the workings of the body and the mind and the freedom to vent her frustrations. It was something about their rapport. She had never felt anything like it before. Not even her friendship with Julie Rosenthal when she was fourteen.

Julie, her fine flaxen hair like gossamer, her face of pale porcelain, her straight little nose and clear blue eyes. So much prettier than herself, Bertha had thought then. She hated her own hair which was thick and dark and springy and took ages to brush. Nor did she like her nose which, when she compared it with Julie's, she found disagreeably prominent.

How she had loved Julie. How they had loved each other, always sitting together in class, holding hands, leaving messages for each other in their lockers. What games they had played that summer! Games that could be played by only two people, no need for others. And the care she had taken in preparing her Purim gift for Julie: a bag of poppy seed candies which Bertha had baked herself, arranged in a basket lined with yellow tissue paper along with a pomegranate. In return Julie had given her a basket of black cherries and a jar of mixed nuts. Bertha had stored the cherry stones in the jar and kept it on her dressing table for months. Until she no longer loved Julie, or rather until Julie no longer loved her. Bertha remembered the pain, when she arrived late for school one day and found Julie sitting beside Heidi Muller. Heidi, of all people! And she wasn't even Jewish. Julie and Heidi were always together after that. For about three weeks, anyway. Renate Grunwald said it was because they both had a crush on Herr Frank, the music master.

But soon Bertha had a crush of her own. When they moved up a class after the summer holiday, Miss Baxter took them for English. Miss Baxter had special friends in each class, a coterie of two or three girls on whom she lavished particular attention. She seemed to cast a spell on them. Bertha was one of the chosen in her class, as were Claudia Hahn and Charlotte Hirsch. It threw the three girls together in a triangle that was at once bonded by shared devotion and riven with jealousy. Bertha secretly believed that she was Miss Baxter's favourite.

85

How else to explain the way the English woman's eyes flashed when she looked at Bertha, a look laden with a barely hidden meaning. '*I and thou, we understand each other*,' it seemed to say.

The name also spoke to her. The sharp, clipped syllables were brisk and no-nonsense, and very English, like the persona Miss Baxter presented to the pupils. But Bertha had also learned the more intimate name; she had seen it on an envelope protruding from Miss Baxter's bag: Lavinia. The perfect name, Bertha thought. Soft and poetic, like the real Miss Baxter beginning to be revealed to her alone. She made it into a song: *Baxter, Miss Baxter, Miss Lavinia Baxter, Lavinia Baxter, Lavinia, Lavinia*. She sang it under her breath on the way to school. If Miss Thomson, who always accompanied her, tried to talk she would tell her that she couldn't engage in conversation as she was mentally rehearsing her homework in order to be word perfect in class.

Bertha always listened entranced when Miss Baxter read poetry to them. One of her favourites had been "Abou Ben Adhem" which told the story of a man who woke from a dream to find an angel in the room, writing in a book of gold. As she learned it by heart – they had been given this to do for homework – Bertha heard the low contralto voice of Miss Baxter saying each line and she found that she had committed the words to memory without effort. She especially liked the couplet

> And saw, within the moonlight in his room,
> Making it rich, and like a lily in bloom

The delicate fervour with which Miss Baxter read those two lines made Bertha's spine tingle. The sound of it ran through her head for days.

Miss Baxter's clothes were the subject of endless debate with the three girls. For their classmates, Mademoiselle Lamartine was the prettiest and most elegant of the teachers. It went without saying, they said; she was French after all. But for Bertha, Claudia and Charlotte, the sober style of Miss Baxter was more admirable, in keeping with the seriousness of her mind, the firmness of her character.

86

Of the three, Charlotte was the first to wear her hair up. Bertha had felt a flash of fury on that first day when Charlotte arrived at school with her hair dressed in the exact same manner as Miss Baxter's. Her own hair, still hanging down her back in thick disorder, struck her as even more unbecoming than usual. She longed for the day when she would be allowed to put it up but now, of course, she would not be able to have it in the style she had secretly intended for it.

Once, when Bertha had come out of class to take a message to the headmistress she saw, approaching from the other end of the long, wide corridor leading to the headmistress's room, Miss Baxter. Bertha had started to feel a warm flush course through her body, a nervousness and an exquisitely acute self-consciousness. The tension in her increased as the distance between them diminished, until she thought she might faint from dizziness. Miss Baxter was striding along, bearing down on her, eyes flashing. What would she say when they passed each other? Bertha's mouth was now so dry she knew she would be unable to say anything. 'Good morning, Bertha.' Miss Baxter's eyes bored through Bertha. Bertha said nothing. Her tongue was stuck to the roof of her mouth. Her face was hot and red. Afterwards she could have cried with vexation. Even now she was beginning to feel hot with embarrassment at the memory.

Bertha ran over again in her mind the words of the day's exchange with Dr Breuer. With her index finger she traced the pathway of the sensory nerves running up her right arm. Strange. She could feel the touch of her right arm on her left finger, but the right arm barely registered the pressure from her left finger.

How Bertha wished she could anaesthetise her other feelings, her sorrow at her father's failing health, her irritation at her mother for her inadequacies, her rage against Willi and against rules that constricted her more tightly than her corset stays. But if she deadened those feelings she would not have the delicious intimacy of disclosing them to Dr Breuer. Bertha started to rerun the morning's dialogue. As she did so, she ran her left index finger over her cheeks and round her mouth, so lightly and gently that she thrilled with each touch, as if the faintest pulse of electricity was coursing through her entire body.

11

20 December 1880

Klara called this morning and spent some time with Bertha. She is engaged to be married, to a lawyer she met in Ischl last summer. She was full of talk of her wedding, her trousseau and the apartment they are to occupy in Wipplingerstrasse. She is delighted because it is not far from here and she will be able to visit more often. It will do Bertha good. Klara is a good-hearted girl, for all her giddiness, and marriage will probably steady her. She brought Bertha a book by Eugenie John. Bertha has no desire to read it. Inferior literature and full of clichés, she said after Klara had gone. I am inclined to agree with her. Those popular novelists do girls a disservice when they fill their heads with romantic nonsense and unrealistic expectations.

I would have liked to ask Klara how she found Bertha but the woman Cousin Inge recommended as a nurse arrived to present her credentials just as she was leaving. Dr Breuer has been most particular about the requirements regarding the nursing. Bertha is to have a programme of massage, two hours of kneading of the affected limbs each day, and for this the nurse must be strong and muscular. Fraulein Gruhle did not strike me as up to the task, being small and slight. This afternoon I received a second candidate, an older woman, vigorous and buxom. I have engaged her on a trial basis. Although she has no experience of massage, Dr Breuer will show her how it is to be done. She is also to enforce the diet prescribed by Dr Breuer. This is to contain large quantities of fish and meat, and as many milky dishes as Bertha can be persuaded to eat.

Dr Breuer is now visiting Bertha every day, except Shabbat. He has warned me that her recovery may be a lengthy process. I am still unsure about the hypnotic procedures but he tells me that she is responding well to their conversations.

I have asked Willi if he could try to spend less time away from home. His studies require him to be in the library, he tells me. That is as may be, but his father would like to see more of him. It does him good to be able to discuss politics and suchlike man to man.

o~o~o

Ilse adjusted the wheeled invalid table and manoeuvred it over the bed so that it was almost at Bertha's chin. It was an ugly piece of furniture, made of oak and cast iron. Bertha hated it. So out of keeping with the rest of her room. Ilse laid on it the bowl of chicken soup which she had just brought in on a tray.

The smell! Greasiness and a sickly parsnip sweetness. Right under her nose. Nausea rippled through her, sweat in its wake. Bertha lifted the bowl and hurled it across the room. The bowl shattered against the tiled stove, soup spilled over the carpet.

'Get out! Take it away.'

Ilse picked up the tray and ran from the room like a startled rabbit. Mrs Pappenheim appeared a few moments later.

Bertha cowered against the pillows, frightened and shocked. How could she have done such a thing? It had not been her intention, she was sure. It had happened without her even being aware of a desire to do it. What could be wrong with her? How could this be?

'Mamma, I'm sorry. I can't believe that I would behave so abominably. What's happening to me? It wasn't me who behaved like that. Truly it wasn't.'

'Bertha dear, we all know that you're not yourself.' Mrs Pappenheim stood in the middle of the room, twisting her hands. She turned towards the door. 'I'll go and tell Ilse to clear up the mess.'

'No. Not yet. I must compose myself. Please just sit with me a little.'

Mrs Pappenheim sat down and took Bertha's hand in her own. 'Now listen, Bertha…'

'Mamma!' A black thing was slithering around beside her head, down over her shoulder. 'Get that snake away from me!' Bertha writhed in her bed, struggling to lift her head from the pillow.

90

'Bertha, there's no snake. What are you talking about?'

'Just now. Beside me on the pillow. I saw a snake. A black snake.' Bertha's right eye darted to each side of her. The left eye remained turned inward.

'Nonsense, child. You're imagining things. Perhaps it was your hair. Look.' Mrs Pappenheim stroked the long dark tress hanging down over Bertha's shoulder. Bertha looked sideways again and saw only locks of hair.

'Perhaps.... you're..... right. I... sorry, I...' Her voice, slow and staccato, faded away.

'Hush, child. Don't distress yourself.' Bertha heard the sounds of her mother's words but made no sense of them. There was only haziness and confusion. She watched as her mother's lips continued to move. Now the sounds no longer reached her. Her mind was inaccessible. She sank into unconsciousness.

When she awoke it was late afternoon and Dr Breuer was sitting at her bedside, Miss Thomson by the door. Bertha was instantly alert. He had been sitting there and she had not been aware of it. She felt cheated out of a portion of her time with him. Not only that, her sleep had deprived her of her usual period of anticipation as she waited for him to arrive,

'How are you feeling today, Miss Bertha?'

Bertha suppressed the petulant response that came first to her mind, the complaint that he should not have been sitting there watching her when he should have woken her and started their work together. Then she remembered the events of the morning – the throwing of the bowl of soup, the shouting – and hoped that Mamma had not told Dr Breuer about it. She was bound to have done, though. Bertha could only hope that he would not want to talk about it.

'I feel... quite refreshed, I think. In my mind, that is. My body is much the same.'

'Very good.' Dr Breuer opened his instrument bag. 'I'd like to check your reflexes first. May I?' He lifted her right arm, flexed the elbow and tapped it with a reflex hammer. He repeated the process with the left arm. Bertha lay still, her eyes fixed on his face. 'And now your legs.' Dr Breuer drew back the bedclothes and raised Bertha's long white nightdress, exposing the knees. He put a hand on her right ankle and slid the foot backwards towards the thigh. He did the same with the left leg. He tested the patellar reflex of each knee with the hammer. He pulled the nightdress down again. He drew the sharp end of the hammer along the sole of each foot, then rearranged the bedclothes, drawing them up over Bertha's chest. All in silence.

Finally Dr Breuer stood up.

'I'd like now to try and loosen up the limbs with some massage.' He put the hammer back in his bag and took out a small vial. 'If I could just turn back your sleeve.' He lifted Bertha's right arm and rolled the sleeve of her nightdress up as far as her shoulder. Then he took a towel from the washstand at the side of the bed and placed it under her arm. Opening the vial he poured some oil onto the palm of his left hand, rubbed his two hands together and ran them lightly over Bertha's entire arm. He began to stroke the arm, starting at the shoulder and moving downwards, again in silence.

Such peaceful silence. Bertha closed her eyes. All she was aware of now was the feel of Dr Breuer's hands on her arm. A faint impression; her arm was almost numb. She wished it were not numb so that she could feel to the full Dr Breuer's touch.

Now there was a stronger pressure. He was kneading the flesh of her upper arm, fingers digging in to the hard resistance of bone.

Still the silence. But it was invaded now by disagreeable little sounds which the silence itself served only to render more conspicuous. A faint squelch as Dr Breuer lifted his palm from her oiled flesh. The sniffs of Miss Thomson who had a slight cold. Worst of all – Bertha could not say why – was a gurgling from Dr Breuer's stomach. She tried to think of something to say.

'Dr Breuer, I'm curious.' Her voice sounded brittle to her ears, as if she was making polite conversation at a coffee-hour. He was kneading her lower arm now. 'Why did you suggest that I should talk to you about my difficulties? I mean in my family life and so on. It's an unusual form of treatment, isn't it?'

Dr Breuer flexed her elbow, rotated the wrist. 'Unusual perhaps, but the thinking behind it goes back a long way, to the ancient Greeks and the work of Aristotle.' He laid her arm down and removed the towel. 'And now – if I may – the leg.' Again he drew back the covers, raised Bertha's nightdress and slid the towel into place. 'It's based on the idea of catharsis.' He poured a little more oil, applied it to the length of her leg and began the same manipulations as he had carried out on the arm.

'You see, Miss Bertha, Aristotle believed that poetry and drama, particularly tragedy, allow people to experience a cleansing of the emotions, a purgation, as it were. The stimulation and expression of the emotions cleanse the mind in the same way that a purgative evacuates the bowels.'

A blush coloured Bertha's cheeks at those last words. Dr Breuer moved smoothly on.

'This concept has now been introduced into medical therapy. The patient stimulates the emotions by talking about the situations which have given rise to them and thus discharges them.

Dr Breuer was now pummelling her thigh in rapid rhythm with the sides of his hands. Looking down Bertha became aware of the nakedness of her leg. For the first time she found the dark hairs on her calves displeasing, felt embarrassed about having them exposed.

She must think of something else to talk about. Dr Breuer had been talking about drama. What plays had she seen recently? Goethe's *Iphigenia* was the last one, just before they left for Ischl in June. She recalled how Iphigenia, the captured daughter of Agamemnon, was forced to act as a priestess for the king of Tauris, and to sacrifice any strangers who entered the kingdom. When her own brother was discovered and condemned she refused to carry out her duty and persuaded the king to release them and let them return to Greece. Bertha thought about it in the light of what Dr Breuer had been saying.

'Do you know the story of Iphigenia?' she asked.

'I do.'

Bertha reflected, frowning. 'I remember feeling a kind of satisfaction when Iphigenia stood up to the king and refused to sacrifice her brother, especially as she wasn't just defying the king but protesting against the whole barbaric system of sacrificing humans for the pleasure of the gods. Is this what Aristotle meant?'

'Well, it's the same kind of idea. Aristotle wrote in particular about pity and fear and how they're aroused by tragedy. But the principle applies equally to other emotions. In your example, you can see how the story of Iphigenia arouses in you feelings of satisfaction about behaviour you think admirable, and because Iphigenia's a woman she's someone you can empathise with.'

Bertha thought some more, and as she did so she became aware of a feeling of her own inadequacy.

'You're right,' she said. 'I do empathise with Iphigenia. I feel as trapped as Iphigenia was when she was forced to become a priestess, to live a life which she didn't believe in and carry out rituals which she thought wrong and cruel. But she did something about it. What can I do? Nothing!'

Dr Breuer stood up and drew the bedclothes back down again. He

'You're still young, Miss Bertha. Who knows what opportunities the future will bring for you? Sometimes it takes just one small thing to transform a situation. In Iphigenia's case, she may well have lived out her whole life as a priestess had the arrival of her brother not prompted her to realise that she couldn't carry on. Continue to think of Iphigenia as a model. Yes, you feel trapped, trapped in your body as well as your mind at the moment, but who knows? Perhaps, like Iphigenia, you can break free.'

Dr Breuer folded the towel and laid it on the washstand. 'Now let's do some work under hypnosis.'

Dr Breuer's carriage lurched out of Liechtensteinstrasse and into the melee of traffic in the Schottenring. How right he had been to ask Mrs Pappenheim to engage a nurse. There could be no question of him massaging Bertha again. The mere memory of it…. No, he must not allow himself. Yet he ached for the thought. Just a few moments then. Till the carriage reached the Am Hof. Then he would put it out of his mind. With a grateful voluptuousness he sank back into the upholstered interior, eyes closed, his fingers on the tenderness of Bertha's calf. The contours of her knee. The swell of her thigh, the flesh yielding under the pressure of his probing fingers. The thrill was too strong now. He must stay his emotions. Concentrate a moment on the anatomy. Here was the femur. Here the path of the sciatic nerve. He opened his eyes a fraction – not too much. Mustn't disturb the balance, the awareness of Bertha. Just enough to see how where they were now. The Schottenstift on the left. Still five minutes then, perhaps a little more. His fingers moved higher. Any more and they would begin to feel tendrils of hair. Oh dear God, this was too much. Quick. The sciatic nerve. What did he know about it? The longest nerve in the body. It runs through the buttocks. No, mustn't think about the buttocks. Mustn't let his hand…. Sciatica. Burning, numbness or tingling. Compression of a lumbar spine nerve root or a sacral nerve root, or of the sciatic nerve itself. Easier now. His fingertips danced delicately on Bertha's thigh. He stretched them outwards, his palm now flat on her body. He stroked downwards, back up again. Oh, the pure joy of it. No further! Stop! Think about the sciatic nerve. It's consumption forbidden in Judaism. *Nikkur* – the process of cutting it away from the surrounding meat. The carriage jolted. He opened his eyes. The traffic more crowded now, coming up to the Am Hof. He was flushed and breathless. He opened the carriage window and shook his head, feeling the fresh chill of the night air.

He left the window open, let the noise and sights come crowding in, the banality of the early evening street scenes. A quarrel between two cab drivers. The hot blaze from the brazier of a hot potato vendor. The advertisements on the side of a horse-drawn tram: soap to make linen whiter and brighter, gout pills, macassar oil, a folding cot together with full layette. A woman selling oranges to a theatre queue.

He could think about Bertha now without the fever of sexual excitement. The strange thing was that he had sensed not a trace of arousal on her part during the massage session. Not that he would have expected any overt demonstration. But he had detected nothing, not the faintest undercurrent of suppressed response. And yet perhaps it was not so surprising. For all her intelligence there was something undeveloped about her, a childishness, an obstinate resistance to reason sometimes. He had noticed it particularly in relation to anything which might cause pain, however slightly, as when he tried to test her tactile sense with the aesthesiometer. In some ways Bertha was like an unripe fruit.

The carriage slowed down. It was turning into the courtyard of Backerstrasse 7. He was home.

It was three o'clock in the morning. Apart from Dr Breuer's visits, night was the best time of day for Bertha. Her mind was at its most alert. So often now in the daytime she was confused or drowsy, hardly aware of what was going on around her, hardly caring. And at night she was alone. Her thoughts raced round her brain.

This catharsis that Dr Breuer had talked of. There was something alluring about it. Talking to him about Willi had assuaged her, as if she had delivered herself of a burden. Of course, there were so many things which she would never ever talk about to Dr Breuer, or anyone else for that matter. Still, if she could.... It was so tempting. But no, there could be no question of it. Bertha thought of the moment when Dr Breuer had compared discharging the emotions to an evacuation of the bowels. She had squirmed with embarrassment, had felt hot blood rise in her cheeks. One did not talk about these things in casual conversation. At the same time, it had been strangely gratifying, suggesting a closeness between the doctor and herself. Then there was the time, during the doctor's first visit, when he had asked about the regularity of her monthly flow. That had been embarrassing too – but she had not

96

known Dr Breuer so well then and her mother was present. Oh, if he should ask her anything about it now! Especially now that she was always almost alone with him! She felt a prickly tingling sensation, but it was not a physical sensation, not of the body – more of the mind.

How peculiar this was, to be getting some kind of pleasure from thinking about talking about disgusting things with Dr Breuer. Even though she was alone Bertha felt her cheeks flush. She thrust the thoughts out of her mind and turned her attention to what Dr Breuer had said about Aristotle. There was something familiar about that name. What was it? Something Willi had said. Yes! That was it! He had been mocking her about her desire to study at university. There was no point, he said, because women lack the reason required to study. Then he had quoted this Greek philosopher, Aristotle, who had described females as being deformed males. They should be ruled by men for their own good, Aristotle had claimed. He had even said that women didn't grow bald because their nature was similar to that of children! Surely Dr Breuer didn't share these ideas? But he agreed with Aristotle about catharsis, so perhaps he did.

A memory sprang up. She was five years old. The new Schiffschul synagogue had just opened and the whole family were to attend the first Shabbat service. It was a great occasion because her father was a cofounder of the synagogue. Bertha wore a dark blue velvet cloak over a blue taffeta dress and a little white velvet beret with a blue feather in it. A white fur muff hung round her neck.

Bertha held Willi's hand as they passed through the doors. She felt herself to be in charge of him as Papa and Mamma were so busy greeting people. She pinched his arm as he tried to pull away from her. 'Stand still. Bad boy.' She pinched him again and looked around to see if the adults had noticed what a good disciplinarian she was. She felt very grown up and important, what with her new clothes and her father's position in the synagogue and being four inches taller than her little brother.

But self-satisfaction turned to bewilderment, and then a

confused shame, as her mother took her hand and led her away to a balcony at the back, behind a metal grill, where all the women and girls were gathered, leaving the men and boys – even Willi – in the main sanctuary of the synagogue. There they stayed, onlookers, throughout the service. Below them, the massed black and white prayer-shawls of the male congregation nodded and bobbed like waves in a choppy sea as their wearers recited the Hebrew prayers. Around Bertha the women chatted. Frau Goldberg invited her neighbour for a coffee-hour the following week. Frau Mahler outlined the menu for her evening meal. A group of women at the back were giggling.

The women fell silent now. Rabbi Herzfeld was removing the Torah scroll from the Ark. He was carrying it through the congregation, stopping frequently for men to kiss it. There was Papa, Willi standing by his side. Rabbi Herzfeld was bending down, putting the Torah to Willi's lips. Frau Heinneman whispered to Mamma what a handsome little man Willi was in his green satin knee-breeches and jacket. Bertha saw the expression on her father's face as he looked down at Willi, the kind of expression he often had when he looked at her, that she had thought was for her alone. She would pinch Willi harder the next time he disobeyed her. Really hard. Make him cry. She felt her own eyes sting with tears.

The feeling of shame recurred each time she attended the synagogue. She felt as apart from the females around her as she did from the men from whom they were physically separated. Everything was so inferior in the women's gallery: the prayer books specially formulated for women's needs, and in Yiddish because the women were not expected to understand Hebrew; the lack of decorum as they chatted about recipes and clothes while the magnificent full-throated chorus of the men's choir rose around them. The women never sang in the synagogue. She felt anger at the other women for their acceptance of all this. Why bother to go to the synagogue at all if it was just to carry on as if they were at a coffee-hour? Was religion only for men, she had once asked her mother. A woman's religious duties were carried out in the

98

home, Mamma had replied.

It was as if the shame was always with her, a sense of self-conscious discomfort, mostly in the background but always ready to blossom at any reminder of her female status. It was similar to the shame she felt about her body, that part of it between her waist and her thighs: a feeling that she wanted to reject those parts of her that made her body female. But she did not want to be a man either.

Bertha wondered why she had this feeling of shame about that part of her body. To be sure, it was involved in disagreeable bodily functions, things which were dirty and smelled bad. But that did not seem reason enough. Everybody was the same in that respect. Perhaps it was because it was the part which most strongly identified her as a woman. And, of course, it was the part involved in that side of marriage. No need to think about it any longer then. That was reason enough to feel shame.

She looked at the clock and saw that she still had a couple of hours of wakefulness before she might expect to fall asleep. She put out her left hand and took up the notebook which lay on her bedside table. Then she picked up a pen and put it into her right hand. The fingers retained some flexibility despite the stiffness in her arm. She started to write.

Her thoughts had kept turning to the story of Iphigenia throughout the night. How magnificently Iphigenia had behaved, particularly in Goethe's rendering of the story. Dr Breuer, who had studied Greek, had told her that in the original version by Euripides Iphigenia had merely devised a plan for herself and her brother to escape from Tauris. Goethe had upgraded her behaviour to a higher plane, allowing her to confront the king in the greater interests of human values and social rights.

Bertha was planning her own version of the story. She transposed the events northwards, to a setting reminiscent of the Scandinavian myths. She discarded the character of the brother, doubting that any brother could inspire a woman to such exalted risk-taking. As she described her heroine, Gertrude, she decided that the victim would be her son, a boy

99

who had been snatched from her when she was captured by raiders from a neighbouring kingdom and taken to serve in the grove of a pagan god.

The priestess and her assistants prepared the stone slab of the sacrificial altar. The man was led in by a team of acolytes, laid on the altar and bound fast. Gertrude stepped forward, dagger raised.

She was flung aside. A tall figure seized the dagger from her and thrust it into the breast of the man lying on the stone slab of the altar, on the bed, the bed of her father, her father who lay with blood flowing from the gaping wound caused by the dagger, by the scalpel of Professor Aschenbach who now stood over him.

Bertha jerked awake in a trembling judder. The notebook and pen had fallen from her hands. She grabbed at the notebook and looked at what she had written. Her story finished in mid-sentence where she described Gertrude stepping forward. Still flooded with the fear of her nightmare she felt a loathing for the story. She tore the pages from her notebook, crumpled them and threw them far from her bed.

12

January 1881

Dearest Anna

It is 3 am and I am wide awake. My nights now are always like this. My mind races. My thoughts tumble over each other. I feel that I could talk for ever, write reams, climb mountains even (were it not for the stiffness of my limbs). Then towards daybreak my energy lapses and I fall asleep. In the daytime, I spend much time dozing and between my naps I feel so sluggish I can sometimes scarcely compose a coherent sentence. I ask myself how this can be, this topsy-turvy change of day and night. And I conclude that at night I am free to be alive, I am liberated from the torments of life in the sickroom which, during the day, make me want to bury myself under the bedcovers like a hibernating dormouse.

Sickroom! How I hate that word! Truly, sickness is a prison, not just for the body but also for the soul. I want only to be left in peace so that I may rest and recover, as I am sure I can with time and the help of Dr Breuer, yet I have to put up with a constant coming and going in my bedroom. Mamma is forever checking to see if the stove needs more wood, if the windows should be opened or closed, if it is the day for changing the sheets, if I need a new nightdress, all the hundred and one things that she thinks are necessary for the proper running of a sickroom. Ilse is forever in and out, bringing and removing trays of food that I have no desire to eat, opening the window if it is closed, closing it if it is open. The sickroom must be properly ventilated, says Mamma. Ilse opens the window. The fire is dying down, we mustn't allow Bertha to catch a chill, says Mamma. Ilse closes the window and fetches more wood.

Now let me tell you about the latest scourge I have to bear. Mamma has engaged a nurse for me, a horrid woman called Agnethe. She is forty years old, a widow with no children, and spreads such an air of gloom with her sagging jowls and ponderous movements. I declare that were it not for her gender she would be more aptly employed as an undertaker. Her principal task is to carry out the programme of massage which Dr Breuer has prescribed for me. For two hours a day she pummels my limbs like a pastry cook kneading dough for matzos. Apart from that, she *assists me onto the commode, gives me a daily bed bath, helps me to sit up or lie down, fetches the things I need and supervises Ilse in the maintenance of room temperature and ventilation. When she is engaged in none of these things she sits on the chaise longue and sews. How I dislike this brooding presence in my room. The only time I am free of it is when she is called upon to help the other nurses in their work with Papa – and, of course, when Dr Breuer is here.*

Forgive me, dear Anna, for this litany of complaints. As you can see, I make a cantankerous invalid. Rest assured that your letters are still a source of pleasure and interest to me, and of comfort too. I cannot tell you how relieved I was to read your response to my confession about wishing Papa's suffering might be over quickly. You have exactly the same views on the matter as Dr Breuer. This does not surprise me, of course, as I consider you both to be such admirably sensible people.

With fondest love
Bertha

o~o~o

Bertha had not been able to rid her mind of the dream of her father's murder on the sacrificial altar. It had played itself out over and over, as if in warning, stirring fears that his health was worsening, that he might slip away without her having the opportunity to talk with him again. She had not seen him since the day she herself became bedridden in early December. For the past few days she had repeatedly asked her mother to allow her to visit him. Her mother had refused; it would not be good for him to see how incapacitated Bertha was. Well, it wouldn't be good for him to think that she was so incapacitated that she couldn't even get out of bed, Bertha had replied. And what was the point of having a nurse if she couldn't help her to do things that she wouldn't otherwise be able to do? Finally she had asked Dr Breuer to intervene. Her mother had relented. Dr Breuer had even arranged for a special invalid carriage to be delivered so that Bertha could be wheeled through to her father's room. It stood by her bed now, a red velvet covered seat mounted on two large wheels, with a small wheel to the front fixed to a steering handle.

102

Agnethe bent over Bertha to raise her into a sitting position. Bertha tried to turn her head to escape the odour radiating from the damp patches under the nurse's arms, a melange of sour sweat and cheap lavender water. But her head would not turn. Her neck was too stiff. She held her breath until Agnethe moved away from her.

Here she was again, putting her arm round Bertha's back to lift her up out of the bed. She could feel the damp patch now, pressing on her shoulder. Bertha squirmed, straining to get herself off the bed as quickly as possible and into the chair, away from Agnethe's armpit.

Mrs Pappenheim held the steering handle to the side as Agnethe eased Bertha onto the velvet seat and draped a shawl round her shoulders. Bertha steered with her left hand as Agnethe trundled her out of her room and along the hallway. Mrs Pappenheim stayed behind with Ilse to see to the airing of the bed.

As Bertha turned in towards her father's door she was seized with doubt, fear of what she was about to see. It was weeks now since she had last seen Papa. He might have changed horribly in that time. Mamma had been right. It would be better not to....

The carriage came to a halt. The front wheel had bumped into the doorpost. Bertha wrestled with the steering handle, venting her anxiety in a frenzy of activity. Agnethe pulled backwards, Bertha thrust this way and that, Agnethe pushed forwards; there was a glancing collision with the door, and Bertha shot into the room.

'Bertha, my darling. Lovely to see my little girl.' Mr Pappenheim's voice trembled with affection. 'I've missed you, sweetheart.'

He tried to smile but his face, the flesh shrunken and pale, grimaced, it seemed to Bertha, in a rictus. Why had she insisted on coming? Her heart hammered. She wanted to flee, to run from this room and its living corpse back to the safety of her bed. But she could not. She was immobile, trapped in the infirmity of her own body. Her mouth dry with fright, she could only whisper to her father in a low rasp.

'I've missed you too, Papa.'

She could think of nothing else to say. She dared not look at her father. The high, canopied bed was like a catafalque.

'What's wrong, cherub? You look so fearful. You mustn't worry. I'm still your dear old Papa.' The words were faint, mere modulations of a stertorous wheeze.

'Where's Mamma?' Bertha gulped for breath, her chest constricted. 'Please call for Mamma.'

'What's wrong, sweetheart?'

'I.... I feel a little dizzy. I'll be all right if Mamma is here. In case I faint, I mean.'

Mr Pappenheim rang the bell at the side of his bed. His wife came in.

'Bertha's feeling faint,' Mr Pappenheim said.

'I'm fine now,' whispered Bertha, buffeted by her terror at staring into the face of death, her guilt at revealing her fear, and her desire to escape.

'Agnethe, the smelling salts, please,' ordered Mrs Pappenheim.

Agnethe hurried out of the room and came back with a small bottle. Mrs Pappenheim opened it and held it under Bertha's nose as the fumes rose.

'Now here's a fine old state of affairs,' Mr Pappenheim said. 'The old papa and his little princess, one as bad as the other. What shall we do with you then? Do you remember, Bertha, when you were little, and you were sick, I would sit by your bed and read to you? I wish I could do that now. But you see, I'm as sick as you are.'

'Papa, please, don't.' Bertha knew that her father was trying to comfort her but his voice – hollow, flat and reedy – tolled like a death knell. She must stop him speaking. 'I know you would. I hope you will, I mean *I* will, read to you that is. When I'm better I'll come and read to you, all day long, all your favourite books.' She babbled on, saying anything at all rather than let her father start speaking again in that awful ghoulish voice. She finally ran out of words.

'I'm sorry, Papa, I'm feeling rather tired now.'

'Thank you for coming, poppet. You've made your poor

104

old Papa feel much better.'

Back in her room, Bertha lay in bed tortured with remorse about her inability to show her father the love and support she owed him. But surely the fact that she felt this remorse was evidence in itself that she loved him? But her father didn't know that she felt remorseful, and it would do him no good to know about her remorse anyway because it would only remind him how very ill he was and that would make him worse. But surely he knew how ill he was. Yes, he knew, but she should be able to behave with him in such a way that he could forget it for a little. Therefore she had failed, let her father down when he was in the most desperate plight and needed her by him.

The restlessness of her mind moved to her body, translated into a need to toss and turn, to plump up her pillows, settle again in an altogether different position. Short-circuited by the stiffness in her limbs, the agitation dove back into her mind, gathering momentum. She would go again tomorrow, offer to read to him. No, she couldn't read to him. Her eyes were too bad. She would talk to him then. Tell him all the things she had often wanted to say but didn't dare. Tell him that, yes, she knew he loved her, but that that wasn't enough. She wanted him to help her. Surely if he really loved her he would help her, help her to do all the things that she wanted to do but couldn't, like confessing that she didn't want to go on pretending that she was happy to spend all day in idle frivolity and pointless pursuits, pretending that she willingly embraced the same kind of life that her mother led, pretending that she didn't hate Willi, pretending that she believed in all those silly Jewish rituals, pretending that he was always going to be there, that he wasn't.... dying.

There was only one balm for Bertha's troubled mind. She switched her thoughts to Dr Breuer and her anxieties dissipated. She projected herself towards the evening. Dr Breuer sitting by her bed. What would they talk about, she wondered. It scarcely mattered. Aristotle's ideas about women, her mother's obsession with domestic details, Willi's bullying, the silliness of the Jewish dietary laws, her lack of education, her illness – all of these shrank into insignificance. All that mattered was the pairing of their minds, a pairing which wafted her far from her mundane cares as if she and he were swept away, soaring aloft in a hot air balloon. Higher and higher. Now they were in the clouds, the earth hidden from view. Her bed was the upholstered interior of the Montgolfier. The white mounds of pillow and eiderdown blended into the snowy mousse of cumulonimbus, the only solidity the mahogany frame. A shadowy form hovered against the foamy backdrop. She had no need to bring it into sharper focus. It was sufficient that he was there. She had no need to speak. Impossible anyway to describe this state, unless with words that contradicted each other: a weighty lightness; a nimble torpor; an anchored freedom to roam; a nothingness and an all. How could….? But no. No need for words to fill this emptiness. It was already full. Bertha closed her eyes and let the feeling course through her, to the tips of her fingers, to the ends of her toes.

'I've brought you a little lunch, Miss Bertha.' Bertha opened her eyes. The door had opened. Agnethe's black plumpness, bearing a tray, invaded the room.

Agnethe laid the tray down on the escritoire. 'Just a poached egg an' some baked rice puddin'. Nice an' tasty, not too heavy.' She turned to the bed and fluffed up the eiderdown, pounded the pillows with a stern briskness. She straightened Bertha into a sitting position, arranged the invalid table over the bed and moved the tray onto it.

Bertha said nothing. How dare this woman burst in on her like this, crashing around, rearranging the furnishings of her fantasy world, bringing it tumbling down? And no, come to think of it, it was not a fantasy world. It was another world. One to which she could return whenever she chose, to which she would return as soon as she could rid her room of this baleful presence. She must try to eat. If she refused to eat, Agnethe would nag her, she would summon her mother, her mother would threaten to complain to Dr Breuer. There would be sharp exchanges and the air of her room would be

106

poisoned with acrimony. She picked up the fork with her left hand and took a mouthful of egg.

Agnethe was straightening the brushes on the dressing table, rearranging the bottles in order of size. Why couldn't she leave things alone? Why did she always have to be fiddling with something, doing things just for the sake of doing? No point in asking her why. She was the sort of person who would say that the devil makes work for idle hands. Now she'd moved over to the escritoire. She was putting the pens away, adjusting the blotter.

No, it was too much. Agnethe had to stop this. The idea of her meddling with her writing things was intolerable. She must leave the room now, even if only for a few minutes. I cannot bear this, Bertha thought. I must find something for her to do elsewhere. Her eye fell on a vase of roses. The yellow petals were browning at the edges.

'Agnethe, those flowers on the windowsill are dying. Would you throw them out, please. Take them to the kitchen now, please, and …'

Agnethe had turned to look at Bertha as she spoke. When Bertha broke off Agnethe saw the fork fall to the eiderdown. Bertha's eyes remained open, but unseeing.

Agnethe moved the invalid table down to the foot of the bed and carried on with her tidying. When she had finished, the egg and rice pudding were cold. She removed the tray and carried it back to the kitchen, along with the wilting flowers. She returned, sat down by the window, and took up some sewing. Now and again she glanced down into the street where rain fell steadily. Few people were out.

'Agnethe!' The voice was querulous, tinged with alarm.

'Yes, Miss Bertha?'

'What's happened to the tray? I was eating a poached egg. It's disappeared.' Bertha's eyes darted round the room.

'Took it back to the kitchen, I did, Miss. The egg had gone cold, the rice puddin' too.'

'It wasn't cold. I was in the middle of eating it. Right now. The fork in my hand, the tray in front of me, and now it's gone. You're trying to trick me. You whipped it away when I wasn't looking.'

'No, Miss. You were in one o' your states, you were. You been like that for about an hour.'

'You're making it up. You're trying to make me believe I'm mad. I'm going to complain to my mother.'

Bertha pulled the bell cord.

'And what have you done with the books that were lying on my bedside table? You've hidden them.' Bertha looked wildly round the room. 'The flowers. Those flowers on the windowsill. Two minutes ago I spoke to you about them. Now they've disappeared too. You said you'd take them away when you took the tray back to the kitchen. But you haven't been to the kitchen. You haven't been out of the room. What's going on? You're trying to drive me mad. You want me to think I'm mad. I'm not mad. You're a wicked woman.'

Bertha seized a pillow and threw it at Agnethe. The door opened and Mrs Pappenheim came in. 'Whatever is….'

Bertha threw a second pillow, and a third. 'Mamma, Agnethe's trying to make me believe I'm mad. Tell her I'm not mad. Tell her to stop her horrid, hateful behaviour.'

'Quiet now, child. Quiet, please.' Mrs Pappenheim turned to Agnethe. 'Agnethe, would you explain to me, please? What's been going on?'

Agnethe related the events of the past hour.

'Bertha, dear,' Mrs Pappenheim said, 'you've just had one of your absences. Don't you see? Agnethe took away the tray and the flowers and tidied up the books while you were in one of your states.'

'I can't understand it,' said Bertha, pale now and trembling. 'How can this happen?'

It was as if there was time missing in her life; time in which things had been happening in the lives of others but not in her own; things happening in her room, in her presence, of which she was unaware. Even the time that they had been happening in had not been there in her life. She was sure of that because she could not remember anything happening in her mind while these things had been happening for other people. She had not been daydreaming because, if she had, she would remember now what she had been daydreaming about. If she had fallen asleep she would know about it because she would have been aware of waking up, but there was no waking up. She was eating a poached egg, there were books beside the bed and flowers on the windowsill, then suddenly there was no egg, no books and no flowers.

'I must be mad,' she whispered.

'No, child, you're not mad, and Agnethe isn't playing tricks on you. She's here to look after you, to help you get better.'

'Well, why not get better? How she help? I want get up, out of bed. Not can.'

'Now there's no need for baby talk, Bertha. That's not going to help.'

'Not baby talk. I talk, I talk... aaaaah....' Bertha's wail ended abruptly. She closed her eyes and lay still. There was no point in talking. No one believed her. Only Dr Breuer.

'You read English novels, Dr Breuer?'

It was evening now. Bertha had dozed throughout the afternoon.

'I've read a few of Charles Dickens' novels. I think they paint an illuminating picture of the social conditions in England. I must confess, though, that I find them somewhat over-sentimental. The French naturalists – Zola and Balzac, for example – are more to my taste. Why do you ask?'

Bertha noticed Dr Breuer's glance turn to her bookshelves. She hoped that none of the titles struck him as frivolous, that he would see no shallow novelettes – presents that she had stowed away in her bookcase unread – which would lower her in his esteem.

'I think about book by Charlotte Bronte. In *Jane Eyre*. Mad woman.'

'Why do you think about *Jane Eyre* and the mad woman?'

Bertha thought about the flowers and the lunch tray and the books.

'That happen to me. Mad. Mad woman.'

'Why do you think you're mad?'

'Things happen. I don't know they happen. People say they happen. Time missing in mind. I frighten. Mad woman in *Jane Eyre* in prison in attic. I too in prison.'

'Do you mean that your mind is imprisoned, Bertha?'

'No, not mind. Me. Put away. Like mad woman in *Jane Eyre*.'

'But you're not mad, Bertha. You're suffering from a hysterical illness. You're not insane and you're not going to be put away anywhere. You need have no fear of that. We've made very satisfactory arrangements for you to be cared for in your home. Don't you agree?'

Bertha said nothing.

'But tell me, Bertha, why are you speaking to me like this, with words missing in your sentences?'

Bertha looked at Dr Breuer, puzzled. 'No words missing,' she said.

'Are you sure? Perhaps you're feeling too tired to talk?'

'No. Not tired.'

'No?' Dr Breuer's gaze probed, telling her she had no need to hide anything from him.

'You know Shakespeare play *Hamlet*, Dr Breuer?'

'I do.'

'I think about Ophelia. Mad. Like me.'

'No, not like you, Bertha.'

'Ophelia's distress. I feel too. I recognise, in her words. Same distress. So I mad too.'

'Why do you think your feelings are the same as Ophelia's?'

'Not know.'

'Why did Ophelia feel the way she did?'

'Hamlet reject her.'

'And what else?

'Father die. Hamlet kill Ophelia's father. By mistake, but he kill him.'

'I think you can see then, Bertha, why you might feel that your feelings are similar to Ophelia's. You know that your father is very ill. Your present anxieties are largely due to his condition and I think all this is preying on your mind more than usual because of your visit to your father this morning. But being worried and upset is very far from being insane.'

Again Bertha said nothing. She ached for a greater comfort than could be formulated in words. It wasn't a matter of explanations or domestic arrangements. She needed a comfort which would strengthen the structure of her being, give solidity to her self.

'Papa! You're late! Where have you been?'

Margarethe came running down the hallway and threw herself into her father's arms.

'Oof, steady, my darling, you almost knocked my hat off.' Dr Breuer laughed and handed his hat and coat to Ida, the maid. He took Margarethe's hand and walked with her into the dining room where the rest of the family were already seated at the table. He bent to kiss Mathilde and took his seat beside her.

'Why are you so late, Papa?' asked Robert. 'We've been waiting for you for ages and now I'm so hungry I'm going to have to eat twice as much as usual.'

'No, you're not,' said Baba, 'because then there won't be enough for the rest of us. You're just a greedy pig.'

'So are you,' replied Robert. 'I saw you in the kitchen just now cutting yourself a slice of strudel. You're a double greedy pig.'

'Children! Stop this name calling or you'll get nothing but bread and water for supper.' Mathilde frowned at her two eldest. The arrival of Ida with the food brought quiet to the table.

'I suppose it was the young Pappenheim lady that held you back this evening?' Mathilde slid slices of brisket onto the plates.

'It was, I'm afraid. A most interesting development. The poor girl, on top of her other disorders she's now suffering from a disruption of her speech faculty. She can only express herself in short sentences, with all but the most basic words missing. Like a telegram, in fact. Her grammar is defective. She no longer conjugates her verbs, she leaves out the definite and indefinite articles and…'

'Papa,' Margarethe stopped eating, her fork halfway to her mouth, 'what does "conjugate" mean?'

'Why don't you ask Robert? Robert, can you explain it to Margarethe, please.'

Dr Breuer turned back to Mathilde. 'It started this morning, according to the mother. She first noticed it when Bertha was upset after a misunderstanding with the nurse but she put it down to childish behaviour, attention seeking…'

'Papa! Robert says he doesn't know what "conjugate" means.'

'Yes, he does. He's just teasing you. Robert, behave yourself.'

'Of course, with it being so difficult for her to find her words, it takes longer for her to communicate, so…'

'Papa!'

'What is it, Robert?'

'Is "conjugate" when you change the end of a noun depending on what the noun is doing in the sentence or is it when you change the verb word depending on who's doing the verb and if it's now, or in the future or the past?'

'It's when you change the verb. You say "decline" when you're referring to changing the form of a noun.'

Dr Breuer turned again to his wife. 'As I was saying about Bertha…'

Mathilde interrupted. 'I think you're saying too much about Miss Pappenheim's language problems and paying too little attention to your children's attempts to learn about language.' She lifted the serving spoon. 'Who wants more potatoes?'

13

20 January 1881

Siegmund had a quiet night. The sleep did him good and he has a little more appetite today.

Bertha's condition is increasingly puzzling. Still no improvement in the muscular impairment or the squint and she still has frequent bouts of coughing. She spends much of the day in what Dr Breuer calls a state of 'absence'. When she is conscious she continues to use a form of baby talk which I find most odd, not to say alarming. Dr Breuer assures me there is no real cause for concern. I hope he is right.

I had a most disagreeable quarrel with Bertha today as she objected to Miss Thomson playing the piano. It disturbed her, Bertha said, as the piano was out of tune. I told her that I could not detect this and pointed out that it was a pleasure for her Papa, one of the few that he can still enjoy, but she would have none of it. I have arranged for the piano tuner to come tomorrow.

Ilse told me this morning that the laundrywoman has been complaining about the amount of washing that needs to be done now that we have two invalids in the house. The woman has said that we must either take someone else on to help her or find a new laundrywoman. I told Ilse that we will send the bed linen out to be laundered from now on, leaving only the smaller items to be done at home.

o~o~o

Bertha lay awake. She preferred the curtains to be left open now so that she could watch the activity of the night sky during her hours of wakefulness. The moon was full tonight. It must be shining in through the window of her father's bedroom. She imagined it casting light on his pillow, illuminating the sunken orbs of his eyes, the waxy pallor of his skin, the spots of fever flush on his cheeks.

Bertha thought of Hans Christian Andersen's *A Picture Book without Pictures*, in which each night the moon transmitted to a poor painter trapped in an urban garret a description of a scene it had witnessed on the previous night so that the artist could paint it. She had not enjoyed the stories when she read them as a child. They were too adult and often pervaded with a melancholy which made her want to weep. But now the memory of them chimed with her mood. There was one in particular, the story of a dying Greenlander, which she called to mind. He lay in a tent while his wife sat beside him sewing animal skins for his shroud. She asked him if he would like to be buried under the firm snow of the mountain or out at sea where the icebergs would be his tombstone. He chose the sea.

Bertha picked up her notebook. A story was forming in her mind. It was that of a dying man whose daughter promised that the material she had been sewing for her trousseau would be used instead for his shroud because her grief at losing him precluded her loving any other man.

Bertha made a few notes and then looked out again towards the moon. How far away was it, she wondered. Australia was at the other side of the world, a very long way away, about 10,000 miles. The moon must be further than that. But how much further? And why did it shine, as if it had gas burning inside it like a street lamp? Why did it change shape throughout the month? Why did it have dark patterns on it like the surface of a pancake as it comes off the griddle? What was it made of? What were the stars made of? How far away were they, how big? Questions crowded in on her mind, each one jostling with the others, crying out for attention. She stared hard at the starry heavens, willing answers to come to her, knowing that they would not. Towards dawn she drifted into sleep.

Bertha felt restless. Ilse had just brought in two stone hot water bottles and wrapped a couple of towels around them. That meant that Agnethe was on her way with the water for her daily bed bath. Why did she have to put up with it? She did nothing, went nowhere, so there was no need for this woman to strip off the bedclothes every morning and scrub every inch of her body, soaping and sponging as if she was as grimy as a chimney sweep. It was just another of those tasks that Agnethe had to be given simply for the sake of having something to do – and another intrusion into Bertha's private world.

The door opened. 'Time for yer bath, Miss Bertha.'

Agnethe was carrying two large pitchers of hot water. She laid them on the marble top of the washstand, beside the white china basin and ewer. She poured some of the hot water into the basin and added some cold water from the ewer.

'Not too hot, not too cold.' She tested the mixture with her elbow. 'Just right. Now where's the soap? Here we are. An' the towels.' She patted the towel-clad hot water bottles. 'Nice an' warm.'

Why didn't the woman stop prattling? No, prattling was too lightsome a word. Her speech plodded, just like her gait, each word leaden and ponderous. Bertha closed her eyes. Perhaps, if Agnethe thought she was sleeping, she would stop talking.

Bertha felt a current of cool air wash over her as Agnethe removed the eiderdown and drew her nightdress over her head, then the prickly fuzz of the blanket which she wrapped around her.

'Face first.'

The wash cloth swept over her forehead, down each cheek and around her nose and chin. Her right eye stung as some of the soapiness seeped in through her screwed up eyelids; there was a bitter taste in her mouth as it penetrated her clenched lips. She heard a dripping noise as Agnethe wrung out the cloth in rinsing water and felt it being passed over again, followed by a patting with one of the warm towels.

'Now yer ears.'

Bertha hated this bit. Agnethe's fat fingers poking around in the crevices and down inside. Sometimes it tickled and made her laugh – as if she had no control over herself, was simply a machine on which a button had been pushed - and then she felt foolish.

Agnethe was doing her neck now, the pressure of her fingers uncomfortable on her windpipe. She was saying

115

something about the refreshment of a daily bath for invalids. She moved on to her right arm, raising it and lathering all round, then under the armpit. The very touch of her was disagreeable. If they would just give her a bowl of water Bertha was sure she could manage on her own. Her left arm was little affected by her illness. She could surely pass a wash cloth over herself. No, Mamma had said when she had protested. The job wouldn't be done properly and Bertha might knock things over, scald herself with the hot water, perhaps.

The right arm was rinsed and patted dry. The hand was last, each finger separated out and rubbed individually. What an unconscionable time it took! Now she was going to have to go through the whole process again with the left arm.

The ignominy of it! As if she were a babe in arms. She must think of something else, anything but this manhandling of her body. Those questions which she wanted to ask Dr Breuer. She started to rehearse them in her head so that she would be able to recall them readily when he was with her later in the day. The distance to the moon. Why it shines. What it's made of. What the stars are made of. Their size. How far away. Wasn't there something else she wanted to know about the moon? Oh yes, why it changes shape.

Imagine. It is Dr Breuer at the bedside now. Not Agnethe. It is his light tenor voice she hears, not Agnethe's ugly Bavarian sounds. His voice. 'How are you today, Miss Bertha?' Not deep and rough and growly like some men. Light, but substantial. Even-toned. There were no sudden changes of register, no stridency or gruffness. She could imagine him singing a Schubert song. She saw him now, standing by the piano in the drawing room, singing. At the piano, herself, her fingers flawlessly picking out 'Evening Under the Lime Tree'.

> Where do you come from, o nameless yearning,
> That presses on my anxious breast?

Bertha played out the scene in her mind several times, always with Dr Breuer singing the same line. Barely aware of Agnethe's ministrations now.

116

The 'nameless yearning' of the song. The 'anxious breast'. Her anxious breast. The song spoke to her. Dr Breuer was speaking to her through it. Back to the beginning. She played the opening chords. Dr Breuer started again.

Where do you come from, o nameless yearning

Hands on her calves now. The blanket rolled up over her knees. Inside it she felt snug. The hands caressed her lower legs, moving, it seemed, in time to the music of the song. Nameless yearning. Dr Breuer's hands. Soothing her anxious breast. Soft warmth enfolding her ankles, her soles, her toes. Enfolding her whole self.

'She was quite awake in the morning, Doctor.' Mrs Pappenheim led the way into Bertha's bedroom. 'For breakfast she took a cup of coffee and half of an orange. She was still alert when Agnethe started her bed bath at ten o'clock, although she didn't speak at all. But then she's been so taciturn lately. Then by the time Agnethe had finished washing her she'd withdrawn into this strange state. As she is now.' Mrs Pappenheim gestured towards the bed. 'She's been like this throughout the afternoon. Her eyes open. Muttering to herself. Making some agitated movements. But she doesn't respond to any of our attempts to communicate with her.'

Dr Breuer looked down at Bertha who was lying propped up against her pillows, seemingly unaware of his presence.

'You say she's appeared agitated, Mrs Pappenheim. Could you describe this in a little more detail?'

'There were repeated hand movements. It's difficult to describe really. Her right arm has such little movement in it. Her fingers have always remained mobile, as you know, and it was the fingers which were moving. I would say that she appeared to be stitching something, although this impression may have been caused by the fact that only her fingers could move and not the rest of the limb. Then there was also the fact that the left hand appeared to be holding something, and holding it close to the right fingers, as if she were supporting a fabric for needlework.'

'You say that she was muttering to herself. Can you remember anything that she was saying?'

'Some of it, yes. She seemed to be talking about a trousseau. In fact, that may have been why I thought she was making sewing movements. She kept repeating something about a trousseau. I couldn't make any sense of it but she seemed to be very preoccupied by this idea of a trousseau.'

'Trousseau.'

Dr Breuer looked down. 'What did you say, Bertha?'

Bertha's eyes were still unseeing.

'Girl sew trousseau. Sew lace. Sew silk. White lace. White silk. Petticoat. Sew all night. Not sleep.' Bertha sighed.

'Who is this girl, Bertha? What's all this about a trousseau?'

Dr Breuer held up his hand to still the mother's questioning. 'I'll sit with her, Mrs Pappenheim. I think you should take some rest now.'

'Very well, Doctor.' Mrs Pappenheim withdrew. A moment later Miss Thomson took up her seat by the door.

'Sew. Always sew.. Soon married. Soon leave home. Silk and lace. Make petticoats. Go to new home. With husband. New clothes.'

Dr Breuer listened attentively. Bertha paused for a while and then started again.

'Girl sit beside father. Father in bed. Ill. Girl sew. All night. Sew petticoats. Girl sad. So sad. Tears drop. Tears fall on silk petticoat.' Bertha moaned, her face contorted. Dr Breuer waited, saying nothing. From beyond the bedroom came faint sounds of household life – the opening and closing of doors, inaudible voices.

'Father speak to girl. "Why weep, my darling? What wrong? You must happy now. We all happy. You married soon."

'"Papa, I swear to you," said the girl, "I will never marry. Never could I love a man as I love you."'

Breuer looked sharply at Bertha. The return to normal syntax had been sudden, but there was no change in consciousness. Bertha was still in her altered state. She

118

continued to speak, now with enhanced fluency, her voice soft and low.

'"You are to be taken from us. We know that. We know that you are to die soon. My grief will not allow me to take another man into my heart. No, papa, my trousseau will be your shroud. I will sit here and continue to stitch lovingly, because this silken garment will be worn by you."

'The girl stooped and kissed her father's forehead, her tears mingling with his hair, running down his pale cheeks.

'Night after night, she continued to stitch. So engrossed was she in her work, determined to create the most beautiful shroud that ever a father had been laid to rest in, that she did not notice, at first, that her father had begun to cough less, to sleep more easily, to speak with a stronger voice.

'"Why are you still stitching, my darling?" he asked one night. "Have you not noticed that I no longer have need of a shroud?"

'"Papa, what can you mean?" the girl asked. "Everyone has need of a shroud, and you will go to your grave in the most beautiful silk shroud that has ever been stitched."

'"That will not be for many a long day," said her father. "The thought of your grief, your sacrifice of married life, of having a family of your own, have given me such strength that I have fought off my illness. Put down that shroud, my darling. We shall buy you a new roll of silk. You are to have the most beautiful trousseau that ever a father has been able to offer his daughter."

'The girl set aside the shroud and started afresh on new petticoats. Shortly afterwards she wed. Years later, when her father died in the fullness of age, she allowed him to slip away. His life had run its full course.'

Bertha stopped speaking. A few moments later her eyes registered a flash of recognition. 'Good evening, Doctor Breuer.'

'Good evening, Bertha. How are you today?'

Bertha breathed in deeply, wallowing in the cocoon of pillows and eiderdown, lulled by the quiet hiss of the gasolier. Rain hammered softly against the window panes, serving only to enhance the warm comfort of the interior.

Bertha considered the question. 'I feel comfortable, more relaxed.' She smiled at Dr Breuer.

'That's excellent news. And how have you been during the day?'

'Oh, I hardly know. I've slept most of the day, I think.'

'Your mother tells me you've been agitated. Do you have any recollection of this?'

'Not at all.'

'She also said you seemed to be talking about a trousseau. Have you any idea why this should have been in your mind?'

'A trousseau?' Bertha thought for a moment. 'Well, last night, while I was lying awake – you know I hardly sleep at all during the night – I was thinking of a story involving a girl who was stitching her trousseau. I made some notes about it. Perhaps I was dreaming about this. I can't recall.'

'Would you like to tell me the story. I'd be interested to hear it.'

Bertha repeated the same story she had recounted earlier.

'Does it surprise you, Bertha, to learn that while I was sitting at your bedside earlier, before you woke up, you told me the same story?'

'But how could I, Doctor, if I was sleeping?'

'Well, I'm not sure that we can call the state you were in sleep exactly. It's more like the state of absence you've been experiencing recently, a state between sleep and wakefulness, a different kind of consciousness.'

The feeling of relaxation ebbed from Bertha at Dr Breuer's words. She had been talking without being aware of it. Telling a story that she had invented the night before. What else might she have been saying? What might she say in the future? It seemed that she was no longer in control of herself. Sometimes it seemed even that she was no longer herself at all.

'I don't understand. How can these things happen?'

'You may find this puzzling, Bertha, but believe me, we doctors have experience of hysterical symptoms like this. You have no need to worry about it. It's all part of your general condition which I've already explained to you. But perhaps

120

you'd like to tell me why you made up that particular story? Why did you have the idea of a girl transforming her trousseau into a shroud for her father?'

'I was looking at the moon, and I remembered one of the stories from *A Picture Book without Pictures*. The one where the moon is looking down on a woman in Greenland sewing animal skins for her husband's shroud. So then I developed a story of my own about a shroud.'

'But why the trousseau? Why was the girl in your story so grief-stricken about her father's imminent death that she renounced all hope of her own future happiness? I wonder, Bertha, if your fears for your father don't play a large part in your story?'

Bertha said nothing. She dared not confess to what she was sure would reveal her to be an unnatural daughter. She knew not when the change had taken place. Was it after she had created the story about the trousseau and the shroud? Had it been a gradual change or had it happened all at once? She was so confused now, with days melding into nights, wakefulness into sleep, and reality into fantasy, that she could no longer be sure of anything. But she realised, with a mixture of appalled guilt and easeful relief, that her father's expected death no longer stood poised over her like the blade of an executioner's guillotine. She was distanced from it, cocooned in the supportive care of the man at her side, a man who she now felt could give her so much more than her own father ever had.

'I expect you're right, Doctor. But please, let's forget about those morbid subjects. I should so like you to tell me about the moon. I have so many questions that came to me last night as I gazed up at it. And when we have finished with the moon, you shall tell me about the stars and why they shine and how they got there and everything that makes up the dazzling splendour of the night sky.'

Dr Breuer stretched out his legs and leaned back into his chair. 'Well, now, Bertha, what would you like to know?'

Bertha again lay awake. She stared up at the full moon with

eyes now open to some of its mysteries. The moon was not, as she had imagined, a lantern hanging in the sky, but a spherical body travelling round the earth at a distance of a quarter of a million miles. An unimaginable distance, but a close neighbour compared with the other heavenly bodies. How omniscient Dr Breuer was. Looking at the stars she tried to guess which of the multitudinous points of light might be planets. The stars twinkled because they generated their own light, Dr Breuer had explained, whereas the planets, like the moon, merely reflected the light of the sun and therefore shone steadily. But there were so many stars and so few planets, looking for them would be like looking for a needle in a haystack. How had they ever been identified in the first place? She made a note of the question in her notebook.

o~o~o

February 1881

Dearest Anna

Again I write to you at dead of night. And again my mind is in a state of exuberance, each thought generating a new one as soon as I formulate the first.

Today I had such an interesting conversation with Dr B. (Need I even write that sentence? After all, my conversations with Dr B are always interesting.) We talked about the stars, which have been a source of much wonder and puzzlement to me. (Is this something which you have studied, Anna? I am sure it would fascinate you.) How gratifying it is to have a learned person like Dr B all to myself, explaining to me mysteries which I had thought unfathomable, and in such a way as to make it all seem clear and simple. Even more interesting than the known facts and figures are the speculations about all the things we do not know. We discussed the idea that there may be people like us – or perhaps very different from us – living on other planets. The very notion conjures up such a myriad of possibilities that I feel I have enough food for thought to occupy my waking hours for all eternity. At times like this I cease to feel wretched and frustrated at my illness because it has brought me pleasures that I had never known before. I am especially intrigued by a story Dr B told me about the moon, written more than two hundred years ago, by a

122

Frenchman, Cyrano de Bergerac. In it, a man travelled to the moon by attaching himself to jars of dew which were drawn upwards by the heat of the sun. But the most interesting aspect of the story was not the scientific one (which in any case was nonsense as evaporating dew could not even lift a man off the ground, much less as far as the moon). No, what was interesting was the society that he found on the moon, whose beliefs and practices were in many ways topsy-turvy to those he had left behind on Earth. Thus for example, for the moon dwellers, to die of old age was a punishment to which they could be condemned for bad behaviour, while those who lived righteously were entitled to what was considered a good death – being stabbed to death by a friend as soon as the infirmities of old age began to appear. At first I was quite shocked by this idea but the more I consider it, the more I wonder if it would not indeed be a better end; one quick sharp pain at a point when there is little left to look forward to rather than the lingering distress consequent upon the gradual loss of one's faculties. What do you think, Anna? Of course, this manner of thinking, this freedom to question, is quite new to me. I am so used to being told that things are so – and that they are so because they have always been so, or because God has decreed it thus – and that is the end of the matter. You, I think, have always been much freer in this respect and I envy you for it.

Please write to me soon, dear Cousin, telling me all the thoughts that this subject has aroused in you.

With greatest affection
Bertha

14

It was well after eleven when Dr Breuer arrived home. The apartment was in darkness, with just a glimmer of light around the door of the bedroom he shared with Mathilde. After his evening visit to Bertha he had gone to a soiree at the Exners. As usual, there was a lively crowd. Dr Breuer had hoped some medical men might be there so that he could discuss his concerns about Bertha's condition. Despite his assurances to the Pappenheims that Bertha was suffering from hysteria he could not rid himself of a nagging anxiety. Some of her symptoms – the hemiparesis, the speech impairment – could be associated with a number of neurological disorders. Was there something he was missing in his examinations?

Mathilde was in bed reading when he entered the bedroom. He bent over and kissed her cheek. She made a moue and carried on reading. He apologized for his lateness and went into his dressing room where he remembered with dismay that he had promised to come back for supper before going to the Exners. It had taken so long to coax Bertha out of her aphasic state and listen to the ensuing story that he had gone straight to the soiree without giving a thought to supper. He took his watch out of his waistcoat pocket and glanced at it. Almost midnight.

The evening at the Exners had nevertheless been a worthwhile one, he thought, as he removed his shirt collar. He had spent much of it in conversation with the author Marie von Ebner-Eschenbach. Now there was a woman who had made the most of her abilities. He must encourage Bertha to read some of her work. It would do her good to see what a woman could do if she set her mind to it. Come to think of it, there was also Betty Paoli. Remarkable how she had been able to make a name for herself as a writer – despite the additional handicap of being born out of wedlock. Her poetry was acclaimed by the Viennese literati, her journalism also. Bertha would certainly enjoy it. He would ask her if she was acquainted with it. He might even give her one of Betty's books. She was ripe for this kind of intellectual encouragement. Dr Breuer paused in the act of hanging up his jacket, thinking back to Bertha's enthusiasm for learning about the stars and her reaction to his recounting of the Cyrano de Bergerac story. If she could only have more of this sort of thing they might well find that her physical illness just faded away. He could not understand the approach of that American fellow Weir Mitchell who deprived his neurasthenic patients of all intellectual activity. For many of those women that was the very thing they needed.

Dr Breuer went through to the bathroom at the other side of his dressing room. He would have liked to take a bath but decided against it. The gas geyser was noisy. It might disturb the family and Mathilde must already be cross with him. He contented himself with a brief rub down with cold water.

His thoughts turned again to the question of diagnosis. It was a week now since Bertha had recounted the story of the trousseau and each day since then her behaviour had followed the same pattern. Somnolent for most of the day, with periods of incoherent muttering. When he arrived in the evening he would encourage her to talk, prompting her with words she had uttered during the day. She would respond by telling a story, first of all in her aphasic style, then gradually improving until she was speaking eloquently in perfect German. After that she spent most of the night awake, apparently, busying herself with writing and thinking up stories. But this in itself was surely enough to settle the matter. If the aphasia was due to an organic lesion, they would not find this regular daily remission of the symptom. Therefore, he could only conclude that it was of hysterical origin. Still, he would have liked to discuss it with someone like Ernst Fleischl or Moritz Benedikt. Pity none of them had been present tonight.

Dr Breuer towelled himself dry, pulled a nightshirt over his head and returned to the bedroom. Mathilde was still reading. As he slipped under the eiderdown he began to apologise for missing supper, embellishing his justification with the latest developments in Bertha's condition. Mathilde snapped her book shut and reached out to extinguish the gasolier by the side of the bed. 'Good night, Josef.'

Agnethe tapped on the parlour door. It was already ajar. Mrs Pappenheim was sitting at the table, writing a shopping list.

''Scuse me, Mrs Pappenheim, mam, very sorry to trouble you but I don' rightly understan' what Miss Bertha is sayin'.'

Mrs Pappenheim looked up. ''I'm afraid we all have that problem, Agnethe. We just have to try to guess from the few words she is able to say what the whole sentence is.'

'This is somethin' different, mam. She's usin' foreign words. She knows I don' speak no foreign, but she looks mighty puzzled that I don' understan' her.

Mrs Pappenheim sighed and set aside the shopping list. 'Very well, then. I'll come and speak to her.' She got up and led the way to Bertha's room. What on earth could this be about? As if she didn't have enough to worry her. The Warburgs were coming for the Shabbat meal and she needed to make sure that everything was in order. Friday was always a busy day. Since Siegmund and Bertha had become bedridden, people had been ensuring that she and Willi never had to celebrate Shabbat on their own. So there were always guests to be catered for, things to be attended to, the household staff to be supervised.

Mrs Pappenheim stopped in the doorway. She saw Bertha's features crease into fretful petulance, her finger pointing to the untouched breakfast tray lying beside the bed.

'*No voglio petit-déjeuner. Enleve. Tired. Voglio dormir. Ne dors pas noche. Je veux dormir adesso.*'

Italian, French, English. Bertha knew all those languages. But why should she want to start speaking them now? And why jumble them all together like this? Mrs Pappenheim clenched her hands and stepped further into the room. 'Bertha, what's all this nonsense? Speak German, please.'

'*I am speaking German,*' Bertha said in English. She closed her eyes.

126

Mrs Pappenheim pursed her lips. She sat down at the escritoire. 'I'm at a loss to know what to make of all this, Agnethe. Each day seems to bring some fresh complication.' She got up again and moved over to the bed. 'Speak to me, Bertha. Is this some silly game?' She reached out to smooth Bertha's hair from her forehead but withdrew her hand without touching it. Bertha said nothing. Her eyes remained closed.

'Ignore this, please, Agnethe. Just ignore it. When Bertha needs something I'm sure she'll find that she can speak German again. And it's too hot in here.' Mrs Pappenheim opened the catch and flung the window wide open. 'It's little wonder if Bertha is confused in this heat.' She bent down and adjusted the stove damper. 'You really mustn't let the heat build up in the room like this.' She pulled the quilt down to the foot of the bed, leaving Bertha covered only by a sheet. Finally she took a shawl out of the wardrobe and laid it over the sheet. 'And now I must get back to my business.'

Agnethe sat down by the open window and took up the length of black bombazine she was stitching for a dress. The sky outside was overcast, the dark grey clouds pregnant with rain.

Bertha lay somnolent throughout the day, often moving restlessly and muttering, sometimes moaning and wailing. At midday Mrs Pappenheim relieved Agnethe so that she could go and eat in the kitchen. When Agnethe returned the rain had started to fall. It was drumming steadily against the windows. Agnethe lit the gasolier and bent over her sewing. Bertha continued to murmur and groan.

By the time Dr Breuer arrived in the evening Agnethe had attached the skirt to the bodice. She folded the half-made dress and stowed it away in the ottoman window seat which Mrs Pappenheim had placed in the room for her convenience. She and Mrs Pappenheim stood at the foot of the bed as Dr Breuer walked over and spoke to Bertha.

'Good evening, Bertha.'

'*Angoisse.*' Bertha whispered, her eyes half-open.

Dr Breuer moved closer to the bed and bent to hear her

words.

'*Angoisse.*'

'Why do you say *angoisse*, Bertha? What do you mean?' He sat down on the low chintz chair at the head of the bed.

'*Angoisse.*'

'*Pourquoi vous parlez en francais?*'

'*Ammalata. Ho paura.*'

'And now I think you're speaking Italian? Can you tell me what's troubling you?'

'*Serpent. Voir serpent.*' Bertha's features contorted with disgust. She shrank back into the pillows. '*Longue. Black. Ho paura.*'

'Where, Bertha? Where is the snake?

'*Voila. Adesso. Look. Go away.*'

'And now you're speaking English. Would you like me to speak with you in English?'

'Agnethe. *N'aime pas. Brutta. Go away.*'

'It's as I told you, doctor,' Mrs Pappenheim said. 'This jumble of languages. If we could even understand what the words meant it might help us. I have some knowledge of English and a little French but that's all and Agnethe, of course, speaks only German.

Dr Breuer stood up and joined the women at the foot of the bed. 'If you could just tell me again what's been happening during the day, in as much detail as you can remember. Mrs Pappenheim?'

Mrs Pappenheim related the events of the early morning, the polyglot speech, the rejected breakfast tray. Agnethe described the lapse into somnolence, the restlessness, the disjointed muttering.

'And have you any idea what she was talking about? Any hint as to what could have been preoccupying her?'

Agnethe reported Bertha as seeming distressed about something. 'Not like she was sufferin' pain, if you understan' me, Doctor, sir. More like she was in a panic about somethin', about not bein' able to find somethin'. Mebbe she was lost. I ain't sure. I don' know why that idea come upon me. Oh yes, lordy, sir, I remember now. Miss Bertha kep' askin' questions

128

about how far, and where.'

'Indeed, I had much the same impression,' Mrs Pappenheim said, 'I didn't attach any importance to it as it seemed all of a piece with the way her mind has been wandering. She also mentioned a desert, although why Bertha should be thinking about deserts I have no idea.'

'Beg pardon, mam.' The talk of deserts had jolted Agnethe's memory. 'Miss Bertha said somethin' about water. I thought she was surely talkin' about the rain hammerin' on the window panes, then she said somethin' about bein' thirsty, an' somethin' about a bottle.'

'Thank you, Agnethe. You may go now.' Mrs Pappenheim turned to Dr Breuer. 'I don't know if this is any help to you, Doctor. I'll be waiting for you in the parlour when you're finished.'

Dr Breuer sat down again beside the bed. Bertha was still muttering. He listened to the potpourri of phrases, trying to piece together some meaning from them. To no avail. He started to interject with questions, latching on to certain of her words here and there. What was causing the anguish she talked of? Why did she talk of fear? What was the problem with Agnethe? No response. Only more of the incoherent speech. He turned then to the details that had emerged in the conversation with the two women.

'You were talking about water, Bertha. What kind of water?'

Bertha sighed.

'Drinking water?' He paused. 'Rain?'

Another sigh. He let a few minutes of silence elapse. Then: 'What is this desert, Bertha?' Bertha moaned and made as if to open her mouth. Dr Breuer repeated his question. 'The desert, Bertha. What is it?'

'Desert.' Bertha repeated the word. 'Desert.'

Then, as on the previous evening, she started to tell a tale, agrammatically at first, and finally quite fluently. The elements overheard by Mrs Pappenheim and Agnethe were there. A young woman, recently married, had set out from her tribal home with a caravan of retainers to travel to her husband's home. They lost their way in the desert. The young woman found a discarded leather bottle. She opened it, weak with thirst, hoping to find a few drops of water. Instead, a genie popped out. The genie offered her the choice of three routes out of her predicament – one to her husband's home, one back to her own paternal home, the third to an oasis. She opted for the route to the oasis. The caravan set out on her chosen road. They never arrived at the oasis. It was a mirage.

~**15**~

15 March 1881

Purim. Normally one of the happiest days of the year but not this year. Siegmund is nearing the end. Doctor Breuer has advised that it cannot be long now and I must admit to a certain relief. His suffering will soon be over. He insisted on hearing the megillah, *however, so I arranged for a reader to come from the synagogue. Willi and I gathered together by Siegmund's bedside for it. Bertha, of course, was absent. She is still in no fit state. Siegmund was upset by her behaviour the last time she visited him. Her obvious distress at seeing him so ill worried him and made him feel it would be better if she didn't visit him any more. I reported this to Bertha, hoping that it would encourage her to rally her spirits. She did not respond. In fact, that was the day she stopped speaking altogether. Not a word for fourteen days now.*

I prepared mishloach manot *for all the usual recipients. Kathe baked* hamentaschen *pastries. I put two in each basket along with a selection of chocolates. Little Cecilia from the Becker family came up with her nurse to deliver a* mishloach *for Bertha — a bowl of walnuts and a tangerine. Cecilia was dressed up as Queen Esther, in a long blue robe with a red sash, and with a silvery crown on her head. It reminded me of how much Willi and Bertha enjoyed this day when they were children, putting on their costumes and masks, running around shaking their* ra'ashan *rattles, singing their Purim songs. I talked to Bertha about this when I showed her Cecilia's present. She seemed not to hear me. I don't even know if she was aware that it was Purim, or even if she would have been moved to pray or to ask to attend the* megillah *if she was. I often feel that Bertha pays no more than lip service to her religion, even when she is well. She does her duty but I feel there is a lack of fervour. I have never spoken of this to Siegmund.*

I have no idea what can be going on in Bertha's mind. Her condition has been deteriorating for three months now, despite Dr Breuer's daily visits. He assures me that it is just a question of time, yet I am beginning to doubt. I am even beginning to wonder if he too has doubts. In any case,

131

what is this illness called hysteria? No one seems to know. Almost anything, it seems, can be diagnosed as hysteria. The only thing that the different cases of hysteria have in common, as far as I can see, is that the doctors can find no other label to apply to them.

o~o~o

Bertha opened her mouth. Her teeth clacked as it snapped shut again. The words. Where were the words? The thoughts were too fast. Gone before she could describe them, before she could tell herself what she was thinking. But she knew. The thoughts were there. Deep down. Like the contents of a closed cupboard.

'I can see that you want to say something, Bertha.'

Man's voice. Familiar voice. Familiar face. Beside her. Like a memory from far back in time. No sense of presence, only a memory, among a flurry of other memories, fluttering around in her mind, like the flakes in a snowstorm paperweight.

Taste of spiced pretzel.

Playing tag in the Prater. Catching Willi. Shrieks of glee. Horses hooves hammering through the chestnut trees.

Smell of chalk dust. Hebrew lesson. Squarish letter shapes.

Ilse, tightening her stays. 'Breathe in, please, Miss Bertha.'

Pinched lips of Miss Thomson. Frown lines between the eyes.

Meadow in Ischl. Apple smell of sweet briar. Klara's laughter. Reverberating. Echoing. Peals of summer thunder. Overlaid with a rumble. Rumble of familiar voice.

'You clearly want to speak but something is stopping you. I think it might be worth trying hypnosis to help you overcome this obstacle. Shall we?'

Dancing lesson. Waltz stilled on second step. Tableau of paired dancers poised on toes, arms arced. Single piano note. Not fading. Not repeating. Just resonating for ever.

'Look at me, Bertha. Keep looking at me. Let yourself relax. You are feeling tired now. Let all your worries slip away.'

The words were coming from far away. The vowels were drawn out, distorted.

132

'Nooow you are feeeling drooowsy. You loong to fall asleeeep.'

Polishing *challah* tray. Spirit of hartshorn spiralling up her nose.

Mama angry with Ilse. Fish not fresh.

Red velvet dress. Willi's Bar Mitzvah.

Red stains of her first monthly flow.

Red sputum gushing from the mouth of Papa.

Split pomegranate! Burst of succulent seeds like bloodied sago.

Stained sky. Rim of flaming ring. Sheets of blood-red cloud.

'Can you hear me, Bertha?'

Bertha's mouth opened and closed. A faint exhalation.

'We are going to work on your speech. We are going to clear the channels of your mind so that your thoughts can pass freely again. Let your thoughts take form, give them words and let the words flow to your tongue. There's nothing to fear. Just let go. Let the words flow.'

Words. There were no words. Only images, flashes of sensation.

The clock in the hallway struck the half hour. One thirty. He had been lying awake for almost two hours. The only other sound was the breathing of Mathilde, rippling with a faint snore.

Confound it all! He was never going to get to sleep without coming to a decision about Bertha. He had been so sure at first that it was a straightforward case of hysteria but over the past three months the illness had branched out into a condition of such unusual complexity he was beginning to doubt his judgement. He needed to have a look at that journal he had ordered, the one Brücke had recommended, a publication specialising in neurology. It had arrived the day before and he had not yet had time to open it. He would do it now.

Dr Breuer slipped out of bed, put on his grey alpaca dressing gown and went down to his consulting room. The

133

package lay on his desk: eight issues, dating back over the past two years. He opened the first one and skimmed over the list of contents. Ha! The first article: *Case of Cerebral Tumour – Symptoms Simulating Hysteria.* The very thing he was beginning to fear. He started to read. A girl of sixteen, of marked intelligence, afflicted with intermittent blindness and deafness. Headaches. Weakness in the lower limbs. Fits in which she laughed, cried, shouted, struck those caring for her. Various doctors consulted could find no organic cause. Ergo a diagnosis of aggravated hysteria, an opinion bolstered by the patient's behaviour. She had always been a wilful child and was suspected of being sexually forward. Too interested in reading novels of an amorous nature. There was also 'abundant evidence that masturbation was practised to a very great extent'.

Good God! What the devil were these doctors about, asking young women about these things! He himself would never dare to broach such a subject with Bertha. In any case, there was no need. No need whatsoever. He began to feel a heat rise in him. He loosened his dressing gown.

Dietary measures, a change of air and moral control were prescribed. Six months after the onset of her symptoms, she suddenly deteriorated rapidly. Totally blind and deaf, no power in her legs, and doubly incontinent. Unconscious and delirious, her pulse mounting to 150, she died.

God forbid that Bertha's illness should terminate in an outcome like this. But how to be sure that she was indeed suffering from hysteria? And what was the root of the problem in the case of this sixteen-year-old? He read on.

An autopsy revealed a tumour in the right hemisphere. The brain was removed and taken to a laboratory for dissection. This was never carried out as the brain was destroyed by mistake.

Dr Breuer slapped the journal down on his desk. What stupidity!

He picked it up again and skimmed the commentary. The author, who had been one of the doctors treating the girl, was at pains to distance himself from those who had classified her as hysterical or malingering. He appeared to think that they had been unduly influenced by her disposition, her sexual precocity and a family history of nervous temperament.

But dash it all, given that no organic cause could be found what else could they do? Examination of the eyes and ears and the muscles of the limbs had revealed nothing. Not only that, her symptoms had waxed and waned in a way that made no sense. Just like Bertha's. Besides, the girl had none of the usual symptoms that might be expected in the case of a brain tumour, such as strabismus, diplopia....

Just a minute! Bertha suffered from both of those.

Breuer stood up and paced around the room. He had examined Bertha meticulously and found nothing to suggest an organic lesion. In any case, it was an established fact that hysteria mimics other illnesses. And the cough was clearly hysterical. Very likely then that the other symptoms were equally so.

But Bertha's aphasia. He sat down again. Such bizarre forms of it. Given the family history, this could possibly be due to a chronic tuberculous meningitis – in the pons, then extending to the left fossa Sylvii and the speech area. It didn't bear thinking of. In any case, if that was the source of the illness nothing could be done. Likewise if it was a tumour. Better just to discount the possibilities and continue with the present treatment.

The hall clock was striking again. Two thirty. He must go back to bed. The reading and thinking had tired him out. He would sleep now.

He closed the journal and went back to the bedroom. Mathilde seemed not to have moved since he left her. He eased himself carefully under the eiderdown.

But still sleep would not come. He could not put out of his mind the tart judgement of a Dr Reynolds quoted in the article: 'to confound hysteria with tumour of the brain indicates either "carelessness, or a prejudiced view of dealing with the obscure affections of women"'.

'Let us go back to the day on which you last spoke,' said Dr

Breuer. Bertha was again under hypnosis. 'Let us try to resume your last conversation. You are talking with your mother. Your mother has told you that your father was upset after your visit to him.'

Voice of Papa. 'How I've missed you, sweetheart.' Faint and reedy. Smell of carbolic acid. Milk-white paper-thin skin.

'He's concerned that you're worried about him and feels it would be best if you didn't visit him at present.'

Choking. Acrid fumes of smelling salts. Anxious eyes of Papa. Making Papa feel worse. Guilt.

'You say nothing. What are you thinking, Bertha? What are your feelings about this?'

Fault. Duty.

'You are back in that conversation, Bertha. Your father doesn't want to see you. He is very ill. What would you like to say?'

Bertha's forehead creased. Her eyelids flickered.

'Yes, Bertha?'

'Papa…..Papa….'

Dr Breuer waited, but Bertha said no more. He brought her out of the trance.

'I think we've made some progress, Bertha. I'd like you to think back to the conversation you had with your mother on the day you stopped talking. She told you he didn't want you to visit him because it was too upsetting for you. How do you feel about this?'

A burning feeling. Shame. Such shame. Her cheeks must be aflame. She burned from within.

'Bertha, you can speak now. While you were under hypnosis you started to talk about this. You said 'Papa'. What about your papa?'

Too ashamed to speak of it.

'Bertha, I know this is difficult for you. Your father is very ill, he doesn't want to see you. Doesn't this make you very sad?'

Not sad. Angry. With herself. Blaming herself. Blaming Papa too. Angry with him. He should know she had to see him.

Dr Breuer got up and walked over to the window. He stood with his back to Bertha. There was silence in the room for some minutes. Then Bertha started to talk, slowly, in English.

'No, I am not sad. I am angry. I am his daughter. I have a right to see him. It's my duty to care for him.'

Dr Breuer turned round. 'But don't you see, Bertha, that in your present state you are unable to care for him?' he asked in German.

'Well, I should at least be able to visit him. How can he refuse that, to his own daughter?'

Bertha lifted her left arm and pushed back a strand of hair which had fallen over her face.

'Bertha, do you realise what you've just done?'

'Nothing. I haven't done anything.'

'You've just raised your left arm. You stretched out from the shoulder, bent your elbow and brushed your hair back.'

'Oh. Did I?'

'Bertha, you haven't been able to make a movement like this for weeks.'

Bertha looked down at her left arm. She flexed the wrist, bent the elbow, then straightened it with the hand above her head as if in salute.

16

It was the fifth of April. Four days previously Bertha had got out of bed and, with Agnethe's help, dressed herself for the first time since early December. Her left limbs had returned to normal, she was able to turn her head from side to side without difficulty, her strabismus was less marked, and the stiffness in her right arm and leg had reduced.

She had not left her room since getting up. Her father must not be disturbed, her mother had said. It was imperative that he be allowed to rest, that an atmosphere of quiet calm be maintained throughout the apartment. Bertha, with her unsteady gait, could not be allowed to stumble along the corridor, in and out of rooms, perhaps falling over or bumping into things.

Bertha had begged to be allowed to see her father. It was such a long time since she had seen him. She did not know how long. The passage of time was confused for her now. Because of her periods of 'time missing', her recent memories were sparse, yet spread out by those vast stretches of unknowing, the mental cloudiness which persisted still.

She tried to remember what she had done in the past few days. On Friday – was it Friday? Today was Tuesday, so it must have been on Friday – she had got up. Yes, of course it was Friday. Ilse had come into her bedroom to do the usual cleaning for Shabbat. How could Mamma let the servants go round the house cleaning, creating commotion, if she, Bertha, was forbidden even to walk along to the bathroom for fear of disturbing Papa? But the Shabbat preparations must take precedence over all else, even the comfort of the desperately ill. And Papa was desperately ill. They were all lying to her.

'He is as well as can be expected,' Mamma kept telling her.

'Much the same,' Agnethe said almost every day.

'There's no need for you to worry, Miss Bertha,' Ilse had

said that very morning when she brought in her breakfast tray.

But there was need to worry. Papa might die without her having the opportunity to speak to him one last time, leaving her with the knowledge that for the last weeks of his final illness she had lain only a few feet away from him, impotent and banished from his sight.

She sat now on the chaise-longue. She had ordered Agnethe out of the room, telling her that she wanted to be alone to read. But she had no interest in reading. There was too much anxiety churning around in her. Her head thrummed with restlessness, frustration and worry.

The front door opened. There was a low murmur of voices. The door closed again. Footsteps – how many? – passed her door and moved on towards her father's room. Bertha got up, stepped over to the door, quietly turned the handle and pulled. As she had expected, the door did not move. Since Friday her mother had locked it from the outside. In case of accidents, she had said. Now that Bertha was out of bed, there was a risk that she might start roaming, like a sleep walker, while in one of her absence states.

Bertha walked over to the window and looked down at the late-afternoon traffic: carriages heading in and out of the city centre, servant girls carrying provisions from the market; an organ grinder stood on the corner of Maria Theresien Strasse, cranking out the *galop* from Offenbach's Orpheus in the Underworld; a costermonger shouted his wares from behind a barrow stacked high with fruit and vegetables; behind him the nursemaid from the Becker family downstairs pushed little Emil in a wicker baby carriage.

It was early spring. The sky was cloudless and the sun radiant. Bertha opened the window. It had been late autumn when she had last stepped outside. She leaned over and breathed in the clean fresh air, thirstily, as if hoping it might flush out the channels of her agitated mind. It struck her rather like an icy douche, bringing her thoughts up short. What was she doing, revelling in the balminess of springtime, when her father lay within, on his deathbed? She recalled with crushing mortification how, after her last visit to him, she had

139

taken refuge in thoughts of Dr Breuer, giving herself over to them with a pleasurable joyousness, thrusting her father and his illness out of her mind. She could not allow that visit to be her last memory of him, a memory of herself shrinking from him, repulsed, fainting even with fear and distaste. She must see him again before he died, to show him the love that she had withheld from him then. She would ask Dr Breuer to persuade her mother to allow it. But no, she did not want to see Dr Breuer. Bertha sank down onto the ottoman. It was Dr Breuer's fault that she was feeling such guilt. If she had never known him she would not have rejected her father in the way that she had. Perhaps if she had not been thinking all the time of Dr Breuer, she would have been able to come to terms with her father's illness, surmount her own maladies, compose herself and support him as a daughter should.

The organ grinder returned to the beginning of his repertoire, the brassy jangle of the cancan cutting like an obscenity across Bertha's remorse over her father. She slammed the window shut. As she did so, a carriage stopped directly below. A man got out and entered the building. It was Reb Goldberg.

Bertha's heart pounded, her mouth suddenly dry. Reb Goldberg was a member of the *chevra kadisha*, the society responsible for the laying out of the Jewish dead. If Reb Goldberg was in the building, it could mean only one thing.

But it may not have been Reb Goldberg. Bertha sat down the bed, perched on the edge, knees pressed together. She could have been mistaken.

Impossible. Reb Goldberg was the smallest man she knew, so small that from behind he could be taken for a child. His face was chubby, rosy-cheeked and somehow innocent, the full black beard almost an anomaly. No one else looked like Reb Goldberg.

Bertha moved over to the door, taking care not to make any noise, straining to hear any sound from beyond her room. Silence.

'Mamma.' She tried to shout. The word came out as a hoarse whisper. There seemed to be no air left in her lungs.

140

'Mamma.'

She reached out and pulled the bell cord beside her bed. At the same instant she heard the ring of the front door bell. A moment later Agnethe unlocked the bedroom door. Bertha seized the handle, yanked the door open, pushed past Agnethe and looked down to the end of the hallway. Ilse had just opened the front door. Reb Goldberg was coming in.

Bertha's legs started to buckle, her breathing fast and shallow. 'Mamma. Where's Mamma. Get Mamma.'

'Now, Miss Bertha, jus' calm down.' Agnethe supported Bertha from behind, one arm round her waist and a hand under her armpit, and manoeuvred her back into the bedroom. She left the room, locked the door and returned almost immediately with Mrs Pappenheim.

Bertha lay on the chaise-longue. She clutched at her mother's skirt, babbling. 'Mamma. Papa is dead. You didn't tell me. You didn't let me see him.'

Mrs Pappenheim took her daughter's hand and sat down beside her. 'No, Bertha, he isn't dead. He's just the same. No change in his condition.'

'You're lying to me. Reb Goldberg is here, from the *chevra kadisha*. You've started the funeral arrangements without even letting me know that he's dead.'

'No, Bertha, don't excite yourself. Reb Goldberg is just paying a visit. He's a friend of your father's.

'I don't believe you. Let me see him, then. If he's well enough to receive visitors, he's well enough to see me.'

'Not today, Bertha. He'll be tired after talking with Reb Goldberg.'

Bertha was silent. She wanted to believe her mother. Could what she said be true? She had never known Reb Goldberg visit before. He was someone they knew from the synagogue but no more than that. She had never heard her father mention his name.

'Tomorrow then?'

'We'll see. You must rest now.'

'I want to write to Papa. I'm going to write a letter for you to give him as soon as Reb Goldberg has left.'

141

'Of course, Bertha. Agnethe will sit with you while you do it and we'll give it straight away to Papa.'

Bertha relaxed. Her mother would surely never agree to her writing to her father if he were, in fact, dead. Reb Goldberg was just paying a social call. She would see him again very soon, in a day or two.

Mrs Pappenheim left the room. Agnethe opened the ottoman and took out a half-made collar which she was tatting. She sat down at the window.

Bertha sat at the escritoire and began her letter.

Dearest Papa

She stopped, unsure that her father would ever read what she was about to write. Her mother could still be lying. Perhaps Dr Breuer had said she mustn't be given bad news because of her poor health. Perhaps even now Reb Goldberg was tending to her dead father's hair and nails, washing him, wrapping him in a shroud. She heard the front door bell ring again. More visitors? Mourners? Some one else from the *chevra kadisha*?

'Please go and see who it is, Agnethe.'

'There's no need, Miss Bertha. Ilse is 'spectin' a delivery from the laundry.'

'I insist. I must know.'

Bertha imagined her father, now in a shroud, a flickering candle at his head, the mourners gathered round reciting Psalm 23. Willi would have been the one to close his eyes and mouth earlier today, drawn a sheet over his face. Willi, who had done so little for their father while he was still alive, was with him in death while she....

'I'm tellin' you, Miss, it's the laundry man.'

Agnethe couldn't know who it was. She was part of the conspiracy. They were all lying to her. They didn't want her to know that her father was dead. They were even prepared to go through the charade of allowing her to write a letter and pretending to deliver it to him. She was imprisoned. There was nothing she could do, no way she could find out the truth.

But wait. If her father was really dead, then she, as a close

142

relative, was forbidden to eat meat during the period between death and burial. Her mother would never allow such an infringement of religious obligation. She tried to recall what had been on the lunch tray which Ilse had brought her. She hadn't eaten any of it, had sent it back to the kitchen untouched. There had been a bowl of mushroom barley soup and an omelette. No meat. Why not? Had her father already been dead then?

'Agnethe, would you call my mother, please.'

Agnethe laid down the collar she was working on, left the room and came back with Mrs Pappenheim.

'Mamma, I'd like to eat now. I couldn't manage any lunch. Ilse mentioned this morning that Kathe was braising some brisket for tonight's supper. I'd like some of that, please.'

'I'm glad to see that you're asking for food, Bertha, but you could have asked Agnethe to attend to it. There was no need to call me.'

Mrs Pappenheim left the room. Had there been any hesitation in her voice? Not that Bertha could detect. And surely, if Papa were dead, there would be some sign of it in her demeanour, some evidence of grief. True, she looked sad and anxious, but she had done for months.

Shortly afterwards Ilse brought a tray with two slices of braised brisket and some fried potato cakes.

Bertha sat at the escritoire, the tray in front of her. She cut a morsel of meat but could not lift it to her mouth. She could not be sure that her father was still alive, and if he was not the consumption of meat would be an outrage to his memory. The pressure of impending grief built up in her. She felt its weight, sensed its ugly heaviness, its corrosive potential, but could not allow herself to experience its full affective force until she knew for certain.

She left the food and lay down on her bed. A feeling of detachment was spreading through her, cutting her loose from her cares. Soon she was detached from all sensory perceptions. She did not hear the frequent ringing of the front door bell, the coming and going of mourners or the psalms of the *shemira*. When Agnethe undressed her and drew the bed

143

covers over her she was unaware of it.

Bertha awoke with a start. Had she dreamt that noise? A bang – as if a piece of furniture had been knocked over – then an agitation of voices. There they were again. In the hallway. She looked at the clock. It was nine a.m. They were male voices, several of them. Then her mother's – asking them to make less noise. What were they doing? Bertha eased herself out of bed and put her ear to the door. The voices were fainter now, as if they were already beyond the front door. She heard the front door close.

'Mamma.'

Mrs Pappenheim unlocked the door and came in.

'Mamma, what's going on? Who were these people in the hallway just now?'

Mrs Pappenheim walked over to the window and opened the curtains. She spoke with her back to Bertha.

'Removal men. They've taken Willi's old writing desk away. He's going to have a new one.'

'Mamma, look at me!'

Mrs Pappenheim turned round. Her face had a closed-in look.

'You're lying to me. It was Papa. They've taken him away in a box.' Bertha could not say the word 'coffin'. She was shaking. 'It was the box I heard.' Her voice spiralled into a breathy squeak. 'The box, banging against the wall. You're lying! You're all lying! Lying, lying, lying!'

Bertha screamed, a long, skirling shriek, then shrank to the floor, heaving with sobs. She filled her lungs with air, and screamed again. She screamed repeatedly while her mother and Agnethe picked her up and laid her on the bed. As she opened her mouth to scream yet again, Agnethe poured in a glassful of chloral hydrate, snapped her jaws together and held her head back until the drug had been swallowed.

It was useless to ask any more questions. Bertha turned her face to the wall and waited for sleep to come.

She awoke in the early evening, unrefreshed and exhausted, but fired anew with the need to know the truth

144

about her father. She opened her eyes. No one in the room. Agnethe's sewing lay on the ottoman, the needle stabbed into it, as if just temporarily set aside. Bertha looked round towards the door. It was slightly ajar. She swung her legs out of the bed and stood up, groggy from the drug, headachy from the weeping. She had to get out of her room and find a mirror. If her father was dead the mirrors would be covered. Her mother would have seen to it. It was a ritual obligation.

There was a mirror above the fireplace in the drawing room, just next to her bedroom. Bertha stepped out into the hallway and turned to the right. She reached out to push the drawing room door. As she did so, her upper arms were seized from behind. Agnethe swung her round and propelled her back into the bedroom.

''Member what your mother said, Miss Bertha. You 'ave to stay in your own room.'

'No, I have to see the mirror. Just let me go into the drawing room to see the mirror.'

'You've got your own mirror, Miss Bertha. On the dressin' table. No need for you goin' anywhere else.'

Her father must be dead then. There could be no other reason for preventing her seeing the mirror.

But perhaps Agnethe didn't know about the mirrors. She wasn't Jewish.

'Agnethe, let me explain….' Bertha stopped. There was no point in explaining. If she did, Agnethe would be even more determined not to let her see the mirror. They were all determined to prevent her from knowing that her father was dead. She wriggled, trying to free herself. Agnethe's grasp tightened. Her mother appeared.

'That's enough, Bertha!'

'Let me go!'

The doorbell rang. Ilse opened the door. Dr Breuer came in.

Seeing him, Bertha felt only a dulling defeat.

'Don't tell my any more lies,' she said. 'I know that my father is dead.'

She lay down on the bed with her face to the wall,

145

repeating the words over and over. Her words began to sound like a chant, as if she were reciting a mourning prayer. After some minutes Dr Breuer took a syringe out of his bag and drew up a sedative. He injected it and waited until Bertha fell asleep.

She slept throughout the night. The following day she drifted in and out of sleep, never quite conscious. In the evening she mumbled for a while in English, incoherently, then awoke to find Dr Breuer again at her bedside. She sat up. '*Buona sera, dottore. E vero che il mio padre e morto?*'

Dr Breuer paused before speaking, as if pondering the effect of what he was about to say. Bertha's gaze was fixed on him, steady. His answering gaze was equally steady.

'You know he is, Bertha. You've known it for two days.'

Bertha nodded. 'Yes, you must be right.' Her features were composed. She nodded again. 'I have a feeling I must have known already. I don't feel inside as if I've only just come to know it.'

She got up, took a shawl out of the rosewood wardrobe, and draped it over the dressing table mirror.

17

13 April 1881

Yesterday was the last day of shivah *and now we must look to the future. It has been good for us to have a constant flow of visitors to condole and pray with us at this difficult time. Willi's behaviour has been exemplary. The realisation that he is now the man of house seems to have given him added dignity. He welcomed guests and organised the reciting of the* kaddish *every day just as Siegmund would have done. I hope that this attitude will remain with him now that he has returned to his studies.*

I feared at first that Siegmund's death would unsettle Bertha yet further and for the first few days it seemed that it was indeed going to have this effect. Then, after Dr Breuer confirmed her suspicions, she became quite calm, as if accepting the finality of the situation. However, although she is clearly much better physically, she has developed some oddities of behaviour. I was pleased to see that she was willing to take part in shivah, greeting family and friends and acknowledging their expressions of sympathy, yet she seemed not to recognise people whom she knows well. At first I put this down to her strange moodiness, a sign perhaps that she did not wish to speak to people she did not like, but she even had difficulty with her cousins Wolf and Wilhelm of whom she is so fond. Only when they spoke, reminding Bertha of things they had done together in the past, was she convinced of their identity. She remembered their voices, she said, and the incidents they recalled, but not their faces. To avoid further embarrassment I asked Bertha to remain in her room, taking only the closest family members in to see her. Even so, after talking with them for a while, she would lapse into one of her strange states, ignoring her guests as if they were not there. When she does speak, as often as not it is in English. Fortunately we have Miss Thomson who is able to translate. I have discussed the whole matter with Dr Breuer. He is to bring a specialist so that we may have a second opinion on Bertha's condition, a Professor Krafft-Ebing from Graz who is an expert on unusual mental states.

o~o~o

Bertha lay on the chaise longue in her bedroom. Papa was dead. It was over. He had been right, she decided, when he used to say that there was no point in fretting over what could not be changed.

She had felt detached throughout the seven days of shivah, more concerned about her inability to recognise people than about her father's death. There had been a coming and going in her room, conversations with familiar voices, talk about shared memories, but the faces themselves were unidentifiable, like mannequins in a dressmaker's shop. At times she had been unable to see the speaker at all, and then it was as if she was talking to a ghost, uncertain whether the person was really there or whether she was simply imagining the voice. Even Dr Breuer's face had begun to waver at times, losing its definition, as if it was immersed in water. Panic-stricken she had clung to his hand as she described those latest symptoms, feeling it all over – the contours of the joints, the texture of the skin, the shape of the nails, the tracery of veins even. It seemed like the only truly solid thing remaining to her. He had spoken soothingly, assuring her that these were all mere manifestations of her hysterical illness and that, by working together, they would soon find a way to eliminate them. When he spoke like that she found herself lulled into tranquillity; energised even by the suggestion that they were embarked on a joint enterprise. But the next time it happened she would be seized again by fears. The experiences were so strange, more like the kind of thing that might happen in dreams than symptoms of illness, and they flagged up yet more areas in which she was losing her sense of control. How could she be in charge of her part in a conversation if she didn't know who she was speaking with? How could she move around a room if she didn't know where people were?

She heard the bedroom door opening. A low hubbub of voices. A rustle of skirts brushing against furniture. Her mother's voice. Telling her a new doctor was here. Bertha did not want a new doctor. Dr Breuer was her doctor.

And here he was. Sitting down beside her, asking how she

was, smiling gravely. He wanted to do some tests, he said, if Bertha would be willing. He would like to demonstrate some aspects of her illness to Professor Krafft-Ebing.

Bertha saw no-one who could correspond to that name but she smiled and nodded. Dr Breuer began his usual tests, flexing her arms and legs, asking her to turn her head from side to side. He commented at each stage on his observations, turning his head to the side as he did so, as if he was talking to someone else. Still Bertha could see no-one there.

'And now, I'd like you to read, if you could.' Dr Breuer reached out and picked a book from the shelves beside the window. It was Hugo's *Les Misérables*. He opened it at random and placed it in Bertha's hand. Bertha looked at the text.

> *Dans les premiers jours du mois d'octobre 1815, une heure environ avant le coucher du soleil, un homme qui voyageait à pied entrait dans la petite ville de Digne. Les rares habitants qui se trouvaient en ce moment à leurs fenêtres ou sur le seuil de leurs maisons regardaient ce voyageur avec une sorte d'inquiétude.*

She began to speak.

> '*In the first days of October 1815, an hour before sunset, a man entered the little village of Digne on foot. The few inhabitants who stood at their windows or on their thresholds looked at this traveller with some anxiety.*'

She looked up at Dr Breuer with a forced laugh, uncertain as to what was going on. 'It's like an examination,' she said.

'You see?' Dr Breuer had turned his head to the side again. 'No matter what language she's asked to read, she renders it into English. And perfect English at that.'

A resentment took root in Bertha. Why was Dr Breuer not giving her his full attention? She was beginning to feel like a prop in a dramatic production.

Dr Breuer was still talking, but not to her. He was taking something out of his instrument case, talking about the degree of anaesthesia in her right leg. He asked her why she had not replied to Professor Krafft-Ebing. The question fuelled her resentment. No question had been put to her. She was sure of that. Perhaps there was someone that she couldn't see but if he had spoken she would have heard it.

They were trying to make her believe that there was someone there when there wasn't. It was all a conspiracy, a game of make-believe. Those people who spoke when she couldn't see them, it was some kind of trickery. It wasn't true what Dr Breuer said about it being part of her illness, it was because they were trying to make her believe that she was crazy. Then they could put her away. That beast Willi must be involved in it too. She'd seen how he'd been toadying to Mamma in the aftermath of Papa's death, swaggering around as if he was now the man of the house. And Mamma had been pandering to him, telling everyone what a young stalwart he was and how she could never have managed without him. He must have been putting ideas into her head, encouraging her to get Bertha sent away.

A sharp jab in her right foot. She cried out.

'It's all right, Miss Bertha,' Dr Breuer said. 'A significant improvement in sensation,' he added. But his head was now turned away from her again.

Her mother was there. She could hear her voice, telling Dr Breuer that she was pleased with the improvement in Bertha's limbs. She could feel her too. Since Papa's death she had been able to sense her mother's presence, even if she could not see her, by a stream of unpleasant heat which seemed to emanate from her as if she were a furnace of burning rubber.

'Bertha, dear, would you answer Professor Krafft-Ebing, please?'

Bertha ignored her mother's request. There was no professor. She wasn't going to behave as if she was being taken in by their play acting.

'Miss Bertha, Professor Krafft-Ebing would like to know…'

Bertha interrupted Dr Breuer. 'There's no professor here. I don't know what you're talking about.' She had to be firm. Make it clear that she wasn't being deceived.

More heat. A different kind now, in front of her. A smell of burning and smoke going up her nose. Bertha coughed, choked. She gasped, screwing up her eyes. When she opened them again she saw a hand holding a fragment of smouldering paper. The hand belonged to a man she had never seen before, a man of about forty with a broad high forehead, a trim pointed beard and stern eyes.

'Ah, now you can see me, I think,' the man said. He turned to Dr Breuer. 'The smoke has done the trick.'

Bertha stared around, her eyes wide, taking in for the first time the group of people standing beside Dr Breuer. The strange man, her mother, Miss Thomson. She jumped up and hobbled to the door. She opened it. 'Out of my room!' Tears ran down her cheeks and her breathing accelerated. 'Coming in here, like ghosts. Voices without bodies. Starting fires. Out. All of you. Get out.'

Her last words were barely audible, submerged in great gasping sobs. She clung to the doorknob and closed her eyes. She dared not open them again for fear of what she might see or not see. She no longer trusted the evidence of her own senses.

Dr Breuer took her by the arm. Bertha's eyes were still closed but she recognized his touch, his odour, and the even tenor of his voice close to her ear as he persuaded her back to the chaise longue.

Now he was escorting the others out of the room, reassuring Bertha at the same time that he would be back immediately. There was a subdued murmur from the doorway, a scraping sound as a chair was put in place for Miss Thomson, retreating footsteps. Then Dr Breuer was beside her again. Only then did Bertha open her eyes. She leaned back, exhausted. She had no desire to talk.

Dr Breuer was speaking to her now, asking how she felt.

Bertha did not know what to say. She did not want to discuss the strange things which were happening to her. If she ignored them, she could pretend that they were not happening. But she could think of nothing else to talk about, and feared that without a subject of conversation Dr Breuer would leave her. And if he left her the strange things might start happening again.

151

She reached out and took hold of his left hand, averting her eyes from his face for fear that she might not recognize his features.

'Bertha, look at me.'

Bertha looked down at the floor, urgently fingering the hand she held, seeking the familiar textures and contours.

Dr Breuer reached out and put his right index finger under her chin, raising it till her eyes met his. And she saw that they were his eyes, the light blue flecked with amber. She saw also the familiar square-cut beard, the high forehead and the fine reddish-blond hair.

She began to cry again, sobbing with relief this time, then telling him how afraid she had been, thinking that people were playing tricks on her so that they could convince her that she was mad and put her away.

'Even you, Dr Breuer. I thought that you too were deceiving me.' No sooner had she said the words than they seemed to Bertha ridiculous. Of course Dr Breuer wouldn't deceive her. The others perhaps, but not him. And even if the others had wanted to deceive her, they wouldn't have done so in his presence. Therefore, it must be as Dr Breuer said. It was all to do with her illness and she was going to get better. It was like the time she had thought the walls were toppling in on her. That hadn't lasted very long. This would surely be the same. She looked up at Dr Breuer, ready to apologise.

'And do you still think I was party to this deception?' he asked, a smile hovering on his lips.

'No.'

'Good. It's as I said. This is due to hysteria and we're going to get to the bottom of it.'

Dr Breuer stood up and looked out of the window. The sky was blue, unmarred by cloud.

'Miss Bertha, you haven't been outside for five months. I think it would do you good to go for a drive. Would you like that?'

Bertha said nothing. What could he have in mind?

'My carriage is downstairs and I've no more appointments this morning. The Augarten is nearby. It would be a pleasure to take you there, and I'm sure Miss Thomson would be happy to join us.'

Dr Breuer raised an eyebrow, coaxing a response from her. Bertha nodded, the terrors of the professor's visit already slipping away.

Dr Breuer turned to Miss Thomson. 'Miss Thomson, would you mind going to tell Mrs Pappenheim what we have planned. And would you ask Agnethe to come and help Miss Bertha into her outdoor clothing.'

Ten minutes later the two-horse fiacre set off down Maria Theresien Strasse. Inside Bertha sat opposite Dr Breuer, Miss Thomson at her side. After being confined to her room for so long, all her senses seemed to be in a state of heightened awareness, making the air fresher, the street sounds louder. Even the swaying of the carriage seemed more pronounced.

Dr Breuer was talking about the Augarten, how lovely it was at this time of year.

Bertha hung on his every word. He was no longer her doctor, tending to her ailments. They were two people, on an outing together. She found that she could disregard Miss Thomson as easily as if she had been eradicated from her presence in the same way as the people she had been oblivious of in her bedroom in the past few days.

The carriage rolled over the Danube and into Leopoldstadt where Bertha had lived as a child. Her school had been in this very street. She pointed it out to Dr Breuer.

The carriage slowed as it turned into the park, the horses skirting round a group of people gathered in front of a one-man band playing a Hungarian folk tune. The crowd clapped merrily and stamped their feet in time to the music, laughing at the antics of the musician as he juggled the sounds of his banjo, harmonica, drum and bells.

Dr Breuer directed the coachman to drive away from the noise and along an avenue of purple-leaved maple trees. He started to describe how the maple leaves changed colour throughout the year. But Bertha had stopped paying attention to his words, listening only to the lilt of his voice, basking in it as if it were a lullaby.

153

Just over there was a spot where she used to play with her school friends. She felt again the wind on her face, her hair lifting as it streamed out behind her, and heard the children's voices as they danced round singing for their favourite game. 'Kling, klang Gloria, who is that sitting in the tower there? It is the king's little daughter.'

The rhythm of the chanting, the fun of the pretending, all building up to a crescendo of jubilation as the princess was liberated. She hadn't appreciated those things enough at the time. She was always in a state of expectation, looking forward to a time when things would be even better. Older girls, even those just one year older, seemed to have a status that was just a degree more desirable. When she was eight, she wanted to be nine; when she was nine she couldn't wait to be ten. Her birthdays were like rungs on a ladder by which she would ascend to ever greater happiness and self-assurance till she became an adult and finally launched onto that high plateau of independence and extended pleasure. But once she left school the colour quickly drained from her horizons. There was never anything which generated the same joyous abandon of the childhood play or the intimacy of the girlish friendships, there was little which corresponded to her anticipation. Apart from little islands of respite, like summer holidays and theatre evenings, there was only monotony and greyness.

She heard her name. Dr Breuer had said her name. But what else had he said? She looked at him, expectant, wondering if she had had an absence.

'I beg your pardon?'

'I was just remarking on the name that you and my eldest daughter share – Bertha. Did you know that it means 'bright'?'

Bertha's heart skipped a beat and then started to thump. Dr Breuer had never mentioned his children to her. Mama had referred to his family, something about children. She hadn't said how many, or whether boys or girls. Bertha had given no thought to them. They were anonymous, not part of her life or of her relationship with Dr Breuer. But now one of them was here, in the carriage. Her name was Bertha, the same as hers. They had called her Bertha, he was saying, because that was

154

his mother's name. But when she was very little she hadn't been able to say Bertha. All she could manage was Baba, and that was what they had called her ever since.

Bertha felt a blade of iciness run through her from head to foot, as if slicing her in two. Her breathing had all but stopped; only a shallow intake now and then, when her lungs could hold out no longer.

She was ten, Dr Breuer was saying. About the same age as Bertha had been in the scene she had just been visualising. Bertha could not speak. She hated her, this little ten-year-old Baba, and she felt a terrible anger against Dr Breuer for having mentioned her, for continuing to talk about her. She must change the subject. But she could think of nothing to say. There was no room in her mind for anything but the monstrous idea of this Baba.

Bertha's features formed into the configuration they acquired during her absence states – eyes fixed, mouth immobile. She retreated behind this façade. It would defend her from any further conversation.

When the carriage arrived back at 2 Liechtensteinstrasse, Bertha still appeared to be suffering an absence. She wondered herself if she truly was in that state. Her face remained static. She felt that she would not have been able to move a muscle of it even if she tried. But she was aware this time. She knew what was happening.

The coachman opened the door and Dr Breuer slid one arm behind her back and the other under her knees. He lifted her out and carried her up the stairs to the apartment. As he did so, Bertha felt herself grow smaller. Her legs no longer extended beyond Dr Breuer's arm, her feet no longer dangled but nestled in the crook of his elbow. Her torso too shrank, till her head fitted under his chin. She closed her eyes, shutting out all sensory impressions which would give the lie to this illusion.

When Dr Breuer laid her on her chaise-longue she wanted to howl her indignation. An inward scream: Pick me up again, pick me up, pick me up. Heels throbbing with the desire to drum her rage.

She felt the heat of Mamma behind her. Dr Breuer was giving her instructions about Bertha's diet and massage programme, telling her that Professor Krafft-Ebing was in broad agreement with his own diagnosis. Now he was saying – no, it was not possible! – that he was going to be away for three days. He was going to Berlin. Today was Sunday, so she wouldn't see him till Thursday at the earliest. Berlin was so far away. Perhaps it would take longer. She might even not see him for a week. Why was he going there? He hadn't said. Would Baba be with him? She mustn't think about it. She must only think about being carried in his arms, the brush of his beard against her cheek, the solidity of the shoulder beneath her head.

They were leaving the room now, their voices fading. She heard the front door open, exchanged goodbyes, the door closing again. Alone, Bertha curled up into the position she had felt herself adopting in Dr Breuer's arms, head under his chin, feet against his upper arm. 'Pick me up,' she whispered. 'Pick me up.'

18

21 April 1881

A telegram from Dr Breuer this morning saying that he returns to Vienna today and will visit Bertha this evening. It is a great relief. Since Sunday she has eaten no food whatsoever, and to drink only water. She spends most of the daylight hours in a state of absence, often disrupted by hallucinations in which she seems to be actively involved, as if she were playing a part in some phantom play. Agnethe continues the massage programme as best she can and I am thankful for the stolidity of her character. She remains unperturbed when Bertha perceives the washbasin to be a skull and Agnethe herself a gravedigger. This has been going on for three days now, and always the same talk about corpses and burials and skeletons. Today she wrapped one of her old dolls in a shawl, referring to it as a shroud, then laid it on the ottoman which she appeared to think was a bier. I am now more than ever convinced that I was right to conceal Siegmund's death from her until the funeral was over. We must protect her from anything liable to encourage morbid thoughts. My anxiety is only slightly lessened by the fact that she returns to a normal frame of mind at night, although Dr Breuer believes this is an encouraging sign with regard to an eventual return to full health. Agnethe and Miss Thomson take it in turns to look in on her during the night and they report that she is reasonably calm and rational, busying herself with reading and writing until about 4 am when she goes to sleep. Last night Miss Thomson found her reading Hamlet. I told her I did not consider this suitable reading for someone already disposed to melancholy. Miss Thomson reassured me by saying that the language of Shakespeare is so obscure that she herself finds it difficult to understand so it is unlikely to be doing Bertha any harm.

A letter from Bella this morning. She proposes to visit with Fritz, Henriette and little Emma before the end of shloshim as they were unable to travel from Karlsruhe for the funeral. I have suggested that it would be better if Henriette and Emma stayed behind as it would not be suitable to bring a two-year old into a house with an invalid like Bertha.

I am even concerned about how she may react to the presence of her aunt and cousin, although she has always been attached to them both.

o~o~o

'*Alas, poor Barta!*' Bertha sat on the floor beside the ottoman on which the doll still lay.

'Who is Barta?' Dr Breuer asked.

Bertha put her hand on the doll. '*This is Barta.*'

'Why do you say poor Barta?

'*Barta is dead.*'

'How did she die?'

'*She drowned herself.*'

'Why?'

'*Don't know.*' Bertha picked up the doll and drew back the shawl to reveal the face. '*Here hung those lips that he hath kissed. He hath borne thee on his back a thousand times.*' Bertha laughed, a crowing laugh of triumph. '*Thou art dead now.*' She covered the doll's face again with the shawl and laid it back on the ottoman.

Dr Breuer said nothing more. He sat in silence, waiting for Bertha to continue the conversation.

The far-away look on Bertha's face faded but when she spoke it was still in English.

'*Good evening, Dr Breuer.*'

'Good evening, Bertha.'

Dr Breuer picked up the doll. 'Does she have a name?'

'*Yes. Hermione.*'

'Hermione? Not Barta?'

'*No. Why should I call her Barta? Her name's Hermione. I've had her since I was three.*'

Bertha took the doll from Dr Breuer and held it to her chest. She laid her cheek against the doll's porcelain head and rocked gently back and forwards.

Aunt Bella had given her the doll. There had also been a little baby carriage for her to put the doll in, just like Mamma did with Willi who was still a baby then, and three sets of clothes. She could barely remember the details but she could remember now – perhaps for the first time – the feelings. So fiercely protective and so proud as she wheeled the doll round the Prater, convinced that Hermione was quite the prettiest doll in Vienna, with her flaxen hair, pink cheeks and blue eyes that opened and closed.

'Bertha, your mother tells me that you haven't been eating.'

Bertha frowned crossly and hugged the doll more tightly.

'Not hungry. Don't want to eat.'

'Perhaps if I have something brought from the kitchen? Just to please me.' Dr Breuer cocked an eyebrow.

The corners of Bertha's mouth turned down and her lower lip jutted out. She looked away. Dr Breuer got up and went over to the door to speak with Miss Thomson. A few minutes later Ilse appeared with a bowl of lentil soup. She set the tray down on the table beside the bed.

'Where would you like to eat, Bertha?' Dr Breuer asked. 'Would you like to sit at your escritoire?'

Bertha shook her head.

'Your dressing table then?'

Again Bertha shook her head.

Dr Breuer got up, lifted the tray from the bedside table and placed it on the ottoman. Then he sat down on the floor beside Bertha. He dipped the spoon into the soup and took it to Bertha's lips. Slowly, and without saying a word, she allowed herself to be fed the entire contents of the bowl.

o~o~o

Dearest Anna

Bertha stopped and bit the end of her pen. For the first time she was at a loss to know what to write to Anna. She should write about Papa, reply to the letter of condolence she had received from Anna. She had only read it once and hesitated to read it again. It made her feel guilty. Anna had talked about the death of her own father, four years ago. Those times are among the most difficult one can experience, she wrote. Bertha could not say this about her own father's

159

death. She simply felt numb when she thought about it. Anna also described how Uncle Veit had been bedridden for six weeks before he died, saying how fortunate she and her sisters had been to be able to nurse him during that time. Bertha could not help but read into this a reproach about her inability to care for her own father.

Thank you for your letter of condolence on the death of Papa. I know that you understand because you have already experienced the loss of your own dear Papa.

Bertha stopped again, troubled by her own insincerity. She did not believe that Anna understood what she was feeling now. Her present feelings could bear no relation to what Anna had felt when her father died. But it would be impossible to express those feelings to Anna. Indeed, she herself could not understand them, could not even say exactly what it was that she felt.

Wilhelm has started to study again now that shivah *is over and Mamma is busy attending to Papa's papers. She is finding the presence of Miss Thomson very helpful at this difficult time.*

You will forgive me, dear Anna, if I don't write any more. I feel very sad.

Affectionately
Bertha

Bertha laid her pen down and picked up her copy of *Hamlet*. She turned this time to the last scene in which Ophelia appeared, just before her drowning. She read the words of the song of lamentation Ophelia had sung for her dead father, trying to stimulate in herself the appropriate emotions. If Aristotle was right in his belief that drama could lead to a cleansing of the mind, then if she could think herself into the mind of Ophelia, allow Ophelia's emotions to become her own, she might experience what duty told her she ought to feel. But the words did not move her.

As she read on to the end of the scene, a memory of Miss Baxter reading Ophelia's lines came to her. Miss Baxter had known the lines by heart and acted them out, running around the room on tiptoe in quick little steps, her arms outstretched as she mimed the distribution of rosemary, pansies, columbines and rue, her normally contralto voice high-pitched and crazed. And as Bertha remembered this, a chord was struck within her – not of filial grief but of impotent despair.

She pictured what came next: Ophelia floating in the brook, singing, until her garments, weighted with water, dragged her under. There was a painting of it by an English artist, Millais, with Ophelia lying on the surface of the water in an attitude of surrender. Bertha imagined herself in the picture, floating, sinking, giving herself up to the water, until she was no more.

There was only emptiness. Then the emptiness began to fill with a sadness, but a sadness without a reason. Bertha looked around the room, as if searching for the source of the sadness. Her gaze fell on the ottoman, and the spot beside it where she had sat being fed by Dr Breuer. The memory sent a thrill through her, like the excitement she had once felt in the company of Miss Baxter, but more mysterious, darker and more profound. She got up, the sadness forgotten, and went to sit in the same spot. She picked Hermione up, hugged her tightly and closed her eyes. This was how she had been, Dr Breuer sitting beside her, lifting the spoon to her lips. She felt the exquisite touch of the spoon on the tip of her tongue, the warm flow of the soup running down her throat, the rough texture of his jacket as his sleeve brushed her chin. She continued to sit, miming her part in the tableau, until late into the night.

Dr Breuer leaned back in the cream damask Biedermeier chair and allowed his mood to yield to the music. Arnold Rosenblum was playing Goldmark's Violin Concerto in A Minor, a piece which the young prodigy had performed with the Vienna Philharmonic a few weeks previously, to great acclaim. Josephine Wertheimstein, the evening's hostess, had immediately booked him for one of her musical soirées. Josephine could always be relied upon to cultivate the most promising talent in any of the arts. In fact, Breuer reflected,

161

attendance at one of Josephine's soirées was always a cultural experience in itself: the guests were usually artists, musicians and men of letters, the paintings and sculptures ranged from Old Masters to the avant garde, and the villa was designed like a classical palace.

Dr Breuer let his gaze rest on a portrait of Josephine on the wall opposite as the music washed over him, the dancing serenity of the violin complemented by the more stately piano accompaniment. Mathilde sat beside him, a far-away look in her eyes as if she was transported by the music. He ought to make more effort to bring her to events such as these, Breuer thought. Yet he was unsure how much Mathilde enjoyed the mingling with the other guests which would begin when the music was over. Even after thirteen years of marriage he did not know whether it was simply a natural reserve which held her back in social gatherings or a belief that she was not the intellectual equal of her husband's circle. Of course, it would not be surprising if Mathilde were intimidated by the likes of Josephine and her daughter Franzi. Born into a family of wealthy Jewish liberals their environment had cultivated them like intellectual hothouse plants and shielded them from the reality that was most women's lives. Mathilde had little in common with them, nor with the male guests with whom the Wertheimstein women were so at ease.

Now if it were Bertha...

Breuer felt exasperated with himself at the thought. He was beginning to resent the way in which this case was encroaching on the rest of his life. Mathilde was clearly irritated by his frequent references to Bertha, and by the fact that the time he spent with her meant that he spent even less time than normal with his family. His conversations with colleagues were often taken up with questions relating to the case and most of his reading now focused on neurological issues which he thought might be relevant. But, like a dog with a bone, he could not let it go.

As the music passed into the slower andante of the second movement Breuer again ran through in his mind the present state of Bertha's condition. Since his return from Berlin a

162

regular pattern had established itself. In the daytime, according to the mother, Bertha oscillated between wakefulness and absence. In the first state she was agitated and aggressive and in the second she seemed to hallucinate fearsome scenes, peopled with skeletons and corpses, to which she reacted with terror. When he arrived in the evening her state of mind would change yet again and, as if in a trance – 'clouds', she called it – she would recount to him the events hallucinated. When she had done so, she would return to what appeared to be normal consciousness.

Her refusal to eat continued. In fact, the only way she could be persuaded to take anything at all was if he himself fed her. During the day she drank, but only water. In the evening, a simple meal was prepared for her – a thick soup or an egg dish, a milk pudding. He would send for it when Bertha had finished her account of the day's hallucinations. She would then sit on the floor beside the ottoman and he, sitting beside her, would feed her. Over the past few days, her demeanour at this time had become increasingly babylike. At first there had only been hints of it. He had felt then that Bertha was ashamed of those little lapses of dignity but as the days passed she seemed to be giving herself over to it with a kind of voluptuousness which he found disturbingly indecent.

Of all the strange symptoms which Bertha had so far manifested, this one perplexed him most. All the others corresponded with symptoms encountered in the course of various organic diseases or with hysterics, but this reversion to infantile behaviour was unheard of – unless in cases of advanced senility. Mathilde had been quite angry when he had talked of it and snapped that if there was any need for Bertha to be fed in this way, then surely the nurse should take charge of it. Did he not think it demeaning to allow Miss Pappenheim to lure him into those undignified charades?

The exuberant third movement was coming to an end. Dr Breuer glanced sideways at Mathilde and smiled at her. At the same time he noticed that Exner was present. Excellent. He had been hoping to meet up with him to discuss this new theory of his about absolute and relative cortical fields. He hoped it might help to throw some light on this business with Bertha. But first he would make sure that Mathilde was firmly established in conversation with some of the other wives.

19

2 May 1881

    I hardly recognize my own child. When I think how I used to reprimand her for her high spirits I feel only remorse. I would gladly welcome the return of those high spirits now. At times I despair of ever seeing them again.

    Bertha spurns all my attempts to help her. She complains about feeling an unpleasant heat whenever I go into her room and responds with abusive language if I try to speak to her. Miss Thomson and Agnethe fare little better, although both assure me that they understand that Bertha is not responsible for her behaviour at present. Mornings are the worst for all concerned as Bertha is quite awake then, and always in a greatly agitated state. Lately she has started to react with physical violence if her will is opposed and I do not know how I would cope without Agnethe. Once again I have to give thanks for her physical strength and her stolidity. Afternoons are quieter although Bertha must still be supervised then so that we can report to Dr B on the content of her hallucinations. When I see her like this I sometimes feel that I would willingly exchange her previous physical ailments for this incomprehensible behaviour. The most alarming development is that she has started to talk about wanting to die and threatens to throw herself out of the window. Dr B assures me that this is merely talk but I feel that with her present unbalanced state of mind we should not dismiss it so lightly.

    Bella and Fritz arrived this morning and will stay for ten days. We held a siyum *this evening in memory of Siegmund. I asked Kathe to make Siegmund's favourite cholent recipe. It was cooked to perfection. A bowl was sent in to Bertha and Dr Breuer managed to persuade her to eat all of it.*

Bertha sat by the window in the drawing room. Ilse was cleaning her bedroom.

    Bertha hated having to leave her bedroom. In it, she could withdraw into her fantasies. She never tired of playing out scenes of being fed by Dr Breuer. She refused all food during the day, eating only in the evening, and only then if Dr Breuer fed her. She took care to ensure that they sat in a different part of the room every time, and in a different position in relation to each other, so that she had a constant supply of fresh imagery to act out in the night hours, after he had gone. It gave her the strangest of feelings, a kind of tickling all over the inside of her body, which made her want to wave her arms and legs and bounce up and down as if she were a rubber ball. But always, sooner or later, thoughts of Baba would come to spoil it, and when that happened she wanted to punch the air with rage.

Mamma was coming – Bertha could feel the heat already – and she wasn't alone; she was talking. Bertha didn't want to see anyone. She just wanted to get back into her bedroom, on her own. Now they were hugging her, kissing her. A man – it must be a man, he had a beard – and a woman. A confusion of speech. The man's voice and the woman's voice. And beside them Mamma. Yes, that was Mamma, because that was where the stream of heat was coming from. But who were the other two? Faces like tailor's dummies. She thought she recognized the man's voice. It sounded like Cousin Fritz. And the woman sounded like Mamma, but she couldn't be Mamma because Mamma was where the heat was coming from. Then she remembered. Cousin Fritz and Aunt Bella had arrived yesterday, and of course Aunt Bella sounded like Mamma because she was Mamma's sister. Bertha wished they would all stop talking. It was so confusing to hear those familiar voices coming from faces which she didn't recognize.

Bertha stood up. She would go back to her room even if Ilse hadn't finished cleaning. She must get away from this hubbub and the horrible rubbery burning of Mamma. She had to go back to her room. It didn't matter if Ilse was still cleaning.

Walking past the mirror. A sideways look.

A white face reflected. Bared teeth, and empty eye sockets.

A death's head!

Alas, poor....

166

Bertha stood still, trembling. Death's head in the mirror. It was her fault. The mirror in her room had remained uncovered for two days after Papa died. Now his dead face was looking at her from the mirror, reproaching her. She must break the mirror, and all the other mirrors in the house. Smash them to smithereens.

She reached out, her hand shaking, fumbling with the silver menorah on the mantelpiece.

Mustn't use that.

Marble bowl beside it. She grasped the bowl, raised her hand, aimed the bowl at the mirror.

Wrist seized from behind, a wrenching, burning grip. Fritz twisting the bowl from her grasp.

Bertha whirled round, grabbing for the bowl, scratching at Fritz's face. She heard a scream. It seemed to come from the mirror. She dared not look again at the mirror. The death's head. The scream must be coming from the death's head. But as Fritz twisted her round, pinioning her arms behind her back, she saw the mirror again and it was her own face she saw, the mouth contorted into a shriek.

Agnethe sat on the ottoman attaching a ribbon to a hat. Miss Thomson was in her usual position by the door, reading *The Englishwoman's Domestic Magazine*.

After the episode with the mirror that morning Mrs Pappenheim had decided that two people must always be in attendance in Bertha's room. 'To prevent anything untoward,' she said. Bertha lay on the bed with her head burrowed into the pillow. If only they would go away. Leave her in peace. Peace! How was she ever to have peace? She no longer had control of her life. So many periods of 'time missing' when she said and did things of which she only knew when others reported them to her. Under constant surveillance, never allowed a moment alone.

How long till Dr Breuer would arrive? She shifted her head to look at the clock on the bedside table. Half past one. Another five hours at least. She closed her eyes again. , Oh no! Agnethe was trying to engage Miss Thomson in conversation.

How long did mourning periods last in England, she wanted to know. Now Miss Thomson was describing the various stages and the rules for mourning dress, the most appropriate materials, the weeping veil, the types of trim used, the colours permitted during half mourning. Talking to Agnethe like a schoolmistress addressing a pupil, of course, querulous and didactic . God forbid that Agnethe should be encouraged to think that they were on an equal footing just because they were engaged in the joint task of guarding Bertha.

How dared Agnethe sit on the ottoman! That was her special place where she sat with Dr Breuer. She tried to think about it now, to imagine how she would sit with him this evening, his hand raising the spoon to her lips. But she could not. All she could think about was the fat bombazine-clad bottom of Agnethe on the ottoman and the voice of Miss Thomson detailing the number of months of mourning required in England for the different degrees of relationship and describing the permissible accessories.

'Jet for buttons and jewellery. No shortage of that in England. The best jet in the world is found in Yorkshire. The hair of the deceased is often….'

Bertha pressed her fingers into her ears.

That evening Mrs Pappenheim reported to Dr Breuer that Bertha had been shrieking and trying to hide under the bed and inside the wardrobe. They had not been able to determine what it was that was terrifying her so. Miss Thomson and Agnethe had been unable to control her. They had had to call upon Willi and Fritz to help them restrain her and force her onto the bed. Then Bertha had begged them to empty all the jugs and kettles containing water, to leave not a drop of water in the house, or they would all be dead.

When Dr Breuer prompted her to talk, asking her why she had been so afraid, why she had talked about jugs of water, she told him a story of a monster, full of eyes, with twelve wings made of black crape and carrying a bloody sword. It was searching for water in which to wash the sword. It must not be allowed to do so because the water would be poisoned and everyone would die.

168

When she had finished her tale, she kept her eyes closed. Whereas on previous occasions her story-telling had assuaged her, now she still remained fearful. It was Dr Breuer's voice she heard talking to her, but was it really Dr Breuer? She reached out and felt the rough cloth of a jacket sleeve. She slid her fingers downwards until they touched his hand. She grasped the hand, feeling it all over. The hand responded with firm warmth. She opened her eyes.

'I think, on this occasion, it's quite clear what's troubling you, Bertha,' Dr Breuer said. 'A monster with many eyes and twelve wings. What does that mean to you?'

Malach HaMavet. The angel of death. Bertha shivered at the thought. She gripped Dr Breuer's hand more tightly, and as she did so she welcomed the frisson of terror that allowed her to seek this comfort from him. She wanted to intensify her fear and began a babbled description of everything she could remember about *Malach HaMavet*: the many eyes that see everything, the seven dragon heads, the poison that drips from the tip of his sword into the mouths of the dying, the poison that will kill everyone if it gets into the drinking water.

Dr Breuer was soothing her, saying that there was nothing to worry about, that really, there was no such thing as the angel of death, not in the way Bertha was talking about anyway.

'Do you know what the great Jewish philosopher Maimonides said about *Malach HaMavet*? He believed that it's merely a representation of the inclination to evil, the tendency to wrong-doing. In fact, he believed that all angels are mythical representations of forces within the human mind. So you see, Bertha, there's nothing to be frightened of. Nothing at all.'

Bertha had believed herself happy during the night. She had lain awake almost until dawn, alternating remembered scenes of Dr Breuer spooning food into her mouth with fantasies in which he snatched her from the path of *Malach HaMavet*, taking her up in his arms in the way he had done when he lifted her out of the carriage, and pressing her close to his breast. But when she awoke in the morning it was to a return

169

to despair, a mood only darkened when she tried to find solace again in the daydreams of the night. The illusoriness of those imagined states of happiness mocked her and the memory of the intense pleasure they had given her filled her with an undefined discomfort.

Agnethe was again on the ottoman, mending an apron. Miss Thomson was still reading *The Englishwoman's Domestic Magazine*.

How ashamed Bertha would feel if they knew the thoughts she had been having during the night. The idea of it reinforced her sense of her own foolishness. A thought struck her. What if she should ever talk of these things during an absence? Or while she was recounting a story to Dr Breuer when in her cloudy state?

The thought flooded her with an embarrassment so intense that she felt her cheeks glow red. She hid her face in the pillows. She must never again allow herself to be overcome by these strange states. But she had no control over them, did not even know when they were about to happen.

Perhaps if she never sat down, kept on walking around, doing something, then she might keep them at bay. She must get up straight away, force herself to stay alert.

Bertha got out of bed and started to get dressed. She managed to pull on her drawers then struggled with her chemise, unable to manoeuvre her stiff arm through the armhole but determined not to ask for help.

'Not so fast, Miss Bertha.' Agnethe laid aside the apron. 'No point tearin' at your clothes when you've got someone here to help you.' Bertha submitted with bad grace as Agnethe eased her into the rest of her clothes.

The day stretched ahead of her, fraught with irritations and danger. How many hours till Dr Breuer would arrive? No, mustn't think of that. She might lose control of her wakefulness, lapse into an absence and start revealing those very thoughts which she must keep hidden.

Read. Something demanding which would require her full attention. She picked up Goethe's *Wilhelm Meister's Apprenticeship*. Anna had sent her some notes she had made for a lecture she had given on it. She hadn't read them yet. If she tried to do so now, concentrated really hard, it would keep her awake.

She sat down on the chaise longue – upright, fearing that unconsciousness might take her unawares if she leaned back – and skimmed over Anna's notes.

We have to be thankful to Goethe, Anna wrote, for making Shakespeare so widely known to German speakers, particularly through his incorporation of the playwright's work in the story of Wilhelm Meister. At the same time, we must remember that the views about Hamlet expressed in the novel are those of Wilhelm Meister, not of Goethe himself, and those views are determined by the character of Meister. Her second point was that, as Jarno, one of the members of the Society of the Tower, told him, the reason Meister was so successful at playing Hamlet was not because he was a good actor but because his own personality was similar to Hamlet's.

Bertha started leafing through the book, trying to find the passage about Jarno. It was such a long book. But she should be able to find it; she knew the book well. She flipped the pages forward, then back again. She must have missed it. But wait. What was Meister saying here about Ophelia? Something about her being unable to conceal her wishes and her longings. And then: 'But at length when all self-control is at an end, and the secrets of her heart appear upon her tongue, that tongue betrays her.'

The very thing that Bertha herself feared. It seemed as if the book was speaking to her, giving her a warning. As if to reinforce this message, a few lines of Goethe's poem 'Epirrhema' came into her mind.

> Nothing is inner,
> Nothing is outer,
> For what is inner is outer.
> Therefore grasp without delay
> The sacred, open secret.

She clutched the book to her chest, repeating to herself the third line, then the fifth. Her sacred secret. Her night-time

171

thoughts. An open secret. Open to everyone. She was going to reveal it. She couldn't help herself. She had no control over her speech when she was in her clouds. Everyone would laugh at her. Dr Breuer would despise her.

She must never let herself go into those clouds.

Stay awake.

Bertha looked down at the book again, turned a few pages and started to read at random. Wilhelm Meister had been invited by Philina to watch a performance of rope dancers. Leaping and somersaulting high in the air, twirling and pirouetting, the crowd applauding….

Agnethe had started talking. She was telling Miss Thomson about the death of her husband.

'Cancer, it was. In his neck. Doctors couldn't do anythin'. The cancer jus' grew and grew. His neck looked like a tree trunk near the end.'

Miss Thomson made a sympathetic noise and gave her magazine a little shake as she turned a page.

'Terrible, the pain was. Couldn't eat nor drink. Hadn't been married very long, more's the pity. A late marriage it was, he bein' much older than me and me not so young myself.'

….. falling, plummeting, with a rope around her neck, hangman cackling, down, down, down…. Bertha jerked and screamed.

A dream. It must have been a dream.

Or – chill dread – an absence. Had she said anything? She bent her head over her book, her heart thudding.

'Now, Miss Bertha, settle down.' Agnethe looked up from her work but turned back to it when she saw that Bertha had already returned to her reading.

Bertha focused on the page but she could no longer concentrate on either the book or Anna's ideas. She wanted to escape into thoughts of Dr Breuer. It would calm her. Yet embarrassment prevented her. She could not understand this compulsion to dwell on fantasies of being small, ensconced in his arms. It reminded her of the stage hypnotist's act where a man had dandled a bundle of clothes on his lap, believing it to be a baby. If such a belief could be brought about in this way,

172

perhaps Dr Breuer had created a similar effect in her, causing her to have the impression that she was now a baby. She visualized the evening feeding scene, herself with her mouth open, ready for the spoon, like a baby bird in a nest waiting for the mother bird to drop the worm in. As she did so, a surge of excitement shot through her body, like a jolt of electricity. Something must have happened to cause her to behave in this way. She couldn't even discuss it with him. It was too embarrassing.

It might get worse. She might get stuck in that state, all the time. Even now she was beginning to feel herself shrink. Her thoughts were trying to formulate themselves in baby talk. She must stop this happening. She must anchor herself in reality.

She got up and walked over to the wardrobe mirror. She looked into it, saw herself fall backwards. The image was horizontal. And it was not herself that she saw, but Ophelia, lying on her back in a stream, drifting on the brackish water.

'All right now, Miss Bertha.' Agnethe's arm was sliding under her shoulders, lifting her up, raising her onto the bed. Miss Thomson stood opposite, making a clucking noise.

Bertha looked again at the mirror. It reflected Agnethe's stooped back and above it, Miss Thomson's head and shoulders. She closed her eyes, unable to contemplate reading, or doing anything at all. How peaceful Ophelia had looked.

She too could have that peace. She pictured herself wading into the Danube, or better still, the River Traun, where it flowed past the base of the Siriuskogel. The current carrying her along, down the valley flanked by the Hollengebirge mountains – she saw the snow-clad peaks towering above her – and into the Traunsee.

Ilse had just brought in the supper tray. It lay on the ottoman. A bowl of cream of mushroom soup and a vanilla milk pudding.

Dr Breuer picked up the spoon and held it out to Bertha. She shook her head with a petulant frown. He waited a moment then put some soup in the spoon and lifted it towards her mouth. She turned her head away. She did not

173

want to start eating. The sooner she started, the sooner it would be finished. He dipped the spoon in the bowl again. This time she would take a little. When he raised the spoon to her lips she parted them slightly and took a small sip. Her heart was beating more quickly. When he brought the spoon again to her mouth, her lips were fully parted.

The soup was finished. The feeding was half over. Too soon. She must try to delay the pudding. But when Dr Breuer proffered it her mouth was already open, the tip of her tongue protruding, flickering out to reach the rim of the silver spoon. Her breathing became more rapid, her cheeks flushed. The last mouthful was accompanied by a feeling of desolation. A night and a day until she could do this again.

In the morning Bertha spoke with no-one. She would not get out of bed. The thought of the spoon on her lips, the warm thick liquids flowing over her tongue was no longer a thrill but a torment. It was all the fault of Baba.

It made no sense.

It didn't matter that it made no sense. That was how it was. If there had been no Baba her joy in being fed by Dr Breuer would have been unalloyed. As it was, the warm thick liquids were running down her throat like a corrosive acid and she wanted to die.

Death. Each time she thought of it now she felt herself being acted on by a force, as if something beyond her own will was pulling her towards it. If she reflected on it, imagined to herself what death would be like, she was overcome with terror and the pull weakened. If she tried to stop thinking about it, made her mind blank, the pull became stronger. Sometimes there was an emptiness within her which made her less resistant to the pull, as if she was a weightless phantom being tossed hither and thither by forces unknown.

The emptiness was taking hold of her now. The fear of death was draining away from her. The corrosive pain also. All the rage and hate, the irritations and frustrations, the dreads, the sorrows – all being gathered up like autumn leaves, rolled up together by gusts of wind, whirled into the air, away.

174

Leaving a gaping hole inside. And with the emptiness she was no longer anchored. Now she was being sucked from life by the same whirlwind which had gathered up her feelings.

The window stood wide open, curtain fluttering outwards, drawn by a summer breeze.

Something external to herself was propelling her towards the window, a force which her emptiness could not resist. There was no hesitation, no fear, only this force of malignant whorls sucking her up, bearing her forwards.

Suspended now, astride the windowsill. So far to fall.

20

5 June 1881

This morning Bertha tried to throw herself from her bedroom window. I can scarcely believe that things have come to this, nor can I begin to understand what can have driven Bertha to such an action. We are all, needless to say, deeply perturbed.

According to Miss Thomson, Agnethe left the room to fetch a jug of water and while she was absent Bertha went to the window, which was already open, and tried to climb out. Miss Thomson – who I believe was reading a magazine at the time although she does not admit to it – did not notice until Bertha had one leg over the sill. Fortunately Agnethe returned just at that moment, seized Bertha by the waist and pulled her back. I think Bertha may even have been unaware of what she was doing. Certainly, when she was brought back in she was overcome by such a storm of agitated weeping we could make no sense of what she was saying. I sent a message immediately to Dr Breuer who arrived within the hour. He has decided that Bertha can no longer remain at home and is making arrangements for her to be admitted to a sanatorium in Inzersdorf. In the meantime Bertha is to be treated with chloral hydrate, as much as is required to keep her reasonably calm.

Bertha reacted with violence to the proposed hospitalization, smashing the chinaware on her washstand and accusing Dr Breuer of betraying her. She believes that it confirms her fear that she is insane and claimed that Dr Breuer had previously assured her that she was not insane and would not be sent away. This afternoon Dr Breuer sent a message to say that he has arranged for Bertha to be accommodated in a separate villa in the grounds of the sanatorium and for Miss Thomson and Agnethe to be in residence with her. She will therefore have a measure of independence and will be apart from the other patients.

I am thankful that Bella and Fritz are still here and able to share the burden with me. Since Siegmund's death I have felt family responsibilities weighing heavily, and Willi is still too young to be of much support. Fritz has been a strong and steady presence in the past few days *and I shall be sorry to see him return to Karlsruhe. Bella has promised to stay for a few weeks more, until we are sure that Bertha is settled satisfactorily in the sanatorium.*

o~o~o

On her fourth day at the sanatorium Bertha stayed in bed. She felt an exhaustion so profound she could not imagine ever getting out of bed again. It was good to be so exhausted. She could barely even think. She did not want to think.

She remembered little of the three days since she had arrived. There had been a struggle when Dr Breuer came to take her to Inzersdorf. She begged and pleaded with him, reminding him of his promise that she would not be put away. The circumstances had changed, he said. He could not allow her mother to have the constant worry that Bertha might harm herself so she must be taken to a place where she would be more secure. She clung screaming to her bedroom curtain when the time came to leave. No-one knew her real reason for resisting the move – her fear that she would no longer see Dr Breuer every day, no longer be fed by him. Only when he promised her that he would visit her regularly at the sanatorium did she allow him to prise the curtain from her grasp and lead her out of the apartment.

After that there were only fragments of memory. People she did not know walking around the grounds. Or did she know them? She could not tell because often she still could not even recognize the people she did know. She thought she had seen snakes in the flower beds, a body floating in the pond. Then there was the shattering sound of smashed glass. Or was it broken plates? Whatever it was, it seemed to her that she had been responsible. Meal trays came from the kitchen. She refused them. A doctor appeared from time to time, asking questions. He said his name was Dr Breslauer. He was a small, fat man, a little older than Dr Breuer. The tips of his moustache were waxed and his hair was closely pomaded to his scalp. There had been warm baths, always followed by a cold douche.

177

At night she refused to go to bed. Her mind was clearer at night. If she did not have this nocturnal clarity she really would believe that she was mad so she must not allow herself to sleep. She sat up through the night reading and writing and worrying about her illness. She still feared that she might be seriously ill, that she might never recover, that other strange symptoms might appear. Dr Breuer had reassured her repeatedly, pointing out all the symptoms that had already disappeared: the loss of feeling and contracture were now much reduced and affected only the right limbs, some of her visual disorders had cleared up, her speech was much better and she was coughing less. But Bertha was not reassured. There was still so much 'time missing' and hallucinations, and she was particularly perturbed by her inability to recognize people. Dr Breuer could not explain these things.

On the third night Dr Breslauer injected her with three grams of chloral hydrate. To help her sleep, he said. Agnethe held her down while he did so.

In the afternoon of the fourth day Dr Breuer visited. He came with the other doctor, Dr Breslauer. She did not open her eyes. They stood by her bedside, talking to each other in a low murmur. Dr Breuer sat down. He took her hand in his, asked her how she was. She said nothing. Afterwards she did not know why she had not spoken, whether it was because she did not want to speak to him, or because she had nothing to say, or because she was too exhausted to form any words.

That evening she accepted a bowl of chicken soup. She did not resist when Dr Breslauer again injected her with three grams of chloral hydrate.

The following day she walked in the grounds with Miss Thomson in the afternoon. When she returned to the villa she lapsed into somnolence. When she awoke Dr Breslauer was sitting beside her. She had been talking while asleep, he told her. Perhaps she would like to tell him what was on her mind. Bertha said nothing. He tried to coax her. She turned her head to the wall.

Thereafter Bertha's days fell into a pattern. She would sleep late in the morning, walk outside in the afternoon and

178

drift into a dreamy state in the evening. If Dr Breuer visited in the evening she would talk, telling stories concocted from thoughts she had had since she last saw him. More often it was Dr Breslauer who came and then she refused to say anything at all.

Bertha liked to sit by the pond in the afternoon. She found the stately glide of the swans soothing and there was a grey heron which often stood motionless in the shallows, its stillness quieting her thoughts. One day as she sat there she heard the piano being played in the sitting room of the sanatorium. It was Schubert's arrangement of Mignon's song from *Wilhelm Meister's Apprenticeship*.

She hummed, then sang quietly along with the music.

> Do you know the land where the lemon-trees grow,
> in darkened leaves the gold-oranges glow,
> a soft wind blows from the pure blue sky,
> the myrtle stands mute, and the bay-tree high?
> Do you know it well?
> It's there I'd be gone,
> to be there with you, O, my beloved one!

Mignon. That strange little twelve-year-old who seemed to be neither girl nor boy. Wilhelm had rescued her from a troupe of acrobats who had kidnapped her from her home in Italy and had taken her into his care.

That night while Miss Thomson and Agnethe slept Bertha pored over the Goethe novel, scanning it for references to Mignon. She read the passage about the egg dance again and again until she knew it by heart.

Mignon, seeing that Wilhelm was sad and hoping to please him, had performed her famous dance for him. She laid out the eggs on a little carpet, summoned a violinist and, blindfold, danced among the eggs, leaping and skipping to the music with clockwork precision. When she finished not an egg had been touched. Wilhelm, entranced by the performance, realized that he wanted to take her to his heart and lavish on her a father's love.

Before she allowed herself to sleep, Bertha wrote a story

179

about a little girl whose father was a valet in the bedchamber of a cruel king. His duties included preparing the tub for the king's bath. One day the water was too hot and the king scalded himself. The king ordered the valet to be executed. The little girl ran to the king and begged for mercy for her father. The king ordered a rope to be strung between two trees and told the girl that if she could walk across it without falling he would consider her plea. The girl walked across. Then the king ordered a patch of burning cinders to be spread on the ground and told the girl that if she could jump across it without burning her feet he would feel more inclined to consider her plea. She jumped successfully. Then the king ordered sixteen eggs to be laid out in four columns of four and told the girl that if she could dance a hornpipe in the square without breaking an egg he would pardon her father. The king summoned a piper, the music started and, as the girl took her first step, she trampled on one of the eggs.

When Dr Breuer next visited he urged her, as usual, to tell him a story. Bertha told him the story of the valet and the cruel king. The sadness of the tale was forgotten when Dr Breuer complimented her on her imaginative prowess. It led to a discussion of *Wilhelm Meister's Apprenticeship* and *Indian Summer*. Bertha found that she could forget herself when reading them. It was as if she was no longer herself, but rather Wilhelm or Heinrich.

'It's like what you told me about Aristotle and catharsis,' she said. 'It's as if I share their experiences and their emotions, the way I did when I was watching *Iphigenia*. The trouble is, the people in these novels are always men. I can't think of any novel which has a heroine whose life I would want to be mine.'

Dr Breuer drew her attention to the Beautiful Soul, the heroine of Book VI of *Wilhelm Meister's Apprenticeship*, who narrates the story of her own personal and spiritual development in a manner that parallels that of Wilhelm himself. He told her also – something which she had not known – that the narrative of the Beautiful Soul was based on an autobiographical manuscript written by Susanna von

180

Klettenberg, a woman who had acted as mentor to Goethe when he underwent a long period of illness.

Over the next two nights Bertha flung herself into a fresh reading of the narrative of the Beautiful Soul, making notes about points she would discuss with Dr Breuer on his next visit. She wrote to Anna, raising those same points and asking for her opinion on them.

But when Dr Breuer next came they did not discuss the Beautiful Soul. Dr Breuer told Bertha that he would not see her again until mid-August. He was going to spend five weeks on holiday with his family in Gmunden.

When Dr Breuer told Bertha that he was going to be absent, she turned away from him, mute, refusing further conversation. She remained sitting on the sofa after he left, unable to get up. There was no longer any solidity under her feet; if she tried to stand she would surely fall away into a bottomless pit.

She still sat there, impassive, when Dr Breslauer came to administer her chloral injection. She allowed herself to be undressed by Agnethe and put to bed.

Her pain was magnified by the way he had said it: so casually, as if it was a matter of no consequence. She would be in good hands with Dr Breslauer, he had said, as if there was no difference between them.

Gmunden. A mere twenty miles from Ischl. At the other end of the Traunsee, a twin resort. She had visited Gmunden last year, on a boat trip along the Traun. She visualized it now, all the things that Dr Breuer would do with his family over the next five weeks – with Baba! – while she was trapped here in this horrible sanatorium with Agnethe and Miss Thomson.

The anger mounted. She took a handful of pillow into her mouth and gnashed at it, a roar rising up in her throat. She could hear it as if from afar like a crash of thunder, unending, a pounding in her ears, on and on, a hammering in her chest and the noise still louder and Dr Breslauer was beside her again with a syringe and gradually the roar faded as she reached out, grasping greedily at the oblivion of unconsciousness.

21

Bertha's day now began with a session in the treatment suite of the sanatorium. Before he left, Dr Breuer had asked Dr Breslauer to draw up a programme of hydrotherapy, starting with intensive treatment for the coldness and oedema in her right extremities. Agnethe escorted her to the sanatorium twice a day and stayed while the nurses applied the procedures. There was no need for her to stay, Bertha told her, but Agnethe said that it would help her to extend her nursing knowledge.

Two minutes with the right foot in a tub of hot water, as hot as she could bear, followed by fifteen seconds in cold water: the procedure to be repeated ten times, with chunks of ice being added to the cold tub. Then vigorous friction of the limb with a mitten dipped in cold water. When the foot was done the process was repeated for the arm. After that Bertha was taken to the gymnasium where she spent thirty minutes swinging dumb-bells and doing exercises on the horizontal bars.

The physical therapy provided a structure for Bertha, a set of experiences which were simple and real. During it she focused her mind on the details, trying to guess how hot or cold the water was, noticing how the hot was hottest and the cold coldest when she moved from cold to hot and vice versa. The longer the limb stayed in the tub, the more the sensation of hot or cold diminished. She tried also to guess how many seconds remained until the next change of tub: five seconds gone in the cold, and she would start counting down from ten, reaching zero as the nurse replaced the cold tub with the hot. It provided a respite from her black thoughts, her worries about her illness and most of all about her disordered emotional state. It held her back at first from what she now thought of as her 'crazy thoughts' – the infantile fancies and the destructive urges.

After a week of the hot and cold tub treatment Dr Breslauer prescribed a twice-weekly wet sheet pack. Bertha hated it the first time. She was obliged to stand naked, squirming with discomfort, while the nurses made the preparations, wringing out a sheet which had been soaked in a tub of cold water and laying it on a bed covered by two wool blankets. She then had to lie down on top of the sheet and raise her arms while the nurses wrapped one side of the sheet tightly round her body, tucking it under her back and around her right leg. The other side of the sheet was drawn over, enclosing both arms and her two legs. Two more blankets were laid on top of her and tucked in, forming a cocoon. A woollen cap was pulled over her head and down over her ears. Bertha felt cold, wet and foolish. After a while she grew warmer and eventually began to perspire but a lurking sensation of disagreeableness persisted.

On the second occasion a curiously pleasurable sensation overcame her once the initial cold dampness had faded and she relaxed into the warm moist tightness. If she closed her eyes she could imagine – well, nothing, really. And this nothingness was good.

The next time she found herself looking forward to the wet sheet pack. There was no longer any inhibition as she stripped off her clothes, preparing her body for the pack. In fact, the curiously pleasurable sensation now even extended to this baring of her body. It increased as she was wrapped, as the cold receded, and when the tight warmth came she sank into it. Her lips started to move. Her mouth was open, her tongue darting in and out. She let its tip caress her upper lip, then the lower. She closed her mouth only to open it again, the tongue now protruding more eagerly. A feeling came over her, as if a swarm of buzzing bees was trapped under her skin, all over her body. The entrapment of her limbs was both a joy and a torment. She ached to fling them wide while at the same time she rejoiced in the constriction. She did not know how long this lasted. It was not long enough. When she began to perspire the nurses plied her with a lukewarm herbal tea,

183

bringing it to her lips in a cup with a spout like a teapot. She drank thirstily.

Since then, the 'crazy thoughts' had grown ever more pressing, as if the treatment had lowered her psychic defences. By the pond in the afternoon she saw, not a small expanse of water in the grounds of a sanatorium, but the Traunsee. At this time last year she too had been in the Salzkammergut. Each activity she remembered was now transformed into an activity Dr Breuer was engaged in. A passing swan became a paddle steamer, crowded with happy holidaymakers. She remembered her daydream of floating down the River Traun like Ophelia, drifting into the Traunsee. She was there now, floating face down past the paddle steamer carrying Dr Breuer. But now, with a lifting lurch of the heart, she saw not her own body in the water but Baba's.

There was a castle on an island in the Traunsee, a square white building with two small onion domes. Bertha peopled it with a succession of evil-doers – goblins and witches and werewolves who inflicted death, disease or imprisonment on those who crossed their paths. She wrote those stories at night, as she waited for her chloral injection to take effect. Try as he might, Dr Breslauer could not persuade Bertha to recount any of these tales.

The writing of the stories seemed only to inflame Bertha with a spirit of malevolence. She found the presence of Agnethe and Miss Thomson in the villa intolerable, but neither did she want to be back home. She would have found her mother and brother even more intolerable; in any case, without the possibility of a daily visit from Dr Breuer there was no point in being at home. She did not want to join the other patients in the sanatorium either. She had nothing to say to them. She didn't want to hear about their illnesses and she didn't want to talk about her own. Each day was just a series of annoyances, bracketed between periods of time-missing. She no longer even worried about her symptoms. It seemed not to matter if she could recognize people or not. She wanted nothing to do with anyone anyway. Nor did it matter if she had periods of time-missing. In fact, she would prefer to have the entire day missing. To have nothing but sleep, and the wet sheet pack.

Anna wrote, replying to her questions about the Beautiful Soul. Bertha set the letter aside. She no longer felt any interest in the Beautiful Soul.

o~o~o

Inzersdorf
August 12, 1881

My dear colleague

In view of your imminent return to Vienna I take this opportunity of bringing you up to date with the condition of Miss Pappenheim.

The patient has responded satisfactorily to the hydrotherapy measures applied in that there has been some reduction of the oedema of the right extremities. The right hand is now fairly free although there is still some contraction of the arm. Anaesthesia is limited mainly to the elbow area.

It is more difficult to ascertain Miss Pappenheim's state of mind as she has become resistant to our efforts to communicate with her. It is unfortunate that she does not seem willing to take advantage of the opportunities for social interaction that the sanatorium offers. She has rejected all attempts to encourage her to take her meals in the dining room with the other residents and she shows no interest in engaging in conversation with either the clinic staff or patients. When she does speak, it is still mainly in English. For the last three weeks she has refused to continue with the prescribed gymnastic exercises.

The patient generally sleeps for about four or five hours each night. She continues to receive three grams of chloral hydrate in the evening. Even with this high dose sleep is always preceded by a period of great agitation. Throughout the day her domestic companions and clinic staff have noted frequent absences, hallucinations and instances of bizarre behaviour.

I look forward to your return and to discussing an adjustment in Miss Pappenheim's programme of therapy.

With kind regards
H. Breslauer

o~o~o

When Bertha came back from her afternoon walk on 15 August she found Dr Breuer waiting for her in the villa, along with Dr Breslauer. They rose to greet her when she entered the salon. Bertha felt her knees buckle. She sat down. This was a hallucination. Dr Breuer was in Gmunden. He would have sent a message if he was really back in Vienna.

She did not acknowledge the two men. If she ignored them they would disappear.

Now there was only Dr Breuer. The other man had left. Dr Breuer was talking to her. Bertha reached out and took his hand. If it really was Dr Breuer she would recognize his hand. She felt it all over. He was still talking, asking her how she had been, if her domestic arrangements were satisfactory, if she felt that the treatment was proving beneficial.

Yes, it was Dr Breuer. It was his hand and it was his voice, and with this dawning realization came a shrinking into herself, a curling up of her soul, stemming from a resentment which she could not articulate. She threw his hand away in a fit of pique. She would not speak to him, no matter what questions he asked. Let him go away. Let him think he had angered her. Her cheeks puffed up in a pout.

Now he was asking her if she had any stories to tell him. Had she written any while he was away? No?

Bertha could imagine the questioning expression on his face, the cocked eyebrow. She kept her gaze fixed on the floor.

He had some tales of his own, he was saying now.

No! She did not want to hear what he had been doing in Gmunden. She shook her head and kept on shaking it till she felt dizzy, so dizzy she was almost unconscious. Then she lay down on the sofa, pretending to be asleep.

After Dr Breuer left, Bertha broke into such a fit of hysterical weeping that Miss Thomson had to send for Dr Breslauer. He injected four grams of chloral hydrate.

When Dr Breuer visited two days later Bertha was again unwilling to talk. She felt as if she was two separate people. She imagined the one persona conversing politely and normally with Dr Breuer, exchanging greetings and news of

186

events since they had last seen each other, discussing her illness and the progress of her treatment, expressing thanks for his care and commitment, in the very way that her mother would speak. She knew the script for this persona as if it was a part in a play but she could not enact it. It was usurped by the other persona, a writhing, snarling, self-centred conglomeration of frustration, bad temper and malice.

If she could just float away. Drifting down the Traun, into the lake.

Dr Breuer was begging her to tell a story, reminding her how this always helped to bring her to a better state of mind. 'Come along now, Bertha. I'm sure you have something to tell me.'

Their eyes locked and Bertha began to talk about a castle on a lake where a werewolf lived. The werewolf was very fond of killing and eating little girls. Then it turned out to be not a werewolf at all, only a man dressed in a wolfskin. She had even seen it here, by the pond in the garden. Bertha did not elaborate any further on the story of the werewolf but went on to complain about a patient who walked in the grounds every afternoon.

'His leg's all twisted and his foot makes a horrible flapping sound when he walks and his speech is slurred and he has disgusting thick white patches around his mouth and on his tongue and he keeps on saying that he's going to die soon and that he's frightened of dying, and I don't understand why I've been brought to this place where I'm surrounded by people like that. He's mad and there are other mad people here. There's a woman whose eyes stick out, and they look in different directions and every time I see her she stares at me as if she thinks that I'm a ghost or something terrifying, and there's another woman who cries all the time. Every time I see her she's weeping and sniffing and blowing her nose. You promised me I wouldn't be put away and now you've put me away with all these crazy people.' Bertha was wailing and sobbing. As she talked the images of the people she was describing became exaggerated in her mind to the point where she imagined herself confined in an asylum peopled by lunatics who might have been created by the brush of Hieronymus Bosch.

But the voice of Dr Breuer calmed her and once she had delivered herself of her grievances Bertha became extravagantly cheerful, full of ideas for the future, and willing even to talk civilly with Miss Thomson after Dr Breuer left.

o~o~o

August 1881
Dearest Anna

I fear I have neglected you of late. Do forgive me. Tonight I feel quite transformed, full of energy and looking forward to a time when I will be quite recovered from this wretched illness.

The past two months have been very trying. I certainly do not enjoy living in this place but I believe the treatment is beginning to have some effect and I must start to make plans for I cannot conceive of returning to my previous life of idleness. I was so interested in your account of the nursing work which your friend Hannelore is engaged in. I should very much like to do something like that. You say she attended a training course organized by the Karlsruhe Women's Association. Is this similar to that run by the Protestant Order of Deaconesses in Kaiserswerth? I believe that Miss Florence Nightingale trained there. I know that Mamma would not approve of me doing such a thing but with the example of the admirable Miss Nightingale I do not see how she can object. I shall discuss it with Dr Breuer and ask him to persuade her.

Now, tell me, Anna, how is your own dear Mamma? You wrote that you are planning another trip to Baden so that she may take the waters for her rheumatism. It must be such an unpleasant condition and so painful but I am sure the baths will do her good. I myself have been following a programme of hydrotherapy here at the clinic and am feeling very much better for it.

My best love to you and all the family
Bertha

22

30 August 1881

Dr Breuer has arranged for Bertha to be brought back from Inzersdorf this afternoon. He has decided that she needs daily doses of what she now calls her 'talking cure' and since he is unable to travel out to Inzersdorf every day he prefers to have her back at home for the moment. I confess to being somewhat puzzled by this form of treatment. Dr Breuer makes much of the fairy stories, apparently of her own invention, which Bertha recounts to him. He believes them to be related to her hallucinations and to events which have upset her. He believes also that allowing Bertha to talk about them unburdens her and is likely to promote her return to health. I can but trust myself to his judgement in the matter. In the meantime, I am concerned as to how Bertha will react to the new apartment as our move was made during her absence. At least Dr Breuer will not have so far to come as we are now only a few minutes from Backerstrasse.

I admit to some apprehension over Bertha's arrival in view of her aggressive behaviour before she left for the clinic. Dr Breuer has always insisted that it would be better not to visit her at Inzersdorf. He felt that Bertha should have a complete break to allow her to reorganize her emotions. It seems, however, that although there has been some improvement in her physical condition she is still overwrought and disturbed. We shall just have to cope as best we can.

Agnethe reports that Bertha is still showing very little inclination for food and often can only be persuaded to eat if fed. She has recently developed a total aversion to water and slakes her thirst with fruit. I sent Ilse to the fruit market today for a supply of oranges and melons. This is just one of a number of obstinate whims which Bertha has developed recently. Another is an apparent inability to eat bread although she asks for it and even raises it to her mouth before laying it aside again. Equally odd is her insistence on keeping her stockings on when undressed for bed at night.

Wilhelm left this morning with some of his student friends for a *hiking holiday in the Salzkammergut. It is just as well that this coincides with Bertha's return.*

o~o~o

Bertha was disoriented in the new apartment. Although she had known about the move, she had nonetheless imagined her bedroom being much as it was in Liechtensteinstrasse: the décor in shades of pink and red, the creamy chintz soft furnishings and the white tiled stove. In the carriage on the way into the city she visualised herself there, resuming her earlier relationship with Dr Breuer, imagined again the feel of his hands as he carried out his tests, the intimacy of the murmured exchanges, and most enticing of all, the spoon-feeding by the ottoman.

As the carriage drew into Neuer Markt, she was put out by the hustle and clamour of the shops and cafes which lined the square, so different from the tranquility of Liechtensteinstrasse. Mamma had fussed in an uncharacteristic manner when she arrived, plying her with questions about her health, trying to ensure that she was comfortable and that everything was to her liking till Bertha's head began to ache and she had to lie down.

The sleigh bed was in her room, and all the rosewood furniture, but the walls were a cold blue, the carpet grey and the satin curtains a chilly white. As she lay on the bed Bertha felt a cramping ache in her eyelids from which she could get no relief. If she closed her eyes, it seemed worse but when she opened them again it was no better. She had been looking forward so much to seeing Dr Breuer again in her own room but it did not feel like her own room and the pain was becoming so unbearable she could not look forward to anything but the cessation of this torment.

The air in the room felt stale. She rang for Ilse and asked her to open the window. With the window open, the shouts of carriage drivers and revelers and music from the White Swan Inn next door filled the room. Bertha told Ilse to shut it again and begged her to go to the chemist for laudanum.

190

Dr Breuer arrived before Ilse's return. Bertha seized his hand, eager to establish intimacy yet now knowing what to say. Everything seemed so wrong and out of place. Dr Breuer enquired about her journey and how she had been for the past few days. Bertha answered impatiently, her irritation at the banality of the questions increasing the pain she felt across her eyes.

'And your new apartment?' Dr Breuer asked. 'Does it please you?' He got up and went over to the window to open it.

'No!' shouted Bertha. 'Leave the window. Don't open it.'

Dr Breuer turned and sat down again by the bed. Bertha seized his hand again and began to talk about the new apartment, how she hated it, hated Neuer Markt and all the noise, hated her new bedroom and hated Mamma for moving without even consulting her about it. She grieved for her old bedroom. She had not even been able to say goodbye to it. When she left for Inzersdorf in June she had not known that she would never see it again. She blamed her mother bitterly and she blamed her all the more because she was unable to express her anger to her because if she did she would feel cruel and unkind. She felt powerless. Everything in her life was decided by someone else. She had no choice about anything.

Bertha talked until she no longer had anything else to say. Then she lay back, opening and closing her eyes. The pain had gone.

'Is there anything else troubling you?' Dr Breuer asked.

Yes, but she dared not say it. She was troubled by her desire to be held by Dr Breuer, to be fed by him.

'I'm thirsty,' she said. 'I'd like an orange.'

Dr Breuer took an orange from the bowl on the dressing table. Bertha watched his slender fingers as he peeled it. He offered her a segment. She did not take it from him. Instead she opened her mouth. He held it as she sucked the juice from it. When it was dry she opened her mouth for another. They continued like this, without exchanging a word, until the orange was finished.

191

After Dr Breuer left Bertha felt first a deep satisfaction, as if a thirst in every nerve of her body had been slaked, and then a surge of energy which galvanized her throughout the night. She sat up till dawn, reading the stories she had written in Inzersdorf till she knew them by heart.

Over the next seven nights Bertha recounted those stories to Dr Breuer until, by the end of the week, she had delivered herself of all the ones written during his absence. They centred mostly on the misdeeds of the werewolves, witches and goblins in the castle on the island in the Traunsee. Their telling was interspersed with Bertha's frustrations about her conditions in the sanatorium, her complaints about Agnethe, Miss Thomson and the other patients, her frustrations with her mother and Willi. She said nothing about the more mysterious movements of her emotions. She would not have known how to express them even if she had so desired.

One evening, while telling Dr Breuer of her irritation with Miss Thomson, Bertha remembered the incident in Ischl when she had entered the governess's room by mistake and found her dog drinking water out of a glass. She recounted the story in detail, experiencing again the revulsion she had felt at the time. Shortly after she had finished she asked for a glass of water and drank it. She had not been able to drink water for the previous six weeks.

On another occasion she told Dr Breuer of the night when Willi had caught her listening outside the door of her father's sickroom. Bertha was already in bed when she told this story as Dr Breuer had been called out to an emergency and his visit was later than usual. She recalled that she had often gone along to her father's room in the middle of the night and had always kept her stockings on in bed for that reason. But the idea that Willi should dare to manhandle her. She was almost choking with rage as she described how Willi had shaken her, treated her like a subordinate when he himself had been out getting drunk and getting up to goodness what with his loutish friends while she, Bertha, had been caring for their father. As she finished talking Bertha ran her hands over her calves and up over her knees. She untied her garters, rolled

192

her stockings down and handed them to Dr Breuer.

At the end of the week Dr Breuer decided that Bertha should return to Inzersdorf. Bertha did not object. She did not feel any attachment to the new apartment and any resistance she may have felt towards returning to the clinic was overcome by the hostility she felt towards her mother and Willi.

23

On her return to Inzersdorf Bertha's daily activities developed into a routine, with her mental states following a pattern. The morning was devoted to hydrotherapy and exercise in the gymnasium. Rest after lunch and then either a walk in the clinic grounds or a carriage ride with some of the other patients. In the evening she lapsed into her cloudy state. Her absences at other times were now much less frequent.

Dr Breuer generally visited every three days, in the evening. She would tell him stories, although those were less well-developed than previously, being rather embellished accounts of her hallucinations or of incidents that had upset her. On the day following his visit she was always extravagantly high-spirited, on the day after that her behaviour was more or less normal but on the third day she would be bad-tempered and rebellious.

She daydreamed constantly about Dr Breuer. But whereas her previous daydreams – about working for *Die Gartenlaube*, or about Ignaz Brull, for example – had been like plays which she invented and in which she acted a part, her daydreams about Dr Breuer were more like states of emotion which she could catapult herself into. All she needed was the stimulus of a memory. She had only to think of him sitting by her sleigh bed and she was again in the hot air balloon, swept up into the snowy whiteness of the clouds, the shadowy figure beside her, the two of them together, as one, detached from all earthly matters. Or the memory of being carried up from his carriage when they returned from the Ausgarten. But in her daydream they did not stop on the third landing and enter her apartment; they continued – up, up and up, for ever, and as she thought of it she felt herself soar, disembodied and all-powerful.

Then there was the memory of the feeding spoon. That

was a different kind of excitement, as if it was anchored in her body, the source deep in her entrails. At times when she thought of it she felt that she was reaching a point where she could bear it no longer, reaching such a pitch of excitement that she felt she would surely shatter. Then she would switch to the hot air balloon and continue to soar, serene. When she felt calmer her thoughts would return again to the feeding spoon.

On the second day after a visit by Dr Breuer, when she was in a tolerably normal frame of mind, it sometimes seemed to her that these daydreams were like emotional hallucinations, as insubstantial as her fleeting visions of snakes. But when she was next caught up in them she could swear that they were in fact more real than any actual experience provided through any of her senses.

She had become accustomed now to her accommodation in Inzersdorf. To a degree she felt protected there, protected from the reality of her life in Vienna, a life to which she felt she could never return. She turned again to thoughts of nursing. Anna had replied to her letter, telling her more about Hannelore's work and also about the voluntary work her sister Rebekka had done with the *Elisabethverein,* a charitable association of women who cared for the poor and the sick. She suggested that Bertha might like to do something like that first, before committing herself to a course. Bertha became quite fired up with enthusiasm as she read about it, imagining herself flitting through the sickrooms of the slums, dispensing comfort and alms.

That was how Miss Nightingale started, after all, caring for the sick in a neighbouring village. She too had faced opposition from her parents but had persisted until they finally relented. Why, she might become like Miss Nightingale herself. Bertha imagined herself in a distant war-torn land, with battle raging all around, busying herself with the wounded soldiers being brought in from the front. And what if Dr Breuer should become an army doctor? She imagined them working together, the two of them bending over a patient, he at one side of the bed, she at the other. They raised their heads and their eyes met. No need to speak. She knew exactly what to do at each stage of the various procedures. They worked as one. Late into the night. It was dark now, just a lamp glowing as they walked round the ward. Bertha was giving him a report on the condition of each of the patients. Now she herself was falling ill. An infectious disease caught from the sick soldiers. Dr Breuer tended her day and night. He fed her when she was too weak to lift her hand. He was doing it now, one arm under her shoulders to raise her up, the other bringing the spoon to her lips. Bertha sighed with the bliss of it.

Bertha had created a story in which a young woman fell ill of a wasting disease. A fairy godmother appeared to her in a dream and showed her three boxes. Each one contained a solution for a cure. All would be effective but not equally so. When the girl opened the first, she could either accept it or open another box. If she decided to open another box she would no longer be able to choose the cure in the first box. The same applied to the second box. She could either accept it or open the third one. If she did so, the third cure would now be the only option open to her.

The girl opened the first box. It contained an incantation. She opened the second and revealed a bunch of herbs. When she opened the third she found the words *bikur cholim*.

'Hm,' said Dr Breuer, when Bertha told him the story. '*Bikur cholim*. Do you really think that caring for the sick will cure you?'

They had already discussed Bertha's desire to undertake some voluntary work with the poor. She had told him about her cousin Rebekka and her work with the *Elisabethverein*, about the sense of purpose it had given her and how sorry she had been to have to give it up when she married. She begged him now to persuade her mother to allow her. 'After all,' she said, '*bikur cholim* is a *mitzvah*, so she can hardly refuse.'

o~o~o

196

14 September 1881

Dr Breuer called this morning. He spoke again about Bertha's desire to do some charity work and I have finally agreed to it. He seems to think that it will be beneficial to her emotional well-being as it will give her both an occupation and a distraction from her anxieties. He reports that Bertha has made much of the fact that it is a mitzvah. I must say, this is the first time I have known Bertha show any enthusiasm for religious obligations and I feel that this kind of work is better undertaken by more mature women. Who knows what the sight of suffering and deprivation might do to someone in Bertha's fragile state. Dr Breuer assured me however that it is more likely to help her get her own difficulties into proportion and I suppose that I must bow to his superior judgement in the matter. I am also concerned about the risk of Bertha catching head lice or impetigo, or worse, if she is to go out and about among the poor. Dr Breuer assures me that the women volunteers are instructed in the necessary hygiene precautions before they begin and that Bertha will be under the supervision of more experienced women at all times. He is to discuss the matter with Josephine Wertheimstein who is herself active in benevolent work and has a wide network of contacts.

Other than that, Dr Breuer reports that Bertha continues to make slow improvement. He thinks it will be some weeks before we can think about her coming home, however, as her mood is so volatile and she continues to lapse into her cloudy state in the evening.

o~o~o

Within a few days Dr Breuer had arranged for Bertha to be taken under the wing of Frau Gottlieb and Adelheid Braun, both volunteers with a small branch of the Israelite Women's Association. Frau Gottlieb was a tall, spare woman of about fifty with a mannish frame and gaunt features. She had a habit of stooping slightly towards whoever she was speaking to as if she was deaf, and a smile which lurked frequently at the corners of her lips but rarely advanced further. Adelheid, who was not much older than Bertha, was Frau Gottlieb's niece and had been accompanying her on her charity work since she was eighteen. She had a surfeit of eagerness, it seemed to Bertha, always ready to snatch at some new opportunity of

197

rendering assistance. Her very hair spoke of eagerness, tumbling over her forehead in a mass of springy curls and sneaking out from the ribbons and pins which tied it up.

Bertha's first outing with them was to one of the orphanages the Association supported. It was a small orphanage, with just fifty girls aged between three and twelve.

Bertha followed the two women inside, into a dingy hall where she was introduced to Frau Fraenkel, the matron. Frau Fraenkel led them into a classroom to meet the older girls.

The girls, all wearing blue calico dresses and blue and white checked aprons, stood up and sang a song to welcome the visitors. They sat down. Frau Fraenkel bade them take out their German primers. They raised the lids of their desks and took out their books. Frau Gottlieb, invited by Frau Fraenkel to test the girls on their work, gave them some questions in mental arithmetic, asked three of them to read from their German primer and asked two more to recite the Shabbat candle-lighting prayer. At a signal from Frau Fraenkel, the girls stood up again and chorused an expression of thanks. They sat down.

Their movements reminded Bertha of a swarm of birds, swooping across the sky, veering and shifting as if controlled by a single psyche. She imagined their entire lives to be like that, conducted in unison from the moment they got up in the morning until they lay down to sleep at night.

After that the visitors inspected the dormitories – two attic rooms with whitewashed walls and brown paintwork and rows of iron bedsteads with white counterpanes, each with a bedside locker, and communal wardrobes at each end of the room. Then they went down to the kitchen where a cook was tending to a cauldron of boiled mutton with the help of several of the girls.

When they had finished Frau Fraenkel asked Frau Gottlieb into her office to go over the accounts and suggested that Bertha and Adelheid might like to spend some time with the younger girls. She stopped a passing orphan and asked her to take them to the playroom. The girl took them down a stair and into a basement room with windows high on the walls, too high even for the adults to see out. Two nursemaids sat at one end chatting with each other while a dozen children played on the floor with an assortment of dolls. The children fell silent when the visitors entered, then a little girl of about four, thin and dainty and with hair like flaxen gossamer, jumped up and ran to Adelheid, holding out her arms. Adelheid bent down and lifted her up, holding her in front of her face, laughing and calling her a little fairy. As if galvanized, more children jumped up and crowded round Adelheid, pushing each other, pulling at Adelheid's skirt, hitting out at anyone who got in the way, shouting 'Me too', reaching up with frantic little arms. One of them, a little girl with black hair, black eyes and a dark complexion, turned instead to Bertha, but more circumspectly, touching her sleeve and saying 'Please, Miss', her voice soft and plaintive like a cuckoo's.

The nursemaids swooped down on the children, ordering them back, smacking their legs and apologizing to Adelheid. Bertha noticed that the little girl who had pulled her sleeve shrank back and ran into a corner, where she sat down on the floor with a doll and hugged it to her chest. The nursemaids, who had introduced themselves as Angela and Bette, herded the other girls into a semi-circle, sitting on the floor. 'Come along, Eva,' Angela said to the girl in the corner. Eva took the nursemaid's hand and allowed herself to be led over to join the group.

Adelheid had decided that she would read a story.

'What story would you like me to read?' she asked the children. The girls said nothing.

'Which is your favourite?' Adelheid looked at the girls encouragingly. 'Come along. You must have a favourite, surely. Who's going to tell me what their favourite story is?'

The girls still said nothing, only looked at Adelheid with a slightly perplexed air, as if they were not used to being asked what they would like. Bertha noticed how the little girl with the voice like a cuckoo sat on the edge of the group, solemn and timid. Or was it timidity? Perhaps she simply felt apart from the other girls. Bertha tried to imagine Eva laughing. It

199

seemed to her that if she did laugh it would be in a self-contained moderate sort of way.

Failing to get a response from the children, Adelheid had started to read the first story in the book that Bette had given her. It was the tale of The Ugly Duckling.

It was the first time Bertha had set foot in an orphanage. Her sewing circle made clothes for orphans, and her mother made donations to funds for food and gifts at the Jewish festivals but it had never crossed her mind to wonder what it might be like to live in an orphanage, to have no parents or family or home of one's own. It must be like being at school all the time, she thought, and much as she had enjoyed school herself she would have hated not to have her home to go to at the end of the day. It was all so regimented and the girls seemed to have their individuality stamped out of them, in their identical dresses, identical beds and even identical hairstyles – parted in the middle and plaited into two pigtails hanging over each shoulder. There was surely little fun in their lives, little lightness or laughter.

And what must it be like to have no Papa? She thought of all the things she had done with her own Papa, little intimate things that you couldn't do with any other man. Holding his hand on walks in the park. Tugging at his beard. Sitting on his knee. She had specially liked that and had continued to do so when really she was too big for it. There was a rhyme he used to chant while she sat astride his thigh, bouncing her up and down in time to the rhythm: 'Bumpety bump rider'. She imagined herself taking Eva onto her knee and singing the song to her, visualizing the little girl begin to smile, then to giggle, finally throwing her head back, shouting her laughter.

A child was crying now. It was the girl with gossamer hair. She had begun to wail as Adelheid described how the ugly duckling was tormented and rejected by the other birds. Angela spoke to her sharply, telling her that she was spoiling the story for the other children and that there was no need to cry because the story wasn't true. Adelheid hurried on to the end where the duckling turned into a swan and lived happily ever after.

200

'More please, Miss,' cried the children when she had finished.

Adelheid handed the storybook to Bertha. 'Why don't you read one now?'

Bertha decided to read Thumbelina. It was a tale her mother's seamstress used to tell her when she came to the house to do the mending. She used to recount it with great flair and Bertha always shuddered at the toad and the mole and the stag beetle and rejoiced when Thumbelina met the fairy prince and sprouted her own pair of fairy wings. Without having consciously willed it, she heard the same dramatic elements colouring her delivery now, and sensed the children being gripped by the story as she had been. She remembered how Frau Maurer used to set aside her sewing and cup her hand to mimic Thumbelina's walnut-shell cradle, and reach out with a snatching motion when she described how the stag beetle captured Thumbelina's lily pad boat. She felt frustrated by the stiffness which prevented her giving full rein to these movements. She held the book in her right hand, leaving the left side of her body to give expression to the story.

After they left, Bertha was still preoccupied by the thought that the orphans had no father. There wasn't a man of any kind at all in the orphanage as far as she could see, and the women were like teachers rather than mothers or even aunts. It was all so unhomely and unnatural. She commented on this in the carriage on the way back to Inzersdorf.

'If you knew what they had come from,' Frau Gottlieb said briskly, 'you would realize how very lucky they are. But perhaps you would like to visit again. The staff are always looking for someone to help supervise the younger ones and keep them occupied.'

Since then Bertha had visited the orphanage three more times with Adelheid. She enjoyed telling stories to the girls. She also enjoyed Adelheid's company and there was a noticeable improvement in her mood. Although she continued to exhibit extravagant high spirits on the day after Dr Breuer's visit she was no longer so irritable on the third day.

o~o~o

Dearest Anna

At last I have some good news to report. Mamma has agreed to my becoming involved with the Israelite Women's Association and already I have started visiting an orphanage where I join with the children in their recreational activities. I think I have you to thank for this, in part at least, for I know that you wrote to her to tell her of all the good work that Rebekka did in Karlsruhe and how highly esteemed she was.

Oh, if you could see these little girls, Anna, I know it would touch your heart. At first I felt a little shy with them. There was something intimidating about the way they stood at their classroom desks, all in the same blue uniform and with such serious faces, as they sang a song to welcome us. Then when I began to join in with their recreational activities I saw that they were all very different and I felt such a – I don't quite know how to say this – a desire to reach out to them, to draw something out of them, the things which for each of them would help them express their individuality, I think.

Of course, when I hear the dreadful stories which lie behind their admission to the orphanage I feel even more that one must try to help these poor creatures. I had always thought that orphans simply had no father or mother, that their parents had died. In fact, it is often much worse than that. Some of the girls were born to women of the street and were abandoned at birth. One little girl arrived at the orphanage full of vermin, covered in bruises and with a broken arm after having been beaten repeatedly by a drunken father. Another was brought in after her parents were imprisoned for selling her older sister into the white slave trade. I have all this from Adelheid Braun, one of the ladies from the IWA that I visit with, who has a fund of frightful information like this.

Since I started this work I have been giving much thought to something which Heinrich's father said to him in Indian Summer. *He believed that man was not on Earth primarily for society, but for himself. This may seem at first glance a selfish idea but he goes on to say that if a person were here for himself in the best way possible, then it follows that he would also be here in the best way possible for society. If a person is born with a talent and a desire to paint, for example, he will be rendering best service to society by becoming a painter, rather than a barrister or a doctor or any other profession. He believed also that we each have an inner impulse which leads us in the direction of this innate calling. Do you believe that this is so, Anna? Did you feel this impulse when you decided to take up the teaching of literature? Do you think Rebekka felt it when she joined the* Elisabethverein?

Tomorrow I have a new adventure to look forward to. I am to accompany Frau Gottlieb and Adelheid on their visits to some poor people in Leopoldstadt. As it is the first day of Rosh Hashanah we are to give them some gifts of clothes and food. I have no doubt that I shall have some very interesting stories to tell you when I next write.

In the meantime, I wish you and all the family peace and happiness in the New Year.

With fondest love
Bertha

o~o~o

The carriage rattled as it rolled over the cobbled street. Bertha sat between Frau Gottlieb and Adelheid. On the seat opposite were piled the boxes and bags containing the goods to be distributed. The cries of the costermongers sounded coarser to Bertha's ears than the ones she was used to, their produce of poorer quality and less varied. The children playing in the street were unkempt, dirty and barefoot. Bertha felt the carriage swing from side to side as the driver manoeuvred the horses around a heap of rubbish. A couple of men staggering out of a grog-shop leered in at the women and shouted an obscenity. The driver turned round and flicked his whip over their heads. The men roared with raucous laughter.

The carriage stopped. A group of boys who had been playing with a rag ball ran over to it, squabbling as to which of them was to have the privilege of opening the door and thus be entitled to a coin from the ladies inside. The driver chased them off with a growl and another flick of his whip.

Bertha stepped out after Frau Gottlieb and Adelheid, lifting her skirts as she put her foot down on cobbles littered with rotting vegetables. She pressed her handkerchief to her nose as they entered a narrow passageway, then a dingy staircase. At the top of the second flight Mrs Gottlieb knocked at a door. Bertha could hear a child crying and a man shouting in the room beyond. She began to dread the scene that was about to be revealed. Why had she ever thought that she would want to do this?

Mrs Gottlieb pushed open the door without waiting for her knock to be answered. Bertha, apprehensive, remained on the threshold. The room was dim, the window half-covered by a piece of sacking. A woman lay on a mattress, her face white and drawn, a baby listless on her breast. Two girls of about seven and nine sat on the floor, surrounded by piles of little boxes, paste and paper. The man they had heard shouting stood up as they entered, leaning on the back of his chair. It was the only one in the room. Bertha noticed that he had a wooden leg.

She stood silent by the door while Mrs Gottlieb and Adelheid gave out a dress for each of the little girls, a shawl for the baby and three bed blankets. On the table they laid a *challah* loaf, some apples and a small pot of honey, wishing the family *chag sameach* as they did so.

'*Chag sameach.*' Bertha's mouth was so dry she could hardly articulate the words. Happy festival. What a mockery to pronounce the greeting in this dreadful place. But not to do so would be unthinkable. They were there for a Rosh Hashanah visit, bringing Rosh Hashanah gifts, and the family would surely be just a little happier because of them. She listened as the man described how his leg had been crushed by falling masonry when he was working on a building site on the Ringstrasse. Following the accident he had had no work for months and now earned a little as best he could as a crossing sweeper. His wife took in washing when she could get it but since the latest baby she had been poorly and unable to do even that. His daughters helped out by making match boxes, he said. 'But it's no life for the lasses, no life at all. They should be at school.'

Bertha tried not to look at the things which inspired revulsion in her: the heap of soiled rags on the floor beside the bed, the yellowish sores round the mouths of the girls, the grime on the man's shirt collar, the black filth under his fingernails. But her eyes kept being drawn back to them, as if

204

by magnets. How could people live like this?

They had more visits to make. She couldn't face it. But what would Mrs Gottlieb think of her if she refused to go? What would Dr Breuer think? She had made such a fuss about wanting to do this there could be no question of backing out now.

She could say that she felt unwell. She was unwell, after all. She was in a clinic, receiving treatment. Perhaps all this was going to make her illness worse. Mamma was right. She wasn't in a fit state for this sort of thing.

Bertha's breathing was shallow. Each intake of air was tainted with the noisome atmosphere of the room and left a sour aftertaste lingering at the back of her mouth.

Mrs Gottlieb was brisk and practical, promising to arrange for a nurse to visit the wife and giving the address of a new soup kitchen which had been set up nearby. Adelheid wrapped the baby in the new shawl and then took it in her arms, murmuring nonsense words to it.

In the carriage on the way to the next family Mrs Gottlieb and Adelheid talked about the family. The nurse would be able to help with advice about diet and to treat the girls' skin complaint. The poor woman had already lost three babies. That was why there was such a gap between the girls and the latest addition to the family. Now that she was away from the scene Bertha began to feel guilty about her feelings of revulsion, to wonder how Mrs Gottlieb and Adelheid were able to cope with it so much better than she could.

The carriage pulled into an alleyway. A group of women gossiping in an open doorway stopped talking and stared in a manner which unsettled Bertha as she got out. She felt more conscious than usual of her dragging foot and her right arm hanging stiff and awkward against her side. She hurried into the building after Frau Gottlieb and Adelheid.

On the second floor a door was already ajar. Inside was a smell of mutton broth and the sound of rowdy laughter. Four small children were chasing each other around the room. The smallest one, a little girl of about three, ran straight into the skirts of Frau Gottlieb and fell over. The mother, who had been standing by the fire stirring a pot bubbling on a hob, picked the child up and apologized to Frau Gottlieb, wiping her hands on her dress. Frau Gottlieb laughed it off. Rosh Hashanah greetings were exchanged. The children were still now, overawed by the sudden appearance of such grand ladies in their midst. The little one sat on the floor with her thumb in her mouth. The other three clustered round their mother, silent, but when Frau Gottlieb laid four apples on the table they pounced on them, yelling. The mother slapped them playfully, telling them not to be greedy. She took three of the apples from them and placed them on a shelf high on the dresser. The remaining one she cut into four and gave a piece to each child. The children ate their apple quarters slowly, sucking them, removing bits of peel and eating it separately. Soon there was none left. The youngest one started crying, her face screwed up with distaste. She spat her last mouthful onto the floor and wailed. Her mother picked her up, asking what was wrong. Then she laughed. The child had eaten the apple pips and was upset by the nasty bitter taste, such a disappointment after the juicy sweetness of the apple flesh. 'She ain't never tasted an apple afore,' the mother said. 'She don't know she didn't oughter eat the bad bits.'

Adelheid took the youngest child onto her knee. She looked at Bertha and nodded to another of the little girls. Bertha sat down awkwardly and drew the child onto her lap.

'What's your name,' she asked.

The girl looked down, her head tucked into her chest. 'Lilli,' she whispered.

'And how old are you?'

The girl, anxious now, looked across to her mother.

'Tell the lady then, Lilli. Tell 'er 'ow old you are.'

The girl looked down at the floor again. 'Four.'

Bertha could barely hear her.

'Would you like me to sing you a song?' she asked. The child looked at her with solemn eyes but said nothing. Bertha started to sing.

> Bumpety bump, rider,
> if he falls, then he cries out

should he fall into the pond,
no one will find him soon.

She balanced the child on her left thigh and jigged her up
and down as she sang, the way Papa used to do when she was
little. Adelheid began to do the same with the toddler and the
other children joined in. At the end of the last verse, when the
rider fell into the swamp, Bertha and Adelheid pretended to
let the children on their laps fall to the floor. The other
children roared with laughter.

'Again,' they shouted. 'Again.'

Frau Gottlieb meanwhile was in conversation with the
mother, asking about her husband's work. He dealt in second-
hand clothes, the woman said, 'So we don't never go without
clothes on our backs. Shoes an' all. We're lucky in that
respeck. He's a good man, my Jakob. Don't take too much
drink neither.'

Bertha could see a second room leading from the one they
were in. A number of garments, adults' and children's, were
hanging from a rope running the length of the room. Two
pallets on the floor were covered with a heap of blankets.

Bertha was beginning to feel better now, and rather
ashamed about how she had reacted on her first visit. She
wished she had been able to join in more there, do something
with the little girls who had been making match boxes.
Perhaps she'd be able to go there again. Take some toys for
them, perhaps, play a game with them.

Their next visit was to a woman in the same house, on the
floor above. She had a single attic room. A few wooden boxes,
broken and splintered, provided rudimentary furniture, a heap
of shavings covered by some sacks the only bedding. The
occupant, a girl who appeared not yet twenty, leaned against
the wall as she spoke with her visitors, holding a baby loosely
on her hip. She thanked the women, yet showed little interest
in the gifts. Her face was gaunt, her hair limp, her expression
one of dull hopelessness. Her right cheek was livid with recent
bruising.

Adelheid opened the pot of honey, dipped a finger into it
and then put it to the baby's lips, smiling and cooing. The

baby turned its head away with a whimpering mewl, like the sound of a wounded animal.

The husband was a brute, Adelheid whispered to Bertha as they went back down the stair, and a slave to strong drink. They were hoping to persuade the mother to allow her baby to be taken into an orphanage, in which case they would try to find a domestic position for her.

That night Bertha was awake till dawn, despite the evening dose of chloral. She wrote copiously. The following evening when Dr Breuer came she told him several stories. They seemed more like dreams than stories, images of sickness and death without any connecting narrative, but Bertha was quite calm when she had finished recounting them. When Dr Breuer suggested that her visits to the poor were having an unsettling effect on her and that it might be better to undertake no more, Bertha was adamant. She wanted to carry on.

Over the next month, Bertha continued to visit the orphanage and to read to the girls. It was satisfying to see how they gained pleasure from this. She also visited more poor families. She became a little more used to the horror of their conditions, less inclined to hang back in the doorway, readier to enter into the reality of their lives. At the same time, she had fewer fairy stories to recount to Dr Breuer and her physical symptoms were much alleviated. At the end of October, Dr Breuer decided that she should return home to Vienna.

24

Dr Breuer ordered his coachman to drive down to the Prater after leaving Neuer Markt. He needed some time alone before returning home. He had so little time to reflect these days. Winter weather always brought with it an increase in his workload and this, plus the intensive programme of therapy which he had embarked upon with Bertha, meant that he was fully occupied from early morning until late in the evening. When he arrived home he had little energy for the children and was often distracted when Mathilde tried to talk to him about domestic matters. Better to go for a walk in the park and try to sort out his preoccupations before he went back.

A sprinkling of crisp snow crackled underfoot as he got out of the carriage in the Hauptallee. He breathed in deeply, taking an icy draught of the night air into his lungs. It felt clean and incisive, like the antiseptic atmosphere of an operating theatre. From the Konstantinteich lake the cries and laughter of skaters carried outwards, as clear as birdsong in spring. A meaty smokiness drifted over from the stall of a sausage vendor.

Dr Breuer walked over in the direction of the lake, his thoughts on Bertha, going over recent events. It was two months now since he had brought her back home. He had believed at the time that she was on the way to recovery and that by providing her with the opportunity to talk away her anxieties with him every day he would be able to prevent the build up of new stresses. He had been struck by the way in which several of her inhibitions seemed to have been resolved merely by the act of her narrating them. There had been the stocking caprice and the drinking phobia back in August. No more had been heard of them since Bertha had recounted events which seemed to be at their origin. And since then there had been a few more incidents. That business with the bread which she hadn't been able to eat, for example. That seemed to have been tied in with some strange idea she had had about Christians and the body of Christ. At any rate, after repeated questioning as to why she felt unable to eat bread she had eventually come up with a story about the Catholic girls at school who used to tease the Jewish girls because, as non-Catholics, they couldn't go to Communion. Once again, after she had put it into words the whim vanished.

He stood for a while as he reached the lake, watching the skaters glide and skitter. A boy of about sixteen came streaking across the ice, skating backwards, knees bent and head spinning to left and right as he checked for obstacles. He skidded to a halt in front of a group of girls who surrounded him, clapping and cheering.

It had started to snow again, thick flakes which fluttered to the ground with mesmerizing slowness. People were coming off the lake, removing their skates and making for the coffee houses.

Dr Breuer turned back towards the Hauptallee, still no clearer in his mind about how he should proceed with Bertha. If the various ailments were to be cured by talking about the symptoms he must really try to find a way of minimizing the time spent in this way. It would be impossible to implement this kind of cure on a regular basis. Few physicians could countenance allowing any one patient to take up so much of their time, nor could most patients afford it. Perhaps he could expedite the memory work by hypnotizing her. Yes, he would try that.

But was this approach really of much help to Bertha anyway? In some ways she was deteriorating again. Since the beginning of December her mood had worsened. She was excitable, gloomy, irritable and depressed by turns. There was nothing new in her evening conversations with him, no narrative inventions or fantasies, simply a rehashing of old resentments and ongoing irritations. Her principal grievance, which she returned to time and again, was against her mother for refusing to allow her to carry on with her charity work. Mrs Pappenheim had been appalled on learning the details of

210

Bertha's forays into the slums and had forbidden any further involvement with the IWA. All very unfortunate as it had seemed to do Bertha so much good. A pronounced improvement in her overall state of mind. The mother would have none of it, however, although he had tried to persuade her to let Bertha at least continue with some orphanage work. 'There's plenty of opportunity for young women to do good work by taking part in committee activities and organizing fund-raising or making clothes and toys,' she had said. 'There's no need for Bertha to go out and about in the slums.' He had not been able to make her understand that it was the direct contact with the poor that had done Bertha most good.

He had begun to think that there was little more he could do with Bertha when, round about Hannukah, her absences became increasingly frequent and prolonged. At the same time he remarked that she seemed to be repeating stories that she had told him a year previously. The first had been a fairy tale based on the story of Iphigenia, and a nightmare she had had about it. He remembered it distinctly because it had been tied in with a conversation which they had had about Aristotle's theory of catharsis. Stranger still, when she finished the story she spoke as if she was still living the events of the previous year.

He stopped under a chestnut tree, to consider again the extraordinary time-warp delusions that Bertha seemed to be under. She had complained to him that her mother was intending to find a nurse to care for her, although Agnethe had now been with them for a year. She complained too about the indignity of having to use a commode whereas in fact she was now quite mobile and able to go about the apartment normally. The other members of the household had remarked on it too. Whenever she was in an absence she spoke and acted as if she was still in the apartment in Leichtensteinstrasse and still confined to bed. What was even more curious, her actions corresponded to ones carried out on the same day of the previous year. It was the mother who had drawn his attention to this after Bertha had complained about a book by Eugenie John which Klara had brought for her. Klara, who was nearing the end of a difficult pregnancy, had not visited since Bertha's return from Inzersdorf, nor had she sent any books. However, Mrs Pappenheim remembered a similar incident occurring previously and, on consulting her diary found that it had been on 20 December 1880, a year ago to the very day. The following day Bertha complained about feeling very cold, although her room was, if anything, over-warm. Checking her diary, Mrs Pappenheim found that they had run out of fuel for the stoves on 21 December 1880. He had never in his medical career come across anything like it. Nor had any of his colleagues been able to throw any light on it. The whole thing was simply a mystery.

A branch above him creaked. A lump of ice fell on his shoulder. The snow was falling in thick flurries now, obliterating footprints and muting all sound, creating an atmosphere of benign eeriness. Dr Breuer felt a chill damp penetrate him. A woman with powdered cheeks and painted lips appeared from behind the tree. She gave him a leering smile. 'Would you like me to keep you warm, sir?' He pulled the cape of his greatcoat up closer to his neck and hurried back to his carriage.

Bertha sat on the edge of her bed. She wanted to lie down. But she couldn't move. The slightest change of position made the pain worse. She must stay still until the morphine took effect. The clock was just to her left. If she turned her head ever so slightly she would be able to see it. It was eleven o'clock when Agnethe gave her the injection. It would be ten past eleven before she could hope for the pain to begin to subside. She couldn't turn her head. It would be too painful. Nor could she ask Agnethe what time it was. She couldn't move her jaws or her tongue to speak. It must surely be at least five past eleven now though. Only five more minutes to wait.

The neuralgia had started again just before Hannukah, and was more severe than previously. Pulsating pain stabbing into her cheekbone like a bolt of lightning, exploding across her jaw, crushing her nose. A moment of cessation and then it would start again, more intense. If she sought relief in screaming it only aggravated her suffering.

Bertha could think of nothing but the pain. Her eyes half-closed now, she tried to turn her head. She must see the clock. It couldn't be long now. It mustn't be long. As she moved a fresh stab of pain, more exquisite than before, ripped across her face. She stayed her head, now turned fractionally to the left. She kept it there until she felt the pain fade away.

Then she lay down, wallowing in the bliss of being pain free, and in the mood of euphoria which was engulfing her, wafting her upwards. Swirling clouds, shifting shapes in shades of white, cradled her. Her nightgown billowed out, giving her buoyancy. She stood now at the prow of a celestial galleon, navigating the firmament, her head thrown back, intoxicated with joy.

Evening again. Which day of the week was it? Which month? Bertha looked at the clock. It was half past six. Dark outside. It must be winter. Of course it was winter. It wasn't long since Hannukah. Or was it? How could she tell? Some days seemed as long as a year. At other times, she felt that a year had slipped by in the space of a second.

Hannukah had been in late December. Bertha remembered the last day clearly. Mamma had accompanied Dr Breuer into her room that evening and Dr Breuer had been telling her how pleased he was that Hannukah would soon be over as his children had been so rowdy in the house with their *dreidel* games.

Baba playing with the *dreidel*! Spinning the top and shrieking with delight as it falls on the *gimmel* and she scoops up the pot of chocolate coins. Dr Breuer sharing in her laughter. Or the top falls on a *shin* and she has to put one of her own coins into the pot. Dr Breuer puts his arm round her and cuddles her in compensation. Scenarios of *dreidel* playing multiplied and flashed across Bertha's mind's eye like the slides of a magic lantern. Baba three years old, learning the game with Papa, stamping her foot in rage because she has lost a chocolate coin, whining because she's exhausted and it's

213

well past her bedtime but she wants to carry on playing. Dr Breuer lifting her, placing her head on his shoulder and carrying her to her cot.

Bertha had refused to speak.

Then she heard the sound of carol singing. It was a mild night and her bedroom window was open. Down on the street, in Liechtensteinstrasse, a group of children were singing *Silent Night*.

'Please close the window,' she said. 'I don't like *Silent Night*. It's such a dreary tune.'

Dr Breuer went over to the window and drew back the curtain. The window was closed, but an accordionist in the White Swan next door could be heard playing gypsy dance music. He let the curtain fall back into place and returned to sit in front of Bertha.

'I don't like anything about Christmas' said Bertha. She continued to speak, telling Dr Breuer about an incident which happened when she was at school. She had asked Heidi Muller why the Catholics were so happy about the birth of Jesus when in three months' time they were going to be wailing and complaining because he had been crucified. Surely it would have been better if he hadn't been born at all in that case, she said. Fraulein Gelber the religious teacher overheard and, before Heidi could reply, had marched Bertha into her classroom and whacked her over the back of the hand with a ruler until her knuckles bled. Even worse than the physical pain was the bewilderment of not knowing what she had done wrong. 'Impertinent girl,' Fraulein Gelber shouted between blows. 'Making a mockery of the religious beliefs of others. Blasphemy! You wicked, wicked child.'

Dr Breuer listened. It was the same story which she had recounted a year ago, when the Pappenheims still lived in Liechtensteinstrasse and they heard carol singers in the street below.

Bertha blinked and frowned. She walked over to the window and looked out, coughing. 'I so dislike this music from the White Swan,' she said. 'Every night I hear it. It was much quieter in Liechtensteinstrasse.'

214

'What about the carol you've just been talking about?' Dr Breuer asked.

Bertha looked at him, puzzled. 'What carol?'

Dr Breuer told her that she had been in an absence and had seemed to relive events of an evening a year ago. He described how she had behaved and what she had said. She had done this kind of thing several times now, he said. He could not explain it.

All that must have been – how long ago? Several weeks now. So it must be January, perhaps the middle of January, or the end of January. Bertha felt too tired and confused to think. What did it matter which month it was? The pain was starting again.

She must have an injection. Now. She rang her bell and waited in a frenzy of impatience for Agnethe to come. She must kill the pain before Dr Breuer arrived or she would not be able to talk with him.

They had a new way of working now. Dr Breuer believed that her symptoms were associated with unpleasant events in the past and that if she could remember what that event was the symptom would be eradicated. At first, she could think of nothing, however hard she tried. Then they found that if she managed to remember each occurrence of the symptom she would eventually find one associated with something unpleasant. That was what Dr Breuer said, anyway. It was usually after she had lapsed into her clouds that she remembered those things. As she had no recall of what she said when in that state she had to rely on Dr Breuer to report back to her. He was visiting her twice a day now. In the morning he hypnotized her and asked her to concentrate on the symptom they were treating and tell him all the occasions she could remember it occurring. In the evening they talked about those occurrences in more detail.

Agnethe. Where is Agnethe? The pain. Shooting across her cheekbone. Bertha reached out to ring the bell again.

Just then the door opened.

'Agnethe. Please. The morphine.' Bertha's lips barely moved as she spoke.

She felt the stab of the needle in her thigh, the inrush of liquid. She could bear the pain now. Very soon it would cease to torment her.

They had been working on her cough for the past few days. Dr Breuer kept asking her when she coughed, what it was that made her cough. She didn't know. It was just a feeling which rose in her throat, a convulsion of the chest and then the choking sound as she opened her mouth. Just talking about it with him had set off the desire to cough again. Even thinking about it now was triggering the need to cough.

But a calmness was soothing her now. The cough died away, unuttered. She was aloft. Floating. Relaxed. She had eaten nothing all day. When Dr Breuer came she would tell him she would like to eat a little food. Nothing much. Just something light. A milk pudding perhaps. But it mustn't be too thick. She liked it to be runny. So that it flowed easily from the spoon. She licked her lips. Then she opened them. Protruded her tongue. Ran it over the open lips, upper and lower, from side to side. Her breath quickened. The milky pudding coursed down her throat, mingling with the morphine. Bertha closed her eyes and yielded herself. She closed her lips around the spoon and let the milkiness dribble down her chin and onto her shoulders. Her hips moved sinuously and her breasts rose as she opened her mouth again to the feeding spoon. She squeezed her thighs together and lifted her hips.

25

15 February 1882

It has been decided that Bertha will have her upper left wisdom tooth removed. Dr Breuer believes that the tooth may be the cause of the pain in her jaw. As the tooth is not essential for dental health I saw no reason to object. I can only hope that it will turn out to have been the source of the pain as I am concerned about the amount of morphine Bertha now requires on top of the considerable doses of chloral hydrate she has been taking since last summer. It cannot be a good thing for a young woman to be consuming such quantities of drugs. I have told Dr Breuer of my fears in this regard. He tells me that as things are with Bertha there seems to be no alternative for the moment.

There appears to be some progress with Bertha's hysterical symptoms, however. Dr Breuer believes he is achieving some success with this 'talking cure'. In addition to the various whims which have been done away with in the past few weeks by this means, it seems that we may now have seen the last of the cough which has so plagued Bertha for more than a year. In obliging Bertha to recall the various situations in which she succumbed to fits of coughing, Dr Breuer claims to have discovered what was at the root of it. It appears that one evening while nursing Siegmund in Ischl Bertha heard the sound of dance music coming from a villa nearby and wished that she could be there. She then felt remorseful for thinking such a thing with her Papa so ill and began coughing. I am at a loss to understand what the connection is. Suffice it to say that there has been no coughing for some time now.

o~o~o

Bertha looked aghast at the black leather chair with its wooden arms and footrest, flanked on one side by a spittoon and on the other by something resembling a spinning jenny. She had never required any dental treatment. Her milk teeth had fallen out naturally and her adult teeth were healthy.

Dr Decker laughed when he saw Bertha's alarmed glance fall on the treadle-drill. 'No need to worry,' he said. 'We won't be using that.'

He settled Bertha in the black chair and explained what he was going to do. There was nothing to be afraid of. She would be asleep throughout the procedure. When she awoke it would all be over and she could look forward to having no more pain in her jaw. His lady assistant would be at her side at all times. He nodded in the direction of the young woman standing by the spittoon.

'If you could just open your mouth, please.' Dr Decker bent over Bertha and introduced a little round mirror into her mouth. He probed the gum with a sickle-shaped instrument.

'Perfect.' Dr Decker straightened up. He reached out to his assistant who put a rubber mask in his hand. As it passed over Bertha's face she caught a whiff of its rubberiness, tinged with a hint of rotten pears.

Two vultures hovering over Papa! Mask over his face. Knives in their hands.

Nostrils filling with chemical smell. Mamma and Miss Thomson sitting side by side on chairs against the wall. Swirling vapours dragging her down in dizzying spirals into a deep black abyss. She is reaching out, clutching – at nothing. Her fists are empty.

Faint voices. Very distant. Metallic taste of blood. Hands on her shoulders, fingers in her mouth. A hand on the back of her head, bending it forward towards the spittoon.

A man's voice. 'Spit, please, Miss Bertha.'

She opens her mouth. A gob of blood like a lump of raw liver falls out.

She wants to go back to her bedroom. She grabs the steering handle of the invalid carriage. She must get away, away from Papa with his ghoulish face, his reedy voice, his bed like a catafalque and the stench of illness. Where is Agnethe? Someone must push her, back to her bedroom. She scrunches up her eyes, not daring to look at Papa, turns her head away from the bed, opens them again and sees Mamma and Miss Thomson, still sitting against the wall, straight-

218

backed and unmoved. She looks at her hands. They are clutching not the handle of the invalid carriage but the wooden arm rests of the dental chair. Her mouth is filling with a warm unpleasant thickishness. She spits.

Dr Decker packs some gauze wadding into the socket. He gives instructions about rinsing her mouth in salt water four times a day. Bertha does not understand what he is saying but she thanks him. '*Merci,*' she says. '*Merci.*'

For the rest of the day she spoke only in French, English and Italian. Mrs Pappenheim's journal entry for the corresponding date in 1881 revealed that this was the day on which Agnethe first reported that Bertha was speaking in a jumble of foreign languages.

Over the next few weeks, the pain in Bertha's face increased, both in intensity and duration. It was managed by regular doses of morphine. Dr Breuer started to visit twice a day. In the morning he hypnotized Bertha and asked her to concentrate on one of her symptoms, noting what she said. In the evening, using his notes, he led her to give a more detailed account of what she had spoken of in the morning.

Bertha sat at her bedroom window looking at the bustle of Saturday activity down in the square. Her facial pain had been much better and she had been able to do without the morphine for the past two days.

A whole day without Dr Breuer; he didn't visit on Shabbat. She was trying to decide what to talk about with him next. She had mentioned to him that she sometimes failed to hear what people were saying. Her mother had spoken sharply to her about it on a couple of occasions, accusing Bertha of rudeness and adding that illness was no excuse for bad behaviour. Bertha had resented the criticism. Sometimes it wasn't possible to hear what other people were saying, for all sorts of reasons. But the more she thought about it, the more she came to believe that it was happening to her too often. There had been things wrong with so many parts of her body it wouldn't be surprising if her ears were also affected. She tried to think of occasions on which she had become aware of not hearing. There was that time on the way to the dentist when she had been so distracted with fears about having a tooth removed that she hadn't heard Mamma ask her if she felt a draught coming in through the carriage window. Or perhaps she had heard her but thought that she was speaking to Miss Thomson. She wasn't sure. Then there were those drunken men who shouted something into their carriage when she was visiting the poor people at Rosh Hashanah. She had asked Frau Gottlieb what they had said and Frau Gottlieb had frowned and said that she preferred not to repeat it. Oh, and there was that awful time in the carriage with Dr Breuer in the Augarten when she realized that he had said something which she hadn't caught. 'I beg your pardon,' she had said. How she wished she had never asked him to repeat his words. If she had not, she might still be unaware of the existence of Baba.

Baba! What could she be doing now? Bertha looked at the clock. Almost midday. And it was a fine morning. Perhaps the family had gone for a walk in the Prater. It didn't bear thinking of. Baba skipping along beside her Papa, holding his hand, chattering and laughing. Bertha felt a flash of pure malevolence. She wished more than she had ever wished for anything in her life that Baba would die. She knew that if she could do so without being caught she would kill her. She looked down at the Donner fountain in the middle of Neuer Markt, its great basin filled with water spouting from the mouths of the fishes surrounding the figure of Providence. How she would rejoice if she could lure Baba here and plunge her into that water, holding her down until her frantic struggles subsided and her limp corpse sank from sight. Obliterated. No more Baba!

How was it possible to hate someone you had never met, someone you couldn't even visualize? She had no idea what Baba looked like. She could ask Dr Breuer, she supposed. No, because that would make Baba more real, and therefore more hateful. Already she hated Baba more, much more, than she had ever hated Willi.

Willi! That beast who thought he could lord it over her. That night when he had actually shaken her – shaken her. She felt again his hand on his shoulder, and saw the nurse in the doorway, her lips moving. She hadn't heard what the nurse was saying. Was this another example of her deafness? Perhaps. But it could just have been that the nurse was whispering, or even just mouthing words. Perhaps she had been annoyed by the fracas outside Papa's bedroom and wanted to chide Willi. She wouldn't have wanted to speak out loud and wake her patient. But it seemed to Bertha that she hadn't even heard the ticking of the clock. That didn't mean anything, she told herself. Mostly we don't hear clocks ticking unless we're all alone and nothing is happening around us.

Bertha sneezed. She sneezed again, and again. She sniffed and took a handkerchief out of her pocket. Her nose had been running all morning and her back was beginning to ache. She must be coming down with flu. A dart of pain flashed across her cheekbone, followed by another, boring deep down inside her brain. A third leaves her shocked, breathless. She dares not breathe for fear of triggering a fourth. The fourth comes, relentless. Bertha groans. A fifth and she screams. She knows the screaming is making the pain worse but she has no control over it. Mamma and Agnethe appear. Thank God. Oh, thank God.

'Agnethe. Morphine. Please.'

26

Dr Breuer had just said goodbye to his last patient of the morning. He should really join Mathilde for lunch now. Instead he returned to his desk and sat down. He needed to give more thought to the latest developments with Bertha.

He was encouraged by the results of their work on Bertha's episodic deafness. He believed that there could be a pattern linking the various situations in which it occurred. Bertha had described a number of events, mostly taking place during a carriage ride, all of them seemingly trivial. Then she had told him a story of being shaken by her brother when he caught her one night listening at her father's bedroom door. At the same moment the door opened and the nurse came out. Although she appeared to be speaking, Bertha – who could see her lips moving – heard not a word that was said. What struck him most was the vehemence with which Bertha had recounted the details of the incident, venting a terrible anger against her brother, her face flushed a reddish purple, spittle on her lips, shrieking her outrage. It still remained to be seen whether her deafness had now been cured, but a second intriguing aspect was the way in which she had experienced the subsequent bouts of deafness. Could there be any link between that business with the brother and those other occurrences she had described? What could possibly connect them?

Dr Breuer got up and paced back and forth in front of his desk, tapping his teeth with his pen. There must be something that he was missing. Perhaps he needed to persuade Bertha to talk about it some more, try to see if there were any other associated memories. He stopped at the window and looked out. Down in the street a couple of boys were playing with hoops, racing each other along the pavement. The smaller boy struck his askew and it veered off into the middle of the road.

A passing carriage swung from side to side as the horses shied away from it.

Dr Breuer sat down again. His eye fell on the journal with the article he had read almost a year ago, the case of the girl with a brain tumour who had been diagnosed as hysterical. He sensed again the fear that he might be guilty of a similar error with Bertha. But no. There was already so much improvement. She was on the road to recovery. It was now simply a matter of hastening things.

But what the devil could be linking the different occurrences of any one symptom? The failure to hear, for example. The image of the swaying carriage he had just seen came back to mind. Wait a minute. The fracas with the brother. He had been shaking Bertha. What if…..? The other incidences Bertha had described had involved carriage rides. Could it be that her deafness had occurred when the carriage was going over rough terrain, cobbles perhaps, or in busy traffic, weaving in and out of other vehicles. The effect on passengers would be one of shaking. Could that be the connection? It was a possibility. But how to test it? Only time would tell.

And in that case, if there was always a link, what could be the connection between the first coughing fit – when she heard dance music in Ischl and felt resentful at having to stay in nursing her father – and all the subsequent ones? Funny to think that the last time he remembered hearing her cough was when she was complaining about the dance music coming from the White Swan next door. It might be worth encouraging her to try to remember if there were any similar instances of coughing.

But time was the problem. He could not continue with this form of treatment indefinitely. He had his other patients to consider, and Mathilde was clearly aggrieved at the prominent position Bertha occupied in his thoughts. She had come to believe that Bertha was taking advantage of him, play-acting in a bid to have him dancing attendance on her. He was beginning to wonder if there might not be some truth in this. Bertha undeniably took pleasure in his presence and the bond which had developed between them now went far beyond the normal doctor-patient relationship. If she truly was feigning some of her symptoms in order to secure his attention he must put a stop to it at once. But how could he be sure?

Midnight. Everyone else in the apartment was asleep. How peaceful it was. The sense of peace was tangible. It was all around her, flavouring the atmosphere, permeating her mind.

Bertha thought of Baba with equanimity and then dismissed her. There was nothing to think of. Baba didn't even exist. There was nothing but this feeling; there was only now, and this space which she could mould into scenes of her own creation. There were no sharp edges in those scenes, no straight lines. Only shifting, curving shapes forming and reforming all around her, like phantoms in a mist. Benevolent phantoms. Tending her, wrapping themselves around her in a protective cocoon, their touch against her thighs as soft as angels' wings. She stretched her legs and threw back her head, inviting more caresses. She felt herself blending with them, being raised aloft, moving in an aerial waltz to ethereal music.

When her right arm began to jerk and flail she scarcely noticed it. She was unconcerned that her face was twitching and grimacing. Let her body do what it liked. She was above and beyond it.

o~o~o

12 March 1882

It seems that no sooner does one of Bertha's symptoms clear up than a fresh one puts in an appearance. The latest is most disturbing to witness, a loss of muscular control resulting in convulsive limb movements and grotesque facial contortions. I first noticed it at breakfast yesterday. Bertha had just started to raise her cup when her arm shot outwards, throwing the coffee all over the table. The arm then began jerking in an up and down motion, while the same time her head made bobbing movements. This lasted for several minutes. Since then she has had numerous similar bouts. Bertha herself does not seem to be unduly worried by these goings-on, although whether or not her attitude is a result of her

224

strange moods it is hard to say. She is either morose, in which case she
says she no longer cares about her state of health, or she is unnaturally
cheerful and then she dismisses it as something of no importance.

Dr Breuer assures me that this kind of thing can be precipitated by
strong emotion and that it is not therefore surprising to find Bertha
affected in this way. He proposes to treat it with increased dosages of
morphine, which I am not altogether happy about it as I feel that the
morphine may in some degree be responsible for her moods. Dr Breuer
tells me I need have no worries on that score and that the morphine will be
discontinued as soon as it is no longer required. He is pleased with the
progress they are making with the 'talking cure' and believes that the
intensive work they are doing along those lines should soon lead to the
elimination of all her symptoms. For my own part, I am less convinced.
He may well manage to eradicate her physical symptoms in this manner
but we still have all the little things which vex her from day to day to deal
with. These must apparently be talked through with Dr Breuer every
evening to prevent any new stresses building up. I feel that this may
encourage attention-seeking in Bertha and, if she is indulged in this way,
could carry on indefinitely

Bertha is also to be purged. Agnethe has been instructed on the
preparation – a mixture of powdered jalap and cream of tartar with a
little oil of cinnamon, to be administered every third day. Her morning
coffee is to be replaced by an infusion of gentian.

o~o~o

Dr Breuer opened the carriage window and stuck his head out.
The carriage had come to a halt just as it was about to turn
into Brandestrasse. A costermonger's cart had tipped over,
spilling cabbages, cauliflowers and bunches of spinach onto
the road. An argument had broken out between the
costermonger and the driver of an omnibus who was trying to
steer his horses over the vegetables. The costermonger had
planted himself in front of the omnibus while his lad went
about picking up the produce.

Dr Breuer noted a feeling of relief in himself. The delay
provided a respite for him, a little more time before he would
have to confront Bertha. For the past few days he had felt

quite drained. Her treatment was taking up about half of his working time – more if he considered the time spent thinking about the case when he wasn't with her. It was like the kind of mathematical problem that he used to wrestle with at school, unable to let it go until he had worked his way to the solution. With Bertha he had believed that he was finally breaking through, identifying not only the source of her symptoms but also finding the means of eradicating them. Now he was not so sure. Although the 'talking cure' seemed to have led to results, it could all be just coincidence. After all, some of her symptoms had disappeared, or started to diminish, before they stumbled upon the method which he now set such store by. Was he perhaps imposing a pattern where none in fact existed? The relentless pursuit of each occurrence of a symptom was proving very wearing. But more than that, there was something about Bertha now which disconcerted him. At first it had been the babyish demeanour she had begun to adopt with him, which had made him uneasy. It was now more pronounced, and at the same time he was aware of an incongruous eroticism mingling with it. He thought back to the times when he had felt erotic impulses himself towards Bertha and recoiled at the memory. This childish seductiveness in her inspired him only with horror.

Outside the feuding became louder as some of the omnibus passengers joined in. A few others dismounted and helped the boy to pick up the vegetables. The sound of laughter now mingled with the angry cries.

By the time his carriage got underway again Dr Breuer had come to a decision. He must start preparing Bertha for the termination of the treatment. If her health still required it, he would then arrange for her to be admitted to a clinic again.

o~o~o

April 1882

Dearest Anna

Forgive me for having remained silent for so long. To tell you the truth, I hardly know what to say to you. I have tried on many occasions

226

to start a letter. I write, and then set it aside. When I come back to it I do not recognize the sentiments I have expressed, or believe that they can ever have been my own. Sometimes I feel deep shame at what I have written, and I cannot understand what process of reasoning or what emotions can have led to them.

For weeks now I have been tormented by this terrible neuralgia. Truly I think I would be out of my mind by now were it not for the blessed relief afforded by morphine, doubly blessed as this precious drug bolsters my mood and frees me from the worry which would otherwise afflict me on account of my parlous state of health. Yet when the drug wears off I then plunge into such an abyss of despair I can see no exit other than a fresh injection.

Dr Breuer says we must now think about bringing the treatment to a close.

Bertha laid down her pen, unable to continue writing after the enormity of the sentence which she had just written. Her life for eighteen months now had been given structure and solidity by his visits. She had given no thought to the idea that it might not continue for ever like this. Yet it often seemed to her that her life with Dr Breuer was like a dream, her feelings for him like the feelings one had in a dream. But what good was it to see it in that light if she couldn't wake up from the dream?

Sometimes it was more dreamlike than at others. Right now it was as if she was halfway been dream and reality. She could allow herself to plunge into the full dream at any time. Just think of the feeding spoon.

She thought of it now. She got up from her escritoire and lay on the bed. She took a square of dark grey woollen fabric out from under the pillow. She had cut it from an old cape. It had the look and the feel of Dr Breuer's jacket. She pressed it to her cheek.   Reaching out, she took hold of the bottle of chloral hydrate which lay on the bedside table. It had a round stopper. She put the stopper in her mouth and sucked, at the same time rubbing her face against the fabric. She removed the bottle from her mouth and brushed her lips across the fabric, making little baby noises, licking its rough surface, licking, licking, her saliva wetting it. Then the stopper was back in her mouth. It felt bigger this time, as if it had swollen. There was a tingling in her hands; she clenched and unclenched her fists. A throbbing spread throughout her body.

She could never tell Anna about any of this.

Bertha took her bible from the shelf and opened it at the Book of Psalms. There was something she had to check, a reference to God striking enemies on the cheek. The half-remembered words had come to her, like a bolt of lightning, the previous night just as she was about to fall asleep, as if they were bearing her a message. She was too afraid at the time to get up and look for them but now that she was feeling stronger – confident and vibrant, she had had a morphine injection only an hour ago – she was prepared to confront them.

She found the lines in Chapter 3.

> Arise, O Lord, save me, my God, for You have struck all my enemies on the cheek; You have broken the teeth of the wicked.

The words which had so terrified her during the night. The striking on the cheek, the breaking of teeth. Such was the intensity of her pain it had seemed to her believable that her neuralgia was God-ordained, a punishment for her lack of religious observance. Now, though, she could read the words with indifference, could even mock herself for her morbid fancies of the night-time.

She read on, entranced by the beauty of the poetry.

> But You, O Lord, are a shield about me, my glory and He Who raises up my head.
> With my voice, I call to the Lord, and He answered me from His holy mount to eternity.

The words infused Bertha with a feeling of power. It surged through her body till she felt that she could take flight. She was Amalia, the winged horse, soaring high, above the clouds, into a dazzle of shimmering incandescence.

Splendid, Beautiful, Radiance of the Universe
My soul is sick for Your love.

Bertha shook her head, momentarily unsure as to where she was. She looked down at the book she was holding: her bible, open at the third psalm. She must have had an absence. Something had happened during it. She did not know what it was, only that it was of great import and that she longed for it to happen again.

27

Dr Breuer looked down at the face of Ernst Fleischl von Marxow, patient, colleague and friend. Ernst was lying in a warm bath, in an effort to ease the pain which ricocheted throughout his entire body. Ten years previously he had infected his hand during an autopsy. The thumb had been amputated but since then neuromas had continued a relentless growth, necessitating repeated operations. The pain was constant, the only relief provided by increasing doses of morphine. Even so, it was difficult to remain in control of the pain, and the morphine consumption brought its own problems. It was difficult to see in him now the handsome, dynamic physician and researcher which he had once been.

Dr Breuer had found him vomiting and sweating when he arrived. Ernst was trying to reduce his morphine consumption. His tolerance to it was growing and he feared that he would soon reach a point at which it no longer had any analgesic power over him. Yet if he tried to do without it, waiting when the drug wore off, forcing himself to endure the pain for at least a little while, the withdrawal from it brought its own intolerable effects. Worse than the physical effects were the mental ones: the despair, which he could understand – he was in a desperate situation – then the undefined emotional agony. As a doctor, he could understand that. It was caused by the drug, or lack of it. But being able to explain it made no difference to the extent to which it made him suffer.

Gaunt and drawn, too exhausted to speak, he made no resistance when Dr Breuer suggested that he might like to get into bed now.

Despite his exhaustion, he knew he would not be able to sleep without the drug. Chloral hydrate was useless in the state he was in. The only solution was morphine. Dr Breuer drew up the liquid into a syringe and injected it into his thigh. The thigh was already covered with abscesses caused by previous injections. It was difficult to find a fresh area.

Dr Breuer sat with Ernst till he fell asleep. He was appalled at the changes in him, the sorry wreck of a man that he had been reduced to. He was appalled too at the thought that a similar fate might lie in store for Bertha. But how to avoid it? When the pain was upon her action was imperative and the only effective option was morphine.

There was still the surgical option to be considered – desensitisation of the painful nerves. But he was unwilling to have recourse to this. It seemed possible that the neuralgia, like her other symptoms, was hysterical in origin, in which case an operation, although curing the existing pain, might only serve to trigger another. In any case, the mother was against it. The removal of Bertha's wisdom tooth had caused a setback, resulting in a repeat of her language disruption.

It was really a battle with time. How to ensure that Bertha recovered from her neuralgia before she became a morphine addict?

But was she already an addict? He should have a word with Obersteiner about it. Morphine addiction was a special interest of his. He'd written several articles about it.

On second thoughts, perhaps better not to talk to Obersteiner. The fellow was so damnably negative about morphine, claiming that it was all but impossible for addicts to achieve a successful cure and that most physicians were blithely unaware of the dangers of the drug. For many patients it was nothing but a godsend.

Ernst groaned.

'What is it, old fellow?' Dr Breuer asked.

A few indistinguishable syllables dripped like slurry from Ernst's lips. He tried to lift his head from the pillow, leaning towards a bowl on the bedside table.

Dr Breuer reached for the bowl and, raising Ernst's shoulders, held it under his chin. Ernst retched, bringing up a quantity of yellow bile. Dr Breuer wiped his mouth and laid his head back on the pillow.

'Bertha, I'd like to consider again the possibility of an operation for your neuralgia.'

'No!'

'But…'

'I said no!'

Bertha was not going to discuss it. If she had an operation for her neuralgia, she would no longer be given morphine and there was no question of doing without that. It was what helped her remain stable. Not just stable but buoyant. Without it, she would teeter and fall, she knew not where, into some dreadful black abyss. She had already experienced this in a small way. When too much time had elapsed since her last dose, she felt herself sink into a grey morass of despair, exacerbated by a host of physical symptoms. She could recognise them all now – the sneezing, the runny nose, the itching, the sweating, the cramps of oncoming diarrhoea. And those were the signs that heralded the emotional dead-weights which followed, dragging her down, deep into the bowels of a very dark place, tugging at her irresistibly like some inexorable force of malign gravity.

'Bertha, I don't think it's good to continue trying to treat you with morphine.'

'But you said – you said yourself – that we have to try to find what causes the pain. You can't find it with an operation. We can only find it by talking.'

'Yes, I know, but if this means that you're going to end up with worse problems – and I assure you that the problems of morphine addiction can be worse than the pain of neuralgia….'

'No!'

Then Bertha shot a sly look at Dr Breuer. Perhaps it would be better to give the impression that she might be prepared to acquiesce at some future date. 'Well, not yet. We can try some more. To cure it by talking, I mean. Let's start again now. I'm going to try to remember all the times I've felt the pain.'

Bertha sat down by the ottoman and lifted Hermione onto her lap.

232

'There was this morning.' She put her thumb in her mouth, sucked for a moment, then removed it. She rocked back and forth, squeezing Hermione to her chest.

'Before that, don't 'member so well.' She frowned and stuck out her lower lip. Despite her fretful demeanour, she was feeling strong and joyous. She had discovered that the morphine also enhanced her experiences with Dr Breuer, and rendered her fantasies about him more deeply satisfying.

'Perhaps then you'd like to tell me a story?'

'Shan't!'

'Just to please me?'

Oh, that cocked eyebrow pleased her so.

She put her thumb back into her mouth. She ran the tip of her tongue, just the very tip – such a sensitive part! – around the nail. That feeling in the tip of her tongue, it was spreading now all over her body, inside and out, occupying its entire volume, until she felt she must surely burst from the pressure of it. She heard herself give an involuntary grunt, and then another. Her face felt hot from the flush suffusing it.

Dr Breuer was standing up.

'We'll continue tomorrow then. In the meantime please try to think about anything which you think might be associated with your facial pain.'

He was leaving the room, saying good night to Miss Thomson sitting in the doorway. Why so abrupt? As if he was offended. What had she done? What if he never came back?

An onrush of panicky questions came at her, only to be repulsed by the bubble of serene elation which enclosed her. It was as if a witch had cast a spell around her, allowing nothing to approach which might disturb her feeling of supreme well-being.

She closed her bedroom door and locked it. Mamma had forbidden her to do so and had ordered that the key should always be kept in the household key basket. That morning Bertha had removed it.

Now she pulls out the hardback chair from her escritoire. She rucks up her skirts and slides herself down astride the chair, facing its back. She closes her eyes. She is sitting on Dr

Breuer's thighs, looking into his face, holding on to his upper arms as he sings and bounces her up and down.

> Bumpety bump, rider,
> if he falls, then he cries out
> should he fall into the pond....

Bertha swoops backwards with a laughing scream as Dr Breuer opens his thighs and lets her fall between them, pulling her back just before she hits the floor, the force of the upward movement throwing her against his chest, her hair in his beard, chuckling in duet.

> ....no one will find him soon.
> Bumpety bump, rider,
> if he falls, then he cries out
> should he fall into the ditch.....

Down again, further this time. A false move and he lets her fall. Bertha hits the floor. She howls although she is not really in pain. Dr Breuer scoops her up and hugs her, murmuring words of comfort. She sniffs and buries her face in his shoulder.

On to the next verse. Bertha rocks back and forward on the chair, tipping it up first on its front legs and then on its back legs, in time to the rhythm. Faster, faster.

> Bumpety bump, rider,
> if he falls, then he cries out
> should he fall into the swamp....

The chair topples over. Bertha lies face down on the carpet, feels the rough texture of it. Dr Breuer's jacket. Her chest again pressed to his, she lets herself lie there, pressing deeper, burying herself.

Later – she does not know how long she has lain on the floor – she gets up, rights the chair, and rucks her skirts up again, slowly this time, savouring the anticipation. There are still too many layers of material in the way. Her drawers, she must take off her drawers. She slides them down, throwing them on to the bed, then sits astride the chair. But this time

234

she is straddling only one of Dr Breuer's thighs, the left one.

'Bumpety bump,' she murmurs, leaning forward, whispering into his ear. 'Bumpety bump.'

She squeezes his thigh with her own, lifting her hips, subsiding again, squeezing tighter. A hot feeling, burning, as if she wants to pass urine; the rough tapestry upholstery of the seat pulling against the hair between her legs. 'Bumpety, bump.' Squeeze, rise, fall, squeeze, rise, fall, squeeze. Breathing harshly into his ear.

o~o~o

7 June 1882

As I have suspected for quite some time, Bertha has become addicted to morphine. Dr Breuer assures me he has done his utmost to persuade her to do without the drug, if necessary by submitting to an operation. Bertha will have none of it. Dr Breuer tells me that he can do no more with her. This 'talking cure' has had some limited success, as far as I can see, but given the state Bertha is in with her addiction it seems pointless to continue it. I imagine Dr Breuer also feels that the demands on his time made by this treatment is having an adverse effect on his workload and eating into the time he should spend with his other patients. He has made arrangements for Bertha to be admitted to Bellevue Sanatorium in Switzerland where more strenuous attempts can be made to wean her from the addiction. She is to be admitted in July as she desires first to travel to Karlsruhe to stay with Anna. She has been most insistent about this. Indeed, it seems to be the only thing which can pacify her at the moment.

o~o~o

Bertha curls herself up into a ball, squeezing her limbs closer to her torso, as if in shrinking physically she might lessen her pain. But the diminution in size triggers a cascade of memories. Carried in Dr Breuer's arms. Sitting on the floor with him. The feeding spoon resting on her lips, tipping its contents onto her tongue.

Forget that those scenes will never take place again. Rejoice in the memory of them.

But she must not, because the memories are followed by intolerable pain, a pain which is starting now.

Stave it off. Wallow more deeply in the memories, relive them, revel in them.

He is offering a segment of orange to her mouth. She takes it lightly between her teeth, closes her lips around it. He holds it as she sucks the juice from it. He withdraws it and offers her another.

She is in the Montgolfier. Being wafted aloft. She loosens her limbs, uncurling herself. Angels' wings caressing her inner thighs. She shivers and spreads her legs. Closes them again – quickly. A brink ahead. Back from the brink!

Astride the chair now, rocking back and forth.

'Bumpety bump, rider'

Buzzing bees, swarming under her skin. All over her body. Stinging her, their barbs charged not with pain but with pleasure.

Bertha moans. She writhes in time with the jolts of pleasure, her cheeks flushed red against the white pillows. She raises her buttocks from the mattress, lowers them again, up and down, as if on the back of Greta the black mare – fully astride her, no longer sidesaddle. Up and down, through the alleys of chestnut trees, the horse's hooves hammering under her, in time with a thudding in her ears, with the blood pounding in her veins. She grips Greta's flanks with her thighs, rising and falling with the gallop.

The rough fabric of Dr Breuer's jacket against her cheek. His hand holding the spoon. Her tongue snakes out of her mouth, quivering, reaching out. Her buttocks heave, her thigh muscles tauten. Bertha groans. A gush of saliva fills her mouth. She gasps, and gasps again. She tosses her head from side to side, uttering incoherent sounds.

Stop! A brink ahead! She seizes the reins, turns the horse's head, falls back to a canter.

The feverishness simmers down to a pleasurable thrill, building up again as she gallops faster. Then the spoon thrusting into her mouth and a shout of joyous triumph as her lips clamp on the spoon and she sucks and sucks. Her back

236

arches. She groans.

Control!

Then riding faster, faster.

She is roaring, her head thrown back. A stirring deep within, a swelling hotness, the pleasure radiating outwards, spreading throughout her body, galvanizing it into a bucking, shuddering recipient of ecstasy, forcing out of her a crescendo of shrieking and screaming that doesn't stop even when Mamma and Miss Thompson come running into the room.

Bertha is delirious, unaware of their presence. Her cries subside but her writhing continues. Up again. Up onto Greta's back, tighten the thigh muscles, buttocks up, up and down, she is spreading her legs further apart, her thighs no longer touch Greta's flanks, and she is screaming again, screaming for more of this coruscating rapture. She is no longer on Greta. She is Amalia, the winged horse. She is flying.

Now she is uplifted, spread-eagled over heaving masses of billowing cloud, a shriek of joy ringing in her ears, echoing in her mind, intensifying, resounding, reforming into a rhapsody of jubilation.

'Splendid, Beautiful, Radiance of the Universe.'

Dr Breuer appears at her bedside. Aghast murmurs between the doctor and Mrs Pappenheim. He injects her with five milligrams of chloral hydrate. She sees and feels nothing of it.

All is eclipsed.

A shattering stillness.

An eternal instant.

'.... all becomes one desire, one togetherness, one bond. A rapturous embracing of all.'

28

Neu Isenburg 1925

'Girls! No slacking, please! This is not the way to prepare the house for Shabbat.'

Bertha frowned at Marthe and Inge who broke off their conversation at once and resumed their mopping of the dining room floor. Bertha paused briefly on the threshold, further words of rebuke on her lips, then withdrew without saying any more. She was aware of her reputation for strictness, prided herself on it in fact, but sometimes she had to curb herself. Marthe was new to the Home. Since she arrived three weeks ago she had been almost mute, saying little more than yes or no when spoken to, rejecting all overtures from both staff and girls, huddling in corners, motionless apart from a ceaseless twisting of her hair between the thumb and forefinger of her left hand. Inge was a kindly girl. If she had succeeded in breaking through to Martha, better to encourage it.

It was seventeen years since Bertha had founded the Home for Wayward Girls, a refuge for Jewish prostitutes and unwed mothers. During that time hundreds of girls had passed through. The Home provided them with shelter, support and security, and a training fitting them for jobs in factories or domestic service. But most important, as far as Bertha was concerned, was their religious education, central to which was the celebration of Shabbat and the proper preparation for it.

Bertha moved on to check the kitchen. Four girls sat at the table peeling and chopping vegetables for *cholent*. Two more were polishing the cutlery and glasses while another was pounding dough for challah. They were talking about a shadow-play they were to perform after the Shabbat meal, based on a Dr Dolittle story about the pushmi-pullyu which Bertha had read to them the previous week.

'Come, Miss Pappenheim, let me show you the puppets we've made,' said Cora, a girl from Galicia.

Cora had been sold into prostitution by her parents at the age of twelve. Three years later she was thrown out of a brothel in Berlin, having contracted a skin disease which repelled the clients. She was like a wild animal then, Bertha recalled, living on the streets, filthy and savage. Now, aged twenty, she was the most willing and reliable of the girls, more like a staff member than a resident.

Cora led Bertha to the recreation room and took from a cupboard a pile of cardboard cut-out animals. She held them up in turn, jiggling them on their sticks and finishing with the pushmi-pullyu, jerking it rapidly as its two heads tried to move off in different directions.

'Perfect,' said Bertha, laughing. 'The younger ones will be thrilled. We'll all be thrilled.' She helped Cora put the puppets back in the cupboard. 'Now run along back to the kitchen.'

It was early afternoon. Bertha decided to go home and spend a few hours dealing with paperwork before the evening meal. As she walked across the road to her house she ran through in her mind the most urgent tasks: a letter to Felix Warburg who was waiting for a report on the cost of updating the bathrooms before sending a donation; a meeting to be set up with the owner of the shoe factory in town to discuss employment opportunities for two of the girls who would be ready to leave the Home soon; the article which Martin Buber had asked her to write for Der Jude, laying out her objections to Zionism.

Bertha had lost count of the number of articles she had written over the past thirty years. No matter how much she wrote, there were always more ideas welling up, as if her mind were a river bed channeling the flow from some inexhaustible source; more wrongs to be righted, more attention to be directed to unaddressed social ills. It was why she had been put on earth, she now believed, and no matter what obstacles lay in her path, no matter what emotional pain she experienced, they were as nought compared to the urge to respond to this demand on her. Occasionally there was a lull,

239

when it seemed that everything had been attended to for the time being, and then, rather than being able to enjoy the opportunity to rest, she felt a lack, a need to go out and search for new claims to impose on herself. She must always be reacting, responding, giving of herself. Her only moments away from that were those she spent in prayer, and those moments only served to fire her with more of that self-giving energy. She emerged from them renewed and regalvanised, with an even more powerful sense of her duty and her ability to fulfill it.

A clock struck three as she entered the house. She hung her jacket on the hallstand and retrieved the morning's mail from her letter box. There was only one item, a package addressed in Cousin Anna's writing. A book probably. Anna often sent her books which she thought would interest Bertha. She laid the package on the table and went into the kitchen to prepare a pot of coffee. She looked out of the window while she waited for the coffee to brew. It was mid-June. The peach trees in the garden were crowned with pink blossom and the cotoneasters bloomed yellow. The Taunus hills rose high on the horizon. For a moment she was reminded of Ischl. How beautiful it would be there now. She must visit again some time. Take some of the girls with her perhaps.

Bertha took the coffee through to the sitting room and sat down at the small round table. She undid the package, revealing a letter and a book. A slim volume, authored by Dr Sigmund Freud.

Bertha opened Anna's letter. It was brief. Anna was eighty-four now and her letters had lately become uncharacteristically short. She was troubled with arthritis in her joints and was finding it difficult to write. She was writing in haste, she said, as she thought Bertha should be aware of Dr Freud's latest book, *An Autobiographical Study*. Not that there was much autobiographical material in it, Anna continued, rather an account of the history of psychoanalysis in which Bertha herself had apparently played a prominent part.

Bertha's mouth was suddenly dry. She was swept back to

1895, to the time of Dr Freud's first publication, *Studies on Hysteria*, produced jointly with Dr Breuer. How horrified she had been to find that her own story featured as the first of those studies and how glad that she no longer lived in Vienna, having moved to Frankfurt with her mother six years earlier. She had raged inwardly against Dr Breuer. What could he have been thinking of to allow himself to be talked into that enterprise by Dr Freud? Mama had told her that rumours were already circulating about the book in Vienna, that people were associating her name with that of the patient described in the first case study, a young woman referred to as Anna O. Bertha bought the book. It lay for three days on her desk before she could bring herself to open it.

Then she had flushed hot with embarrassment as she read the first few pages, believing that anyone in Vienna who read it, who knew her family, would surely know that the patient referred to was herself. Her symptoms, her age at the time, the dates of her father's illness and death, the dates of her own illness – all pointed in her direction. Hers was such a small social world: the well-to-do Jews of Germany and Austria. Everybody knew each other, even if only by name and reputation, and what a reputation *Studies on Hysteria* must have given her.

She had been appalled by the description of her strange moods and aggressive behaviour, her suicidal impulses, the reference to her sexuality as 'astonishingly underdeveloped'. An inexcusable intrusion, an unforgivable revelation about her private self.

Mama had been shocked. She could scarcely believe that Dr Breuer would have agreed to such a flagrant breach of confidentiality. Dr Freud had undoubtedly been the driving force behind it, in her opinion. It was all the more scandalous in that Dr Freud had a very dubious reputation in Vienna at the time. Few people took him seriously. His obsession with attributing all nervous ailments to sexual causes made him a source of titillation and amusement. Not that Mama mentioned that, of course, but Bertha knew she was aware of it.

It had pained Bertha to read that account of her illness, all laid out so objectively, distantly, as if she were the subject of some laboratory experiment, a 'case' rather than a person. It felt like a betrayal of her personal relationship with Dr Breuer.

She also felt used, as if a means of professional advancement had been built on the foundations of her own suffering. As she read and reread the case study it seemed to her that a pattern had been superimposed on her illness. She recognized the events described, the states she had been in, but in her own memory it was all far more disorganized than in the published version. As if Dr Breuer, or Dr Freud more likely, had wanted to create his own story, using elements of her illness as one might put together a patchwork quilt, picking and choosing, matching for best fit of colour and design to give the most pleasing overall effect. And of course his account of her cure was an outright lie, claiming that she was more or less better in June 1882 whereas in reality she had spent the next five years in and out of sanatoria, struggling with morphine addiction and recurrences of other symptoms.

Bertha sat for a while, recalling all those emotions. Did she really want to stir it all up again by reading what was being said about her now? She filled her coffee cup and drank it slowly. Better perhaps not to read the book, to remain in ignorance about Dr Freud's latest speculations.

But she felt much stronger now than she did in 1895. For all her anger about *Studies on Hysteria*, she had later come to feel that she was in some ways indebted to Dr Breuer. He had taken her ambitions seriously, had encouraged her to think independently, shown her that her horizons were less limited than she had come to expect. Without his backing, Mama would never have allowed her to do the charity work she undertook while in the clinic at Inzersdorf. This had primed her for the work she began to do once she was restored to health.

Already by the time *Studies on Hysteria* appeared she had been doing social work in Frankfurt for several years and had just taken up a position as director of the Israelite Women's Association Orphanage for Girls. Since then she had gone

242

from strength to strength professionally. After taking her first steps as a published writer with two volumes of her fairy stories she had gone on to write plays and articles, always with a strong social and feminist content. In 1902 she founded Women's Welfare, a Jewish social welfare organization, finding in the needs of the refugee Jews from Eastern Europe a ready outlet for the exercise of what she thought of as her 'social imperatives'. Two years later she set up the League of Jewish Women, the first national organization of Jewish women in the world. She campaigned vociferously against the white slave traffickers who had been luring so many destitute Jewish girls to a life of vice, an area of concern which had led her to set up the Neu Isenburg Home.

But then again, might she not have achieved all this without Dr Breuer? There was also Anna who had been such a powerful influence, who had been a source of constant encouragement and shown by her own example that life for a Jewish girl was not necessarily limited to husband, children and home-making. One could never really know for sure the cause of anything, one could only surmise.

Bertha picked the book up. Of course, there had been many other books by Dr Freud over the past thirty years. She had not sought them out, although his theories and the practice of psychoanalysis were subjects often bandied about in general conversation. There had been talk also of a rift between Dr Freud and Dr Breuer. Something to do with Dr Breuer not accepting that hysteria was rooted in difficulties associated with sexuality.

She started to read. The first few pages outlined Dr Freud's family background, education and early medical work. Bertha scanned them quickly, stopping when she came to Dr Breuer's name in association with 'a case of hysteria which, between 1880 and 1882, he had treated in a peculiar manner'. There was only the briefest mention of her symptoms: 'a variegated picture of paralyses with contractures, inhibitions and states of mental confusion'. Bertha read on. Much of it was a repetition of material already contained in *Studies on Hysteria* – the idea that her symptoms were caused by unpleasant events which occurred during her father's illness.

It had always seemed to Bertha that the two doctors had put their heads together and invested incidents with far more causal significance than they merited. That business with her occasional experiences of not hearing, for example. Dr Breuer had tried to make her believe that it was linked to the time Willi had shaken her outside Papa's bedroom door and that it was brought on by subsequent shakings. Even at the time she had doubted his reasoning. And here was what they made of it:

> When the patient recalled a situation of this kind in a hallucinatory way under hypnosis and carried through to its conclusion, with a free expression of emotion, the mental act which she had originally suppressed, the symptom was abolished and did not return. By this procedure Breuer succeeded, after long and painful efforts, in relieving his patient of all her symptoms.

If only it had been so easy!

To be sure, it had been such blessed relief to talk to Dr Breuer about her sorrows and resentments, her frustrations and anger. It was true that he had helped ease her mental anguish in that respect. She had been able to express herself more freely to him than she could have done to anyone else, even Anna. However, that was a separate issue. As far as she could see – and she had given the matter a lot of thought since then – those things had nothing to do with her illness.

She was finding it easier to read *An Autobiographical Study* than *Studies on Hysteria*. She was more detached, could think about it objectively. It was almost like thinking back over a dream, or even something which had happened to someone else – which in a sense it was; she could barely identify herself now, aged sixty-six, with the inexperienced, immature girl she had been then.

What was this though? Dr Freud was now writing about a 'veil of obscurity' which rested over the final stage of the treatment, one which Dr Breuer had never raised for him.

Bertha puzzled over the words. What could Dr Freud

mean? A veil of obscurity? Perhaps he was only referring to Dr Breuer's reticence about discussing the case publicly. On the other hand, Dr Freud seemed to believe that this veil had hidden an 'invaluable discovery' which could have enriched science had not Dr Breuer preferred to keep it secret. She could make nothing of it.

And now here was Dr Freud on his favourite hobby horse, discussing the emotional dynamics of hysteria and attributing it all to a disordered sexuality in early childhood.

Bertha stopped to reflect on what she was reading. Dr Freud's reasoning puzzled her. On the one hand he claimed that she had been cured by the process of recalling the cause of her symptoms, each one being associated with an emotional event occurring during her father's illness; on the other hand he maintained that all causes of hysteria were associated with childhood sexual experiences. He couldn't have it both ways. And why had Dr Breuer never spoken up to contradict Dr Freud's theories about the sexual origin of hysteria if he himself believed that the cause of her own supposed hysteria was connected with things that had happened during her father's illness? She skimmed the next few pages, pausing every time she came across Dr Breuer's name. Ah, now here Dr Freud was himself admitting to being surprised that Dr Breuer had not made that very point, tying it in with the remark made in *Studies on Hysteria* about her underdeveloped sexuality. Dr Freud had a ready explanation for this.

> After the work of catharsis had seemed to be completed, the girl had suddenly developed a condition of "transference love"; he had not connected this with her illness, and had therefore retired in dismay.

This, Dr Freud confessed, was only something which he had reconstructed on the basis of some remarks made to him by Dr Breuer. Yet from this confection of surmise and conjecture Dr Freud concluded that Dr Breuer had indeed recognized the sexual origin of neurosis but was unwilling to admit it. This must be what Dr Freud meant by the veil of obscurity which he had referred to earlier.

245

Bertha could not deny that she had felt an intense attachment to Dr Breuer. Had her feelings exceeded what could be accounted for by the actual situation, as Dr Freud claimed was true of this 'transference' which seemed to be crucial to his thinking? That too she could not deny. But was it so significant? She recalled her feelings about Miss Baxter, the English teacher. Those too had been out of proportion to the reality. Perhaps Dr Freud would say that they had a significance of their own.

There was just one memory from her illness which still made her uncomfortable: the fantasies and play-acting of sucking and gurgling as she was fed by Dr Breuer, of basking in his arms, rocking on his knee. It embarrassed her all the more in that she could sense that voluptuous pleasure even now if she allowed herself to think about it.

So she understood the words that she was reading now. Here undoubtedly Dr Freud had hit upon a truth: the idea that erotic feelings were in existence even at an early age, and distributed throughout the body, giving rise to indiscriminate pleasure.

> Thus at first the sexual function is non-centralized and predominately auto-erotic.

She read the sentence again. Yes, indeed. She herself had experienced it.

But she had experienced more than that, much more, and with it had come a knowing, a recognition of something which she felt she had always known without being aware of it, which had lain hidden in the deepest part of her being and which had been brought to light in those spring days of 1882 and had stayed with her ever since.

Shekhinah! The divine presence. Shadaj! Mighty One.

Again the reference to a veil of obscurity came back to her. There was a veil of obscurity in her own mind about the ending of her treatment with Dr Breuer. He had been called back to the house urgently, that much she knew. Something powerful had been happening to her. She had hardly been aware of what was going on around her. What had really happened? What had the others heard, seen? It had been like a dream. Was it really a dream? But something must have happened for Dr Breuer to be called in. He had already finished the treatment, said that he wouldn't be continuing his visits. So something had happened. She had never talked about it with Mama; it was too intimate. It was something momentous. How much of it had been evident? How much just in her head? She would never know.

But there had been something in it apart from her fantasies about Dr Breuer, apart from the pleasure which her own body had begun to give her, which seemed to have been associated with her absences during the latter period of her illness. She would come to, knowing that she had experienced something which she didn't understand or even quite remember, an instant of rapture which had lasted an eternity.

Since then her life, her mind, her soul had changed – even though she had remained ill for some time. Yes, she still had difficulties, often felt lonely, but there was a bedrock of assuredness, in her, a feeling that she was standing on solid ground; also a compulsion to the practice of *tikkun olam*, the holy injunction to heal and repair the world. As she thought about it now, she began to be flooded with waves of desire, a desire which sought not its own satisfaction but which powered her ever onward. It was the fount of her energy.

Bertha sat in silence for a while, emptying her mind of all thought, creating mental space, preparing herself.

The clock struck. Twenty minutes to sunset. Time to go back to the Home. Bertha got up, then stood for a moment in front of the silver menorah which stood on the black Biedermeier cabinet, murmuring a prayer of her own composition.

> My God, you are not a God of meekness, of the Word and of incense, no God of the past. You are a God of omnipresence. To me you are a demanding God. You sanctify me with your "Thou shalt"; you expect me to decide between good and evil; you demand that I prove that I am strength of your strength, that I strive to rise to your heights, to carry others with me, to help them

with all my being.Demand, demand, so that I feel in my conscience with every breath of my life, that there is a God.

When she finished, she draped a shawl round her shoulders and left the house. Her girls were waiting for her.

AUTHOR'S NOTE

Bertha Pappenheim is better known as 'Anna O', and is generally believed to be the patient whose treatment gave rise to the ideas on which psychoanalysis was later based. Shortly after terminating her treatment in 1882, her doctor, Josef Breuer, discussed the case with his friend, Sigmund Freud, who began to treat some of his own patients in a similar manner. 'The Case of Anna O' is the first study described in *Studies on Hysteria*, one of the founding texts of psychoanalysis, published jointly by Freud and Breuer in 1895. Although Breuer claimed in this study that Anna O was cured, subsequent research has revealed that this was not the case and that Bertha Pappenheim spent several years in a wretched condition, with recurrence of her symptoms and spells of hospitalisation.

In the 1880s, neuroscience was in its infancy and the diagnosis of hysteria was often applied to symptoms which would now be identified as of organic origin. Since the concept of hysteria began to fall into disuse during the last century, various attempts have been made to diagnose Bertha Pappenheim retrospectively.

My own belief is that many of Bertha's symptoms could be accounted for by a form of temporal lobe epilepsy, as hypothesised by Alison Orr-Andrawes. Taking this further, it seemed to me feasible that this could explain Bertha's shift from religious indifference as a young woman – as documented by Breuer – to deep devotion in later life, experiences of a mystical and profoundly meaningful nature being symptomatic of this condition.

A number of historians of psychoanalysis have also found fault with Breuer's and Freud's reporting and analysis of the Bertha Pappenheim case, pointing to inconsistencies, improbabilities, flawed reasoning, and outright falsification.

Since the publication of *Studies on Hysteria* in 1895, much has been written about Bertha by academics and psychoanalysts but nowhere do we hear the voice of Bertha herself. This is what I have tried to provide.

After finally recovering her health, Bertha moved to Frankfurt with her mother in 1889. Shortly after that she embarked on what was to become a long and highly successful career in social work. She also gained prominence, both in Germany and internationally, as a feminist and writer. In 1954 she was honoured with a German postage stamp bearing her image in the series *Benefactors of Mankind*.

My research focused primarily on a case report written by Josef Breuer in 1882 which remained undiscovered until unearthed in the Sanatorium Bellevue in Switzerland by medical historian Henri Ellenberger in the 1970s, and on associated documents found by Albrecht Hirschmüller shortly afterwards. Other principal sources are listed in the Bibliography.

BIBLIOGRAPHY

Bennett, A. Hughes, 'Case of Cerebral Tumour – Symptoms Simulating Hysteria', *Brain* 1 (1878) 114-120

Borch-Jacobsen, Mikkel, *Remembering Anna O: A Century of Mystification* (New York: Routledge, 1996)

Breuer, Josef, 'The Case History of Bertha Pappenheim (Anna O.)', in Albrecht Hirschmüller, *The Life and Work of Josef Breuer: Physiology and Psychoanalysis* (New York: New York University Press, 1989), pp. 276-292

Breuer, Josef, 'Fraulein Anna O' in Josef Breuer and Sigmund Freud, *Studies on Hysteria*, trans. James and Alix Strachey (London, Pelican 1974), pp. 73-102

Breuer, Josef and Sigmund Freud, *Studies on Hysteria*, trans. James and Alix Strachey (London, Pelican 1974)

Dormandy, Thomas, *The White Death: A History of Tuberculosis* (London: The Hambledon Press, 1999)

Ellenberger, Henri F., *The Discovery of the Unconscious: The History and Evolution of Dynamic Psychiatry* (New York: Basic Books, 1970)

Flanders, Judith, *The Victorian House: From Childbirth to Deathbed* (London: Harper Perennial, 2003)

Freeman, Lucy, *The Story of Anna O* (New York: Walker, 1972)

Freud, Sigmund, *An Autobiographical Study* http://www2.winchester.ac.uk/edstudies/courses/level%20t wo%20sem%20two/freudautopdf.pdf (accessed 10 October 2012, first published 1925)

Gauld, Alan, *A History of Hypnotism* (Cambridge: Cambridge University Press, 1995)

Greenberg, Blu, *How to Run a Traditional Jewish Household* (New York: Simon and Schuster, 1983)

Hirschmüller, Albrecht, *The Life and Work of Josef Breuer: Physiology and Psychoanalysis* (New York: New York University Press, 1989)

Hollender, Marc H., 'The Case of Anna O: A Reformulation', *American Journal of Psychiatry* 137 (July 1980), 797-800

Hurst, Lindsay C., 'What Was Wrong With Anna O?', *Journal*

of the Royal Society of Medicine 75 (February, 1982), 129-131

Kaplan, Marion A., *The Making of the Jewish Middle Class: Women, Family and Identity in Imperial Germany* (USA: Oxford University Press, 1995)

Martineau, Harriet, *Letters on Mesmerism* (London: Moxon, 1845)

Masson, Jeffrey M., ed., A Dark Science: *Women, Sexuality and Psychiatry in the Nineteenth Century* (New York: The Noonday Press, 1988)

Micale, Mark S., *Approaching Hysteria: Disease and Its Interpretations*, (Princeton: Princeton University Press, 1995)

Orr-Andrawes, Alison, 'The Case of Anna O: A Neuropsychiatric Perspective', *Journal of the American Psychoanalytic Association* 35 (April, 1987), 387-420

Playfair, W. S., 'Remarks on the Systematic Treatment of Aggravated Hysteria and Certain Allied Forms of Neurasthenic Disease', *The British Medical Journal* (August 19, 1882)

Porter, Roy, 'The Patient's View: Doing Medical History from Below', *Theory and Society* 14 (March, 1985), 175-198

Reuter, Gabriele, *From a Good Family*, trans. by Lynne Tatlock (New York: Camden House, 1999) First published Germany 1895

Ritchie, Douglas, *Stroke: A Diary of Recovery*, 2nd edn. (London: Faber and Faber, 1974)

Rosenbaum, Max and Melvin Muroff, eds., *Anna O: Fourteen Contemporary Reinterpretations* (New York: The Free Press, 1984)

Schachter, Steven C., ed., *Brainstorms: Epilepsy in Our Own Words* (New York: Raven Press, 1993)

Skues, Richard A., *Sigmund Freud and the History of Anna O: Reopening a Closed Case* (Basingstoke: Palgrave Macmillan, 2006)

Teale, T. Pridgin, 'An Address on the Surgical Treatment of Abscess of the Lung and Empyema', *The British Medical Journal* (October 13, 1888)

Thornton, E. M., *The Freudian Fallacy: Freud and Cocaine* (London: Paladin, 1986)

Veith, Ilza, *Hysteria: The History of a Disease* (Chicago: University of Chicago Press, 1965)

Made in the USA
Charleston, SC
12 November 2013